Manchineel

For Mercedes

MANCHINEEL

John Ballem

A Castle Street Mystery

THE DUNDURN GROUP
TORONTO · OXFORD

Editor: Marc Côté
Copy Editor: Barry Jowett
Design: Jennifer Scott
Printer: Webcom

Canadian Cataloguing in Publication Data

Ballem, John
Manchineel

ISBN 0-88882-217-0
I. Title

PS8553.A45M36 2000   C813'.54   C00-930054-6   PR9199.3.B36M36 2000

1   2   3   4   5   04   03   02   01   00

Canadä

THE CANADA COUNCIL | LE CONSEIL DES ARTS
FOR THE ARTS | DU CANADA
SINCE 1957 | DEPUIS 1957

We acknowledge the support of the Canada Council for the Arts, the Ontario Arts Council, and the Book Publishing Industry Development Program (BPIDP) for our publishing activities.

Care has been taken to trace the ownership of copyright material used in this book. The author and the publisher welcome any information enabling them to rectify any references or credit in subsequent editions.

J. Kirk Howard, President

All the events and characters in this book are fictitious. Any resemblance to actual people, places or events is purely coincidental.

Printed and bound in Canada.

✿

Printed on recycled paper.

Dundurn Press
8 Market Street
Suite 200
Toronto, Ontario, Canada
M5E 1M6

Dundurn Press
73 Lime Walk
Headington, Oxford,
England
OX3 7AD

Dundurn Press
2250 Military Road
Tonawanda NY
U.S.A. 14150

Manchineel (man-chi-neel) — a tropical American tree of the spurge family with a blistering milky juice and apple-shaped poisonous fruit.

Webster's Dictionary

Chapter One

T he Grenadines stretched to the southern horizon in
a long, graceful arc, a necklace of jewel-like
islands adrift on a turquoise sea. At four thousand feet,
the Cessna 180 was well below the white cumulus
clouds that dotted the Caribbean sky. St. Vincent was
coming up on the port wing and Skye MacLeod eased
back on the throttle. Bequia passed beneath him and he
altered course slightly to line up with Manchineel, the
distinctive hump of its Mount Morne still blue in the
distance. The airstrip was directly beneath Mount
Morne which, although it was more of a hill than a
mountain, was still high enough for the winds to create
a dangerous lee-wave turbulence as they flowed over it.
The 2,500-foot runway terminated abruptly at the edge
of a small cliff that dropped straight into the sea. The
Caribbean is notorious for its dicey landing strips and
Manchineel had the reputation among pilots of being
the diciest of all of them.

It was time to make contact with the airport. "Manchineel radio, this is November 115 Charlie. Position report, 20 out at 3,500 feet. Transponder squawking at 1,200. Landing at Manchineel. Request advisory."

"Welcome home, November 115 Charlie." Skye recognized the warm Caribbean accent of Henry Armbruster, the manager of Manchineel Air who doubled as the flight service operator. "Active runway 07, winds 130 degrees at 20, gusting to 30."

Gusting to 30. Jesus Christ. The Cessna 180 was a high wing monoplane and very susceptible to crosswinds. Closing in on the northwest tip of the elongated, amoeba-shaped island, and dropping the vintage Cessna lower, Skye saw the figure of a man kneeling beside what appeared to be three bodies lying on the sand. It looked like there had been a multiple drowning. The man looked up and waved as Skye banked for another look. With the wind throwing his airplane around, he didn't dare fly low enough to see who it was. He raised Armbruster again to ask what was going on. "Shark attack," was the answer. "Bodies washed up on the beach. Haitian refugees most likely. Some kid found them about a half hour ago. We're trying to keep a lid on it until we know more about it. Look, Skye, the wind velocity is increasing. You better bring her in."

"Roger." Skye gained altitude and headed for the airstrip. Landing the airplane in wind conditions like this required all his attention. He overflew the airstrip midfield at 1,500 feet. When he first started to take flying lessons, he wondered why anyone would fly directly over the field until an instructor pointed out that when other airplanes were taking off or landing, they used the ends of the runway, not the middle. On the downward leg, he dropped to one thousand feet. Up ahead the wind was really tossing the palm trees around on the top of Mount Morne. Armbruster had been right, the wind was stronger than 30 knots. He put on 10 degrees of flap. It would increase the airplane's vulnerability to wind gusts but the short runway gave him no choice.

Over the water, he turned onto his final approach. The wind was playing havoc with the windsurfers in Maggins Bay, their rainbow-coloured sails lying flat on the water. As the Cessna 180 swept over Mount Morne, its wheels almost touched the tops of the towering coconut palms. Grazing goats didn't even bother to look up as its shadow passed over them. As soon as he had the runway made, Skye retarded the throttle, but still kept some power on and held the 180's nose down to prevent a stall. The wind buffeted the airplane, tossing it up, down and sideways. Skye dipped a wing and crabbed into the wind to stay lined up with the runway. Over the runway numbers he pulled the nose up. A stronger gust broadsided the Cessna as the wheels touched, pushing it toward the verge of the narrow runway. Skye applied power and the nimble 180 lifted off the ground, then immediately bounced back into the air. Skye held the control column as far back as it would go and the 180 touched down once more. But he couldn't keep her on the ground. The wind was too strong, and she bounced once again, although this time only a few feet in the air. The bounces were using up too much precious runway, and as soon as she touched down again Skye rode the brakes, praying that he could bring her to a stop before they ended up in the drink. It was too late to abort the landing and take off again. Skye expelled a pent-up breath as the 180 slowed to a stop just short of the end of the runway. As he had so often in the past, he blessed the short landing capability of the ancient tail dragger.

She wasn't officially listed as a STOL airplane but she could handle short runways with the best of them.

Skye could feel the sweat trickling down his ribcage. He tried to persuade himself it was simply because of the heat that quickly invaded the cabin now that he was on the ground. Propping the door open, he taxied back to the small, thatched-roof building that served as both an open air passenger terminal and customs and immigration.

"I should charge you four landing fees for that one." Henry Armbruster was smiling; but his large, blotchy freckles stood out more than usual. He was from Bequia, where many of the people were of mixed race, and he had lightly pigmented skin.

"It was more of a controlled crash than a landing," Skye agreed ruefully as he jumped down onto the tarmac. "But I'll take it."

The airport manager nodded. When conditions were almost outside the envelope, the wise pilot didn't try to paint his airplane onto the runway, he was content to get it on the ground without bending it. "Andy Foster needed three tries before he made it," he told Skye. "Lord and Lady Fraser chartered the 421 to fly over from Barbados. His Lordship kissed the ground soon as he got out and she swore they'd charter a boat to go back. I had to help her walk to the terminal."

"The Frasers will get over it," he assured Armbruster. "A few stiff whiskies and Lord Fraser will be dining out on it." Skye was considerably cheered by this news. Foster was a commercial pilot with Manchineel Air. He flew in and out of the strip every day; and the twin-engine 421 was a lot more airplane than the 180. "Tell me about this shark attack."

"There's not much more to tell. All I know is what

I've been told over the radio. Kids. Teenagers. Pretty well gutted."

"I haven't heard of shark attacks in these waters."

"Probably happened well north of here."

Skye walked over to where Overfine waited on the tarmac to help with the luggage. "It's been a long time, Overfine," said Skye as he shook his servant warmly by the hand.

"Too long, Mister Skye," Overfine replied, a hint of reproach in his voice. Lifting two large soft-sided suitcases out of the luggage compartment, he placed them on the tarmac. He started to reach for a small black plastic case further back in the compartment, then withdrew his hand. Staring at Skye with a look of almost superstitious dread, Overfine asked, "Be that Mistress Jocelyn?"

"Yes. It's okay. I understand your feelings. It's best I handle her remains, anyway." Skye reached in and picked up the black case with both hands.

Jason Carmichael was on duty behind the customs and immigration desk and Skye knew he was in for the full treatment. Jason took himself and his responsibilities very seriously and insisted on going by the book, despite pleas from the Manchineel Company that this was no way to welcome the rich and famous to the island. Skye had been coming to Manchineel for six years, but it was as if Jason had never seen him before. He peered suspiciously back and forth between Skye and his passport photo before stamping the passport with a loud thump. Overfine, who knew the drill, had already opened Skye's suitcases for inspection. Jason sifted through them with expert thoroughness, held up the two bottles of vodka, glared accusingly at Skye before putting them back and nodding to Overfine to close the cases. When Skye placed the small plastic case

John Ballem

on the table, Jason glared suspiciously at it and demanded to know what was in it.

"My wife's ashes," Skye replied evenly.

Jason recoiled, crossed himself, and waved Skye through.

Toting the suitcases, Overfine led the way to a Land Rover in the airport parking lot. Like all the other Land Rovers on the island, this one was Brazilian-made. It was ideal for coping with the steep and winding tracks that passed for roads on the island. In any event, the Manchineel Company, having struck a favourable deal with the Brazilian manufacturer, had decreed that it was the only passenger vehicle that would be allowed on the island. The edict also specified that all of them were to be painted white. Henry Ford in reverse. Although technically they were Land Rovers, they were never called anything but jeeps. A green tree frog painted on the doors and the hood identified Overfine's vehicle as belonging to Skye's rambling villa, the Whistling Frog.

Adrienne Jones, "the lady who fished for the hotel," as she described herself, was walking up the road from the sea wall, balancing a basket of sea urchins on her head. Skye had been aimlessly thumbing through a dictionary of first names one day and had been struck by the aptness of her name. Adrienne's brown eyes had blazed with excitement when he told her that her name meant "woman of the sea." It confirmed her own belief that she was a special person. She was wearing a black one-piece bathing suit that so closely matched her skin that from a distance her taut, shapely body appeared to be nude. Skye hastily stowed the black case in the back of the jeep where it was out of sight. It was common knowledge that Adrienne was a mambo, a high priestess of voodoo who presided over the ceremonies when the drums began to beat in the native village. As she drew closer, Skye could see that she was visibly excited. Omitting any words of welcome, she demanded, "Hear about the bodies?"

Skye nodded. "I saw them on my way in."

"I want you to take Adrienne there."

The peremptory request didn't surprise Skye. He and Adrienne had developed a sort of working relationship in that he sometimes did favours for her in return for her letting him observe the voodoo rites over which she presided. Their friendship had been cemented four years ago with the incident of her only daughter's almost fatal appendicitis attack. Penelope had come down with an attack of acute appendicitis that Adrienne — sure that she could cure it with white magic — had let go far too long. A panic-stricken Adrienne had finally asked Skye for help. He and Jocelyn had immediately flown the adolescent girl and her distraught mother to Barbados where an ambulance waited to rush Penelope to the hospital. They operated immediately and the surgeon said that the appendix had started to leak and would have perforated within the hour. Two weeks later, when Penelope was fully recovered, Skye had ventured to reprove Adrienne for relying on her magic and having put her only child at risk.

"You was my white magic," she retorted.

"I will be happy to take you there, Adrienne. I was intending to go there myself. But what about your catch?"

"We drop it by the hotel on the way."

"Let me put it in the back. The guests at the hotel will dine well tonight," Skye said as he took the heavy basket from her and placed it in the rear of the jeep, re-arranging the suitcases to hide the black case. She jumped nimbly over the tailgate and sat on the bench seat, her wet bathing suit leaving a mark on the plastic cover.

Catching Skye looking at her, Adrienne smiled wickedly up at him and slid a strap off one smooth shoulder. "Adrienne miss you, Skye. You stay away too long."

"I missed you too, Adrienne."

Besotted with his beautiful wife, Skye had managed to ignore Adrienne's blatant sexuality and tempting body. But with Jocelyn gone.... He brushed the thought aside and climbed into the driver's seat.

The road from the airstrip passed directly in front of the one-storey office building of the Manchineel Company. The Company ran the island with an iron hand. Everything was directed toward protecting the privacy of those holidaying on the island and preventing the outside world from intruding. To achieve that end, no cruise ships were allowed to call, private yachts had to receive special permission to anchor, and supply boats had to be on their way within four hours of docking.

Like many Caribbean islands, Manchineel suffered from a chronic water shortage. The landscape Skye gazed upon with such affection was mostly brown grass interspersed with clumps of coconut palms, banana trees, and a magnificent poinciana, whose bare branches would be laden with brilliant red flowers at the end of the dry season. Down by the beach manchineel trees grew, from which the island took its name. The manchineels produced a green fruit resembling an apple that was extremely poisonous, as were its leaves and its milky sap. The Company had posted signs warning of the dangers of the tree and painted red rings around the trunks to identify them.

Overfine brought the Land Rover to a halt at the Sugar Mill, a converted stone warehouse that was now a small but luxurious and very expensive hotel. Penelope, who worked there as a waitress, came out to greet Skye and take the basket of sea urchins from Adrienne. In the two years since he had last seen her, her budding beauty had more than fulfilled its promise. That much-maligned word "nubile" was the only one Skye could think of to describe her slender, long-waisted figure.

"She's beautiful, Adrienne," said Skye as they drove away from the hotel towards the site of the accident.

Adrienne sniffed. "She think she too big for this island." Normally Adrienne spoke fairly grammatical English, but when she was upset, it fell apart. Among her own people, she spoke the patois that only those born and raised in the islands could understand.

Skye pulled in beside a jeep and a bicycle parked on the edge of a small cliff overlooking the beach. The jeep had a small red cross painted on the side. That was the medical clinic's vehicle, fitted out as an ambulance. But there was nothing that Manchineel's resident physician, Sir George Glessop, could do for the bodies splayed out on the sand. Sir George rose to his feet, dusted the sand from his tropical slacks, and came forward to intercept the little group. His eyes behind round pebble glasses were concerned, and his face was red and perspiring. He held up his latex-gloved hands as if to explain why he couldn't shake hands with Skye.

"I wouldn't come any closer," he said. "It's quite ghastly."

"I think the damage has been done already," Skye replied, looking past the doctor's portly figure. He gagged as the cloying smell of putrefied flesh reached them. Overfine abruptly turned aside and was violently sick in the eelgrass growing at the foot of the cliff.

True to form, Adrienne, black mambo eyes glowing with excitement, brushed past Sir George and walked over to where the bodies were splayed out on the sand and squatted beside them.

Sir George stood aside, muttering, "Well, I did my best to warn you." He fell into step beside Skye. "Welcome back, Skye. It's good to have you back on the island." Skye, struggling to hold back the gorge rising in his throat, nodded his thanks. Up close, he smelt the usual mixture of whisky and peppermint on the surgeon's breath.

The three bodies were little more than skeletons, and two were missing a leg. Looking down at them, Sir George said, "They must have gotten hung up on the reef. The crabs have almost stripped them clean. But the sharks got them first. Look at this." He pointed to a serrated wound on a strip of flesh that still clung to the chest of one of the bodies. "She's a female," he added, "although you might not know it at first."

Skye nodded mutely. The initial shock had passed and he could look at the mutilated remains without revulsion. He leaned over to inspect the wound that Sir George was pointing out. Straightening up, he asked, "Where's Edwina? Is she still with the clinic?"

"Of course she is. I couldn't function without her invaluable assistance." That was true enough, thought Skye as Sir George continued, "Today is her day off, and she flew down to Grenada to see some relatives." Calling out to the policewoman who had been standing guard on top of the cliff, he said, "There's nothing more to be done here, Constable. If you agree, we should remove the bodies."

Constable Phillips came down to join them. As always, she eyed Adrienne with suspicion. She said she would contact Mr. Armbruster once more and he would kindly radio the message to the authorities in Kingstown.

"There's a body bag in the ambulance," said Sir George. "Unfortunately, I only have one, but it should hold what's left of this lot."

"I'll get it, Sir George." Overfine, eager to make amends for what he thought had been a display of weakness, volunteered.

Sir George smiled approvingly, handed him the keys and told him where to find the body bag.

There was no way the portly, sixtyish doctor could handle the cadavers by himself. Swallowing hard, Skye took hold of the largest one, supporting the shoulder blades with one hand and holding the skull with the other. Walking backwards, gripping the pelvis and the one remaining leg, Sir George tripped and fell down on the sand. Wordlessly, Overfine took his place. As he and Overfine were laying the smallest cadaver on top of the other two, Skye bent down for a closer look. A pale white piece of gristle was still attached to the rear of the ribcage. Beckoning Sir George over, he said, "Look at that cut. That doesn't look like a shark bite to me."

The surgeon smiled patiently. "I can see why you might think that, Skye. It does look like a sharp and clean line. But no, I wouldn't say surgical incision. I know them well, as you know."

There was a bad moment when the body bag refused to close. "Press down on them a bit," said Sir George. "If need be, I can sort them out later."

The body bag had handles and Constable Phillips helped them carry it up to the ambulance. It was disturbingly light.

"You will keep the remains under lock and key, Sir George?" said Constable Phillips with a meaningful glance at Adrienne.

"Of course. When will the authorities collect them?"

"In the morning."

"We better go back down and wash our hands off in the sea," Skye said to Overfine.

"I can do better than that." Sir George reached into

his medical bag and took out a plastic vial. "Use this. It's a mild disinfectant. That was quite a homecoming, Skye," he went on as the three of them rubbed the disinfectant on their hands. "I'm very grateful to you and Overfine."

"This is bound to keep people from swimming in the ocean. They'll be thinking of Jaws all over again."

"Not after I put out the word that the attack took place hundreds of miles from here. Most likely between Haiti and the U.S. mainland. There's no cause for alarm."

* * *

Word about the bodies that had washed ashore spread. As the little cavalcade of jeeps with its gruesome cargo drove away from the beach, they encountered jeeps coming in the opposite direction. "They're too late," Skye said to Overfine. When they dropped Adrienne off at the hotel, guests were clustered on the front lawn, talking excitedly among themselves.

As usual, a smooth-billed ani was perched on the stone wall by the school. Skye smiled as he remembered how thrilled Jocelyn had been when she finally identified the strange-looking bird with its glossy black plumage and large, parrot-like beak. She had refused to let him tell her what it was, insisting on tracking it down herself. The two ladies who ran the vegetable stand under a huge, fern-like jacaranda tree were doing a brisk business and Overfine frowned in concentration as he steered around the parked vehicles. Traffic on the island drove on the left in the English fashion, although all the jeeps were left-hand drive, which made things a little awkward. Most of the shoppers were staff from the villas; some of them wore T-shirts bearing the name of the villas they worked for. Overfine had once hinted that he wouldn't mind wearing a T-shirt like that, but neither Skye nor Jocelyn had cared for the idea. Instead, Jocelyn designed a neat little logo of a green frog. Overfine wore it on his shirts with great pride.

"How were the last guests? The ones who just left," asked Skye. Like most villa owners, he rented out Whistling Frog during the tourist season when he was not in residence himself. Whistling Frog, which was one of the smaller villas, was also one of the most popular, and rented for more money in a week than a New York apartment in a month. That meant Skye could own and run the villa virtually free of cost. For the past two years, Whistling Frog had been rented out for the entire season.

"They be good tippers," Overfine muttered, his tone making it clear that that was the only thing that could be said in their favour. "You know they be two men?" he asked as he geared down for the road that led up to the large villas perched high in the hills. Whistling Frog was about a third of the way up. It overlooked the airstrip, a feature that had done much to sell Skye on it.

Skye shook his head. "I had no idea. The Company looks after renting the place. My God," he exclaimed as he suddenly thought of Agatha, his fanatically religious cook. "How did Agatha take it?"

"She very vexed. She make them sleep in different rooms."

"The hell she did!" Skye grinned to himself; he could picture the formidable Agatha terrorizing the two hapless guests into doing what she thought was proper. As they approached the island's riding stable, he asked Overfine to pull up. Elizabeth Mallory, who managed the stable on behalf of the Manchineel Company, was watching as her groom, a Rastafarian complete with wool cap and dreadlocks, led a small group of inexperienced riders out through the gate. Her full breasts moved underneath her thin cotton shirt as she dogtrotted across the paddock to greet Skye. Elizabeth was a small, blond Englishwoman with a slender waist and astonishing breasts. Skye sometimes wondered if they had been augmented. Augmented or not, he was acutely conscious of them as she gave him a welcoming hug. "It's so good to have you back," she said a little breathlessly. "I was beginning to think we had lost you."

Skye gave her a reassuring squeeze, but said nothing. He didn't know the answer to that himself. Not yet. He dropped his arms and she stepped back. Looking at her, he was struck anew by the flattened bridge of her nose. It gave her otherwise attractive face the look of a boxer who has absorbed too many blows. It could have been a riding accident, but more likely it was a memento from her succession of ill-chosen lovers. Elizabeth was an expert sailor and a superb horsewoman, but she was loosely wrapped when it came to men.

Smiling up at him, she said, "I've got a new horse who is perfect for you. I just brought him over from Barbados. He's an ex-race horse but he's got lovely manners."

"Great. I'll try him out the first chance I get."

"Skye." She looked up at him. "I want you to know how sorry I am about Jocelyn. Everybody is. She was awfully well-liked on the island."

"Thank you. And she loved it here."

Wrinkling her nose, the stable manager said, "What's that hospital smell? Did you have a fall?" Skye knew she meant over a jump.

"Nothing like that," he said and told her about the bodies, emphasizing that the attack had taken place hundreds of miles away. Then assuring, her that he would come around in the next few days to try out the new horse, he climbed back into the jeep.

Agatha and the new housemaid, who had been hired

since Skye was last here, had heard the jeep grinding in
low gear up the driveway and were waiting, in freshly
pressed and starched uniforms, outside the front door to
greet the "master." It was a bit too baronial for Skye's
taste, but that was how things were done on the island.
It was the first time he had arrived at the villa alone,
without Jocelyn. Agatha's eyes studied Skye as he took
both her hands in his. Satisfied, she pronounced, "You
look good in de face."

Myra, the housemaid, dropped a little curtsy and
shyly welcomed Skye home. With Agatha leading the
way and Overfine bringing up the rear with the
luggage, Skye was ceremoniously ushered into the villa,
fragrant with oleander blossoms.

Like most villas on Manchineel, Whistling Frog
was built out of the local coral stone. Jocelyn had the
pale stone painted a cool yellow, except for the corners
where alternate stone blocks had been left unpainted to
provide contrast. The roof line consisted of a series of
individual tiled roofs over each section of the villa,
creating an attractive tented effect. Like the servants'
quarters, the master bedroom suite stood apart in its
own separate building. While Overfine unpacked the
suitcases and hung Skye's clothes in the closets, Skye
went back to the jeep to retrieve the black case that
held the bronze urn containing Jocelyn's ashes. He
waited until he saw Overfine leaving the bedroom suite
with the empty suitcases. As soon as Overfine was
safely out of sight in the main building, Skye cut across
the lawn and entered his bedroom. With reverent care,
he placed the plastic case on the top shelf of a closet.

The staff had taken all the things he kept there —
lightweight tropical shorts and shirts, riding clothes and
boots, scuba equipment, and other personal items
necessary for island life — out of storage and put them in

the closets. He had left instructions that Jocelyn's belongings were to be distributed where there was the greatest need for them. But not on Manchineel. He didn't want to encounter someone wearing one of the outfits she wore with such casual elegance. Skye waited for the sudden stab of longing to subside before stepping out of his clothes and walking over to a closet for his bathing suit. As he opened the door he saw himself reflected in the floor-length mirror. He paused for a moment to take stock. At thirty-eight, his hair was still thick and brownish-red. Jocelyn had loved to run her hands through it. His six-foot-one frame was lean and toned. He could probably thank the horses for that. The face that looked back at him was Hollywood handsome. He would have to be blind not to be aware of the burning second looks many women gave him. Jocelyn, who attracted more than her share of second looks herself, had taken it in stride. Turning away from the mirror, he pulled on his swimsuit and stepped out onto the lawn.

The stubbly grass was rough on his bare feet as he headed for the pool. Another week and he wouldn't notice it. Myra came out of the villa to intercept him and give him a note that had just arrived from Star Spray.

Louella Harper owned Star Spray and her note welcomed Skye back to Manchineel and invited him to a party she was giving at Casuarina Bay that night. "Sevenish" was the appointed time. The "sevenish" made Skye smile. Louella had been born and raised in Iowa and had lived all her adult, married life in Grosse Pointe, Michigan. She had been left a wealthy widow when her workaholic husband, a top executive at Ford, dropped dead from a heart attack in his office. The year before his death they had purchased Star Spray, and Louella spent six months of every year there. Except for last year when failing kidneys made her a slave to the dialysis machine and she had to remain at home. Consciously or otherwise, she had adopted some of the mannerisms and speech patterns of the English aristocrats who flocked to Manchineel every winter. It didn't quite come off, but nobody minded. Everybody liked Louella. Besides, she threw great parties.

Skye frowned slightly as he read the postscript. "Princess Helen has graciously consented to attend." So "The Highness," as Princess Helen was invariably referred to, was in residence. The easy-going ambience of the island was always a little diminished when the Royal Flight arrived. Security officers from Scotland Yard lurked about — Skye wondered if Inspector Foxcroft was still in charge of the security detail — one of the best swimming beaches was cordoned off, and a certain protocol was imposed on the casually elegant social events that were so much a part of the island lifestyle. Weighting the note down on a table with a chunk of coral, Skye dove into the pool. Twenty brisk laps later, he hoisted himself onto a submerged concrete seat and smiled at the whistling frog painted on the end wall of the pool. Although the island was semi-arid, the pool overlooked a sea of green — rows of palm trees, their fronds rustling and tossing in the wind like the manes of spirited horses. Skye's smile faded at the memory of the eviscerated remains of the three young people.

Chapter Two

The narrow band of cloud just above the horizon meant there would be no green flash that night. Doves came in to the pool on whistling wings for a final drink, then a black swift flew past at an incredible rate of knots. Skye didn't bother to check his watch — it was always 6:10 when the first swift appeared. At 6:20 the sun dropped below the horizon with dramatic suddenness and the swift tropical night descended. A whistling frog, hidden in a croton bush by the garden shed, began its harsh bleeping. Skye leaned back in the chaise lounge and smiled to himself as another frog answered. The tiny tree frogs were very territorial; unlike other frogs, they never joined together in a chorus, just individual bleeps that ceased abruptly if one ventured too close. The insistent, piping call was the most familiar sound of soft tropical nights, and it expressed the quintessence of everything that was Caribbean. When he and Jocelyn heard them on the first night they spent in their newly purchased villa, they knew they had found its name.

It was time to get ready. Louella's invitation had said "sevenish" but, with Princess Helen attending, that meant not later than 7:20. The Princess made a practice of arriving thirty minutes after the appointed time and protocol required that all the guests be present when she appeared. Worse still, protocol also demanded that no one leave until she did. The Princess was a confirmed nighthawk with an awesome capacity for alcohol, and many parties turned into endurance contests as exhausted and bleary-eyed guests tried to stay awake while the chain-smoking royal downed one gin after another, growing more voluble and animated with each drink. She was invariably sullen and morose the following day and wasn't fit to look upon until she had her "elevenses" — a mid-morning gin and tonic.

* * *

The lights of the jeeps crawled over the dark hills like glowworms on parade as the party-goers headed for Casuarina Bay. Skye glanced up at the star-filled night and decided he could safely lower the jeep's canvas top. The procession of identical white vehicles inched their way over the rocky outcrop that led down to the beach and parked side-by-side under the feathery branches of the casuarinas, whispering in the breeze. When Skye switched off the engine, he could hear the pounding roar of the surf. Alighting from his Land Rover, he suddenly felt naked. This was the first party he'd attended on Manchineel since Jocelyn's death. As Skye paused to collect his thoughts before heading towards the throng, he looked down the path and smiled ruefully as he saw the familiar faded red flag that warned of dangerous swimming conditions. The red flag seemed never to come down, regardless of the size of the waves. Eventually visitors concluded that the Company simply couldn't be bothered checking out the beach every day and the more daring ones made their own decisions as to whether or not it was safe to swim. Last year a teenager had been caught in the undertow and swept out to sea. His distraught parents threatened to sue, but the Company complacently pointed out that their son had ignored the warning flag and had gone swimming at his own risk.

As Skye made his way towards his hostess, an overpowering miasma of sweet and cloying perfume announced the presence of Nick, the island's black entrepreneur, with his blonde of the year. He was wearing an embroidered white guyabera and a small fortune in gold chains. Nick was the proprietor of a bar that bore his name — Nick's — and he would be catering the party. He catered all the parties on the island. Skye and Nick shook hands perfunctorily and with an obvious lack of enthusiasm. Skye found Louella standing by the bonfire, her plump softness enveloped in a flowing muumuu. She greeted Skye warmly. He was a favourite of hers ever since he had helped her overcome her fear of flying by explaining exactly how airplanes managed to stay in the air. She had listened intently as he described how when air is bent around the top of the wing it pulls the air above it down. The pulling down of the air causes the pressure above the wing to become lower which creates lift that keeps the plane in the air. She thought about it for a moment then nodded acceptance. The cure was complete on one unforgettable afternoon when he let her take the controls of the forgiving 180.

"You look wonderful, Louella," said Skye, kissing her on both cheeks. They were warm and powdery. She did look immeasurably better than when he had last seen her, two years ago at Jocelyn's memorial service. Louella's colour was good, and her eyes, once dull and cloudy, were clear and shining. "You must have had the operation," he said.

She nodded happily. "It's like a miracle. Not to be chained to that machine and to be free to go where I want. I feel alive again."

"Where did you have it done? Detroit?"

"Heavens, no. It would be another two years before I got to the top of the list for a kidney transplant. I had it done at a very posh private clinic in Florida. It's almost like a spa."

Louella turned away to greet another guest as a waiter appeared at Skye's elbow and handed him a vodka tonic without being asked. Skye smiled his thanks. There was something comforting about a place where your every whim was known and catered to. Lord Fraser, resplendent in a kilt, mess jacket and sporran, came up to greet him, hand extended and a delighted smile on his rather craggy face. The Scottish nobleman was Skye's closest friend on the island. Skye sometimes thought of him as a living oxymoron. Robert Lovat Fraser had inherited a title that had been conferred on his family by the English crown in the early 1800s and spoke in the tones of the classically educated Englishman, yet he was Scottish to the core. Skye would never forget the first time he was introduced to him. On hearing Skye's name, Fraser had given a great shout of delight, uncharacteristically clapped him on the back and immediately launched into a long dissertation on the MacLeods of Skye. Skye knew the basic elements of the story from his father — also called Skye, as had been his grandfather. An ancestor had fought in a Highland regiment on the side of the British during the American Revolution and somehow, probably by deserting, had contrived to stay on in the new country when the war ended.

All this Skye knew, but Fraser was able to fill in the details, and describe the places that still resonated in Skye's tribal memory. He spoke of Dunvegan, a castle on a rocky cliff overlooking the sea that was the seat of the clan chief on the Isle of Skye. One night, while taken grandly with wine, Lord Fraser tried unsuccessfully to convince Skye and Jocelyn to change the name of their villa to Dunvegan. Jocelyn's face had been a study of horror and amused incredulity. Fraser's own villa, one of the largest on the island, built on a rocky promontory on the windswept Atlantic side, was called Beaufort after a castle near the river Beauly. When at home in Scotland, the Frasers lived in another ancient castle called Airdwold, on a small island in the same Beauly River. Fraser often complained that the cost of its upkeep was slowly bankrupting him. "And we don't have any Rembrandts or Gainsboroughs to sell off, either," he had added, "Celtic chieftains weren't much into culture back in those days. They were too busy feuding with each other." But he was scandalized when Skye had once innocently asked him why, if that was the case, he didn't simply shut the place down.

"Simon Fraser built Airdwold in 1746," His Lordship had spluttered, "and Frasers have lived in it ever since. Besides, the villagers depend on the estate for their livelihoods and I can't abandon them. Noblesse oblige, and all that."

Soon after building Beaufort, Fraser had brought over a piper, a member of the famous MacCrimmon clan of hereditary pipers, to instruct the villa's black butler in the art of playing the bagpipes so that His Lordship could awaken each day to the skirl of pipes. Fiona, Lord Fraser's serenely patrician wife, came over to greet Skye. "It's wonderful to have you back, Skye. We've missed you terribly. Especially Robert. Now you two can go back to having your learned discussions about everything under the sun."

"I already have some topics in mind," Skye grinned, pleasantly aware of how much he enjoyed the company of these two.

Over in the parking area, Nick cleared his throat noisily. A cavalcade of three jeeps was advancing slowly down the rocky trail. It was time for the "entrance." Inspector Foxcroft was riding in the passenger seat of the first jeep while one of his men drove. There were two other Scotland Yard detectives in the third vehicle. Except for the royal standard flying from the left fender, or "wing" as the English called it, the second jeep was identical to all the others. Curious to see who the royal companion was this year, Skye stared at the man climbing out from behind the wheel. With a faint sense of shock, he realized that he recognized him. Although his involvement with the horse show world had waned considerably in recent years, Skye still subscribed to the International Journal of the Horse, and the exploits of Harry Downing-Harris had been featured in recent editions. Downing-Harris was the youngest member of a revitalized English equestrian team that had recently won a World Cup in Dublin. The lanky horseman was at least a foot taller and more than twenty years younger than Princess Helen, but that was the way she increasingly seemed to like them.

Princess Helen occasionally went horseback riding with Skye and had always been fond of him, and she made her way directly to him, ignoring her hostess. He inclined his head in a modest bow and murmured, "Your Royal Highness." After one "Your Royal Highness," it was permissible to address her as "Ma'am." She hadn't

attended the memorial service but she had written a
thoughtful letter of condolence. The chances were that it
had been written by one of her ladies-in-waiting, but at
least she had signed it. Now she held out her hand to be
kissed, and Skye kissed the air just above it in the
prescribed manner. "We were so sorry about Jocelyn.
She was such a lovely person."

"Thank you, ma'am. And thank you for your letter."

Turning to Downing-Harris, she introduced Skye
as a fellow horseman. The young Guards officer
greeted this news with bored indifference. Skye had
intended to congratulate Downing-Harris on his
brilliant wins in the show ring, but the words died
unspoken in his throat. Was it possible the guy was
jealous? It seemed inconceivable that the dowdy, thick-
waisted Princess could inspire such feelings, but being
her acknowledged companion could have many
advantages in the Byzantine social world they
inhabited. As Downing-Harris turned to follow
Princess Helen over to greet the Frasers, Skye was
amused to see he had a badly receding chin.

Lady Fraser swept low in a practised curtsy and her
husband bowed from the waist. Finally, Princess Helen
deigned to greet her hostess. Louella Harper almost
stumbled as she attempted a curtsy, then uttered a
flustered "Oh, dear," as another jeep pulled into the
parking lot.

"Trust the Rastoks to make a gaffe like that,"
muttered Lord Fraser. The Rastoks were a wealthy
couple from La Jolla who rented Banyan every
February and March. The jeep jerked to a halt and a
slender figure sprang lithely over the tailgate.

In the flickering light of a torch, Skye saw with a
sudden lurch of his heart that it was Erin Kelly, the ex-
wife of the man who had killed Jocelyn. There was no

mistaking the face that had been splashed on the front page of every newspaper in America since the day she married Patrick Sullivan Kelly, the handsome, dissolute scion of a powerful political family. The drunken brute who, his belly full of Scotch, had raced out of control down a ski trail and smashed into Jocelyn, leaving her unconscious and broken. Without stopping or even looking back over his shoulder, he sped on, hoping to lose himself in the anonymity of the crowded ski hill. He would have got away with it too, except for a young skier who chased after him and followed him into the ski lodge. The same young man who later changed his story and refused to identify Kelly so that the charge of criminal negligence, which would have netted him a substantial jail term if convicted, was dropped. The same ambitious young man who subsequently found the means to enroll at a very expensive and prestigious university.

"Why didn't somebody warn me?" Skye demanded.

"Because nobody knew she was on the island," answered Lord Fraser, who, while no reader of the tabloids, had also recognized her immediately. "She must have just arrived today."

"I'm out of here!" Skye hissed.

"You can't do that. You have to deal with it now. You're bound to meet her sooner or later. Let's take a stroll on the beach while you come to terms with it." Fraser laid a fatherly hand on Skye's arm as they walked along a sandy path, bordered by sea grapes, to the beach. "She wasn't the one who killed Jocelyn, you know. She wasn't there. In fact, she probably hates that drunken boor as much as you do."

Skye realized that his older friend was probably right. Erin had no reason to love the Kellys. Skye, who had made it his business to look into the Kelly dynasty, knew how poisonous the relationship between the Kellys and their erstwhile daughter-in-law really was. Because of all the publicity, the whole western world knew it too. At first, the union between the beautiful blond socialite and the man who one day might be president had captured the imagination of the American public. In a way, the golden young couple became a substitute for the royalty the country never had, but subconsciously craved.

The honeymoon, both with themselves and with the press, was soon over as Patrick Kelly continued his philandering ways and his young wife, shaken by his blatant infidelity and intimidated by his domineering family, took refuge in the bottle and fell into alcoholism. While the honeymoon with the press might have ended, the troubled couple still made wonderful copy, and the media reported with glee that Erin had been charged with driving while intoxicated and that she had twice checked herself into a detoxification centre. Glossy magazines delighted in running photos of Patrick, his good looks fast deteriorating with his dissipated lifestyle, living it up in nightclubs with one interchangeable blonde after another. Erin bore his philandering with stoic silence until *Truth* ran a colour photograph of her naked husband making love to an equally naked woman on the deck of an anchored yacht in the Mediterranean. The day after the photo appeared, she filed for divorce. Some said it wasn't his adultery that bothered her, it was when she saw the photo and realized just how gross and bloated he had become.

The divorce quickly turned into one of those messy domestic sagas that hit the front pages and stay there. The marriage had produced a son, also named Patrick Sullivan Kelly, who was three years old at the time of the divorce and was already being groomed by the family as the heir who would continue the dynasty. The Kellys were determined to keep control of the child so that he could be brought up with a proper sense of his destiny. They also sincerely believed that Erin, whom they held in contempt for her drinking and her failure to stand up for herself, would be the worst possible influence on the boy. They were determined not only to maintain custody of young Patrick but, if they weren't able to eliminate Erin's visitation rights entirely, to restrict them to the barest possible minimum. The way to do that was to prove that Erin was an unfit mother, due to her alcoholism and depression. Her lawyers countered by attacking her husband's character. Thanks to his lurid lifestyle they didn't lack for ammunition. They also attacked the Kelly family itself, claiming that its oppressive, domineering atmosphere would smother the child's individuality.

When it was over, Patrick was to live with his father and Erin was to have visiting rights that would increase if she stayed sober. To the dismay of the family, she announced that she intended to give up alcohol, and then when enough time had passed, she would reapply for custody under the "changed status" rule. All that would have been nearly three years ago.

As Skye and Lord Fraser rejoined the other guests, it was apparent that a rapport had sprung up between Princess Helen and Erin Kelly. They probably felt a sense of kinship because of the way the world press treated them. Someone must have told Erin about Skye because her expression became guarded as she saw him approaching.

"I guess we both know something about each other," she said. In person, she was much different from what Skye had expected. From her photographs he expected her to be tall, statuesque and rather withdrawn. She was fairly tall all right, but she was slender rather than statuesque, and the expression on her attractive face had been open and friendly when she was conversing with the Princess.

"I'm afraid so." Skye hadn't intended to be so curt, but the words just popped out as the bitter memories came flooding back.

Erin, who had been about to extend her hand, dropped it as if she had been burned. The green eyes frosted over, and she smiled gratefully as Lord Fraser intervened and introduced himself. Then she turned away to continue her conversation with the Princess.

"I know what you're thinking, Robert. But when I think of ..."

"I understand, old boy." Fraser accepted a glass of whisky with a splash of water and no ice from a white-jacketed waiter. It was Glenlivet but Fraser bridled when anyone used the term "Scotch" instead of just "whisky." Whisky distilled in the highlands of Scotland was the only true whisky, and to describe it as "Scotch" was to confer an unwarranted recognition on the lesser liquors.

The four security officers were standing off by themselves at the edge of the lighted area. Still unsettled by his encounter with Erin, Skye went over to shake hands with Foxcroft. The detectives from Scotland Yard didn't mingle with the guests on the island, but Alan Foxcroft was a competent horseman and he was the one who accompanied the Princess when she went riding with Skye. In that way the two men had come to know and like each other. Once Skye had caught the inspector gazing at the Princess with a quizzical expression, as if pondering the workings of an inscrutable fate that had led to his playing nursemaid to this spoiled and willful creature. But Foxcroft's normal demeanour was one of cool professionalism. He introduced his fellow officers; Skye recognized one of them, whose name was Goodwin, as having been there in the past, but the other two were new. After exchanging a few cordial words with the inspector, Skye rejoined the party, now in full swing.

Down on the beach someone pointed out to the dark sea. The lights of three small boats were drawing steadily closer. Skye smiled in anticipation. The purring sound of throttled-back outboard motors drifted in with the onshore breeze, then a steel band burst into a highly stylized version of a Chopin polonaise, the music rolling in from the sea and crashing against the shore in a solid wall of sound. The steel band from neighbouring Union Island was making its entrance in its usual inimitable style. Next to the call of the whistling frog, the lively music of a steel band spelled Caribbean for Skye. At home in Bridgeport, Connecticut, he had every steel band CD the record store could locate, and on raw winter nights he and Jocelyn used to light a fire and play them one after another, letting their imaginations drift languorously down to their favourite islands. Joining the crowd streaming onto the beach, Skye could almost feel Jocelyn walking beside him, lips parted in excitement as the spine-tingling music grew louder and louder, until it seemed to fill the sky. But no one stood beside him as the members of the band, still playing their drums, leapt nimbly out of the pirogues.

The barbecue was buffet style, with the guests helping themselves and then sitting down at long trestle tables. There was no seating arrangement, but Detective Goodwin had come over to inform Skye that Princess Helen would like him to sit at her table. Erin must have received a similar command for she brought her plate over to the same table. Princess Helen, who was not above using her position for her own mischievous entertainment, had seated Erin next to her at the head of the table, directly across from Skye. Erin glanced at Skye as he sat down, then studiously looked away. She was explaining to the Princess that she and Mary Rastok, née Godfrey, had been classmates at Smith and had remained close friends. Skye liked Mary Rastok but had little use for her husband. It was Mary's family that had the money, and Gordon Godfrey was her trophy husband. Handsome, a superb tennis player and scratch golfer, Gordon devoted his days to his two favourite sports. He would have liked to have expanded his interests to include the pursuit of attractive women, but his wife kept him on too tight a rein. Gordon had lusted after Jocelyn, but from a distance. Jocelyn had dismissed him as a lightweight. The Rastoks hadn't been invited to join the Princess's table, but had tagged along after Erin.

A string of low-wattage bulbs shed their light on the scene and Skye saw that Erin's hair wasn't pure blond; it was softened and warmed with strands that had a brownish tinge. It was straight and bobbed chin-length to frame her small and exquisite features. Her complexion glowed and her eyes flashed green in the light of the torches. Princess Helen swallowed the last of her gin and tonic, nodded at a waiter to fill her wine glass and raised it in a toast to Skye. "It's good to have you back on the island, Skye."

"Thank you, ma'am," murmured Skye, genuinely touched by this unexpected gesture.

"Skye MacLeod," the Princess went on in a musing tone. "Such a perfect name for someone who flies airplanes."

"Strictly amateur," said Skye with a deprecating smile.

"Damn sight better than some commercial pilots I know," Lord Fraser, who was sitting beside Skye, muttered darkly. "Did you hear that we nearly bought the farm this afternoon?"

"The wind conditions were pretty tricky," Skye replied soothingly. "I think Andy just wanted to make sure he had things under control before he committed himself to a landing."

"You think so, do you? Well, I think the man was frightened out of his skin. The sweat was positively streaming off him by the time we finally managed to land."

The subject of the shark attack was brought up, but quickly derailed when Lord Fraser announced, "As Chairman of the Manchineel Corporation, I hereby forbid further discussion of shark attacks. I have stockholders to think of."

After Princess Helen added, "As one of those shareholders, I second that motion," the subject of the shark attack was dropped.

"What's the latest on the Prime Minister?" The Princess looked anxiously at Lord Fraser.

"Not good, I'm afraid," he replied gravely. "And getting worse by the day."

"Surely they're not going to let the poor man die? He must be entitled to some kind of priority."

"Apparently not. One gathers that to do so would be undemocratic and un-American. But that's not the real problem. The real problem is finding a match for his heart. Sir George tells me that in the case of a heart transplant, it's absolutely essential to have a perfect match. To make matters worse, the PM's blood type is not all that common. It's B-negative which, while not the rarest type, is still quite rare." Lord Fraser looked across the trestle table at Skye. "Do you know what we're talking about?"

"Only what I've read in the papers stateside. And that's not very much. All I know is that the Prime Minister is hospitalized somewhere in the States waiting for a new heart." Over the years, Skye had met Marcellus

Thomas, the popular Prime Minister of St. Vincent and the Grenadines, including Manchineel, on a number of occasions. The pragmatic Thomas who easily won every election was well-disposed towards Manchineel because of the revenue it brought in, and followed a strictly hands-off policy.

"He's in a New York hospital waiting to be flown to wherever and whenever a match shows up on the computer. If it ever does." Lord Fraser rubbed the side of his long, aristocratic nose. "Sir George also tells me that the chances of success in a heart transplant are much greater if there is a blood relationship between the donor and the recipient."

"That does tend to narrow the field a bit," Skye remarked. "It's one thing to donate a kidney to your sibling, but donating your heart is something else again."

"Precisely," said Lord Fraser with an amused smile.

"We can't afford to lose him, Robert," the Princess fretted. "He's such a pleasant man. So co-operative. If he dies, that odious little man, Gilbert Humphreys, will likely succeed him. I'm afraid Mr. Humphreys doesn't approve of our playful little ways. Humphreys is no friend of this island, Robert."

"I'm only too well aware of that, ma'am. We must all pray that a match is found before it's too late."

The deep, hypnotic beat of voodoo drums interrupted the Princess's sarcastic rejoinder to that pious platitude. The guests fell silent, looking at each other. Erin was the only one to glance in the direction of the sound. The others all knew it was coming from the native village, Sterling Hall, high up on the hill overlooking Maggins Bay. The Manchineel Company had recruited many of the labourers and household staff from the impoverished island of Caroun where the inhabitants were mostly descended from members of the Fon tribe imported as slaves from Benin in the late 1700s. With them, the slaves had brought their African religion and, over the years, elements of Christian rituals had been incorporated into their ceremonies. Many of the voodoo worshippers were also devout Christians, belting out fundamentalist hymns with great fervour, or attending mass, in the little white church on the hill that served both the Baptist and Roman Catholic congregations. This commendable ecumenancy was brought about not by brotherly and sisterly love between the two faiths, but rather because the Company would allow only one church to be built on the island. Despite the sinister aura that surrounds the practice of voodoo, the homeowners had learned that the worst to expect was to have some members of their staff carrying out their duties on the following day in an exhausted, half-dazed state.

Skye felt the skin on the back of his neck grow warm. He turned around on the bench to find Edwina staring at him. Tall and elegant, her extraordinarily long fingers, café au lait skin, and slender neck showed her Amharic ancestry. It had been Skye who had told her that she must be a descendant of that aristocratic Ethiopian tribe. Edwina Stewart was the nurse who, for all practical purposes, ran the Manchineel medical clinic. Skye looked away. Princess Helen had drained her glass, which was immediately filled by a hovering waiter. Other guests were also downing their drinks. While the residents of Manchineel had come to realize voodoo did not pose any danger to them, the incessant, atavistic beat of the drums did unsettling things to their nerves. Nick quickly rounded up the members of the steel band and the stirring strains of The White Cockade, which they had learned to please Lord Fraser, soon overrode the distant drums. But the voodoo drums could still be heard pulsing beneath the surface.

Skye finished his coffee, bowed to the Princess and walked over to where Edwina was standing at the far edge of the firelight, the light reflected redly in her huge brown eyes. She had removed her sandals, and barefoot in the sand, was almost as tall as he was.

"I thought you were in Grenada."

"I came back on the last flight."

"You missed the excitement."

"I know. Sir George said you were very helpful."

"Is that what this is all about?" Skye turned to look in the direction of the village, three valleys away.

"No. It is because of what you brought on the island."

"What are you saying?"

"It is not good, Skye. They know you brought your wife's ashes with you."

"How do they…? Oh, Jason, of course."

"Yes. He tell everybody." Edwina paused. Out here on the beach the sound of the voodoo drums was clearly audible. "The loa they are summoning tonight is a dangerous one."

"Baron Samedi." Before Skye could say more than the name of the loa, they were interrupted by Sir George Glessop, who was lurching across the sand toward them, glass of port in hand. Sir George Glessop, FRCS (Lon.), had once been chief of surgery at St. Michael's Hospital in London. Skye and Jocelyn had long ago decided that if they ever suffered from anything more serious than the common cold they would fly back to the mainland for treatment, rather than entrust themselves to the care of the once-eminent doctor. Alcohol had finally gotten to Sir George, to the extent that the medical profession, notoriously tolerant and protective of its members, had reluctantly decided that he should be eased out of the practice of medicine. It was rumoured that some sort of a scandal had finally forced the medical governing body to act, although no one, except Lord Fraser, of course, seemed to know what it was. Through the good offices of Lord Fraser, Sir George had landed an appointment in Manchineel where his responsibilities were undemanding and where Edwina Stewart did virtually all the work. That didn't prevent the Company from making much of the fact that the distinguished former chief of surgery at St. Michael's was on hand to look after whatever medical problems might arise.

Swaying on his feet, Sir George repeated his thanks for Skye's help that afternoon. Skye scarcely heard him, his thoughts were on the implications of what Edwina had said. He had to get back to the Whistling Frog. Turning on his heel, he strode across the sand to thank his hostess and make his excuses to the Princess. To everyone's relief, she decided to leave as well. "That damn drumming is really too barbaric."

Downing-Harris hastily finished his drink and draped a fur wrap around her bare shoulders as she stood up.

Chapter Three

T he black case was no longer on the top shelf of the closet. Skye cursed his stupidity in not realizing that the case and its precious contents would be irresistible to voodooists. Adrienne. Damn her black heart! He had to retrieve the case before all that was left of Jocelyn was subjected to some hellish ritual. Maybe it was already too late. Probably not. Jocelyn's ashes would be destined to play a starring role in tonight's obscene ceremony and the climax wouldn't come for some time yet.

Cursing Adrienne and his own stupidity under his breath, Skye raced across the lawn to the staff quarters. Although the night was warm and the breeze had died away, the windows were closed and tightly shuttered to keep out any spirits that might be roaming the night. Could Overfine have been in on it? No way. He and Agatha were both from St. Vincent and would have nothing to do with what Agatha scornfully called "them heathen orgies." Rubbing his eyes, Overfine cautiously opened the door to Skye's insistent pounding.

Skye told him to get dressed and explained what had happened. Overfine paused with one foot in his right pant leg and looked over his shoulder in wide-eyed disbelief.

"You ain't planning on goin' down to that place, are you, boss?"

"I am. And I would like you to come with me. But you don't have to. Not if you don't feel up to it. But I can't let them do this to Mistress Jocelyn's memory."

That was the clincher, as Skye knew it would be. Overfine finished pulling on his pants.

"Don't use the lights," Skye said as Overfine's hand reached for the switch on the jeep's dash.

The native village sprawled down the far side of a hill. Ironically, it commanded the best view on the entire island. The Company had once considered moving it, but that came to naught because no one could agree on where it should be moved to. At the foot of the hill, Skye told Overfine to pull over to the side of the road and cut the engine. The sound of the three Rada drums was much louder now and grew steadily louder as Skye and Overfine walked up the hill, keeping well clear of the narrow asphalted road. Reaching the top, they skirted the darkened village. By Company decree, all the small wooden houses were identical. They were all painted white with green trim and were built on stilts to counteract the steep slope and to permit air to circulate underneath the floor. All were tightly shuttered. Those belonging to believers and non-believers alike. There were no non-believers, just non-practitioners. All believed completely and fearfully in the power of the voodoo gods.

The path branched off into a grove of casuarina trees, their jointed, leafless branches hanging motionless in the still air. Skye touched Overfine's elbow and they stepped off the path and into the trees as they saw lights up ahead. A few yards further on, Skye whispered that Overfine was to remain there, out of sight. Overfine made as if to protest, then, seeing the determined look on Skye's face, a look he knew well, nodded a reluctant acceptance.

"If things start getting out of control, you can run in and take the case from me," Skye said as he moved away.

Reaching the edge of the clearing, Skye crouched behind a tree. There was little need of concealment. The worshippers were transfixed, intent only on what was taking place within the temple. Nor would there be any sentries. White people never ventured near the village after dark, and those natives who were not voodoo worshippers could be counted on to remain indoors, no doubt praying to their own god. The temple was a thatch-roofed shed with walls that extended half-way to the roof. Ostensibly it was a storage shed, but the items it stored, wheelbarrows, carts and wagons, were all designed to be easily removed when it was time for it to serve its true function as a tonnelle.

Skye nodded to himself as he spotted the old man with a pipe between his teeth, sitting on a chair outside the entrance to the temple. That was Papa Legba, keeper of gates and crossroads. Papa Legba was summoned early in the proceedings since his presence made it easier for the other gods to enter the temple.

The scene was lit with the harsh, baleful light of two gas lanterns, leaving large areas in shadow. Some fifty worshippers sat on the earthen floor, chanting in unison. Closer to the altar, young women dressed in white sat cross-legged. One of their number lay on her back, twitching and moaning. Those next to her stroked her as if praising her and seeking to share in her trance.

The altar was crowded with bottles of rum and

wine, mounds of cornmeal, chunks of raw meat and cakes. Candles burned with clear, straight flames and wicks floated in coconut shells filled with oil. Adrienne, resplendent in a scarlet robe and feather headdress, traced a pentagram and other cabalistic signs in front of the altar with cornmeal poured from a bottle. Skye focused his binoculars on her as she straightened up and faced the audience. If he had not witnessed it before, he would have been shocked at the transformation. Her attractive, rather youthful face, with its air of good-humoured sensuality, was now a rigid mask beneath the black and scarlet plumes, lips drawn back in a ferocious snarling grin. The chanting rose and fell, interspersed with voices that soared above it in ululating solos. A shape in the semi-darkness to the right of the altar caught Skye's eye and he zeroed in on it with the binoculars. It was Penelope dressed in a white tube top, rocking gently from side to side, her eyes closed. She seemed to be crooning to herself.

With the co-operation of Adrienne, Skye, who had a restlessly enquiring mind, had been an unseen witness to a number of voodoo rites. But tonight was different from the others. Tonight there was a palpable current of ecstatic fear, of deeper and darker mysteries that would unfold if the gods were willing. Skye knew only too well what would be used to tempt the most powerful of gods. He swept the area around the altar with the glasses. There was no sign of the plastic case. He knew it was there somewhere and tensed himself for action as soon as it appeared.

A man with a seamed, stubbly face approached the altar, holding a black cock out to Adrienne. While the altar servants held it, she drew a cross on its back with white flour. Another assistant crumbled a cake into the palm of her hand and she held it out to the cock. A moan of ecstasy went up as the cock pecked at the food. Adrienne stroked the fowl gently, then snatched it up and began a wild dance, whirling, holding the bird high over her head, its wings frantically fluttering, while the Rada drums beat an insistent tattoo. Then in one swift motion, she bit off its head and danced through the crowd, spraying the acolytes with the blood spurting from its neck, splattering their spotless white gowns with crimson.

Another black cock was brought in, and after a long suspenseful wait for it to peck at the food, was similarly sacrificed. This time Adrienne collected some of the spurting blood in a small bowl which she handed to a blood-splattered acolyte crawling on her belly across the floor. The girl took the bowl, drank from it, and slithered across the floor, offering it to the supplicating hands reaching out for the bowl. Damballa, the great serpent god, had arrived and mounted his "horse."

A brown goat, tethered to a post at the far end of the temple, suddenly bleated in terror. With the intelligence of its kind, it realized that death was in the air. The altar servant helped the half-dazed Penelope to her feet and led her toward the altar, holding her tightly by the arm to keep her from stumbling. Her mother held out her arms to her, crying, "Damballa calls you! Come to the great Damballa!"

As Penelope half fell into her mother's arms, another assistant led the little goat to the altar. The assistant knelt before it, rubbed its small hooves with oil, and traced a cross and circle on its forehead with blood from the cocks. Then he bowed low and held out some green leaves for the little goat to eat. Adrienne, meanwhile, was hugging Penelope, moaning and weeping as though they were to be parted forever. The altar assistant forced them apart, pushed the girl to her knees and held a bottle of rum to her lips. Her mother, once again the high priestess, her face a rigid mask, began to pour oil and wine over Penelope, working it into her hair and smearing her face and bare shoulders with it.

Penelope was on all fours, the palms of her hands flat on the ground, facing the goat. Adrienne, her arms outstretched, stood over them chanting over and over, "Damballa calls you. Damballa calls you." Gradually the girl and the young goat grew quiet, staring into each other's eyes, their foreheads almost touching, while red ribbons were tied on the goat's horns and woven into the girl's hair. As the priestess continued her monotonous chant the girl began a low, piteous bleating and the goat cried with a voice that was eerily human. The goat's penis slipped its sheath and became fully erect and the girl's nipples hardened under the thin cotton of her shift. She raised her eyes heavenward, exposing the curving line of her neck. A long, oblong bowl was slipped between the two heads and an assistant squatted on his heels and held out a branch covered with tender green leaves. He jiggled it slightly as if to attract their attention and a long sigh went up from the congregation as the girl began to nibble the leaves.

The mambo, holding a machete honed to a glistening edge, turned from the altar. The goat didn't flinch as she touched its neck with the razor sharp blade, nor did it cry out as she deftly slit its throat. As the blood gushed into the wooden bowl, the girl, her body as taut and tight as a bowstring, leapt into the air with a strangled cry of agony, then sprawled senseless before the altar.

Skye left the shelter of the trees and sprinted across the clearing in a crouching run. A sacrifice such as this was intended to invoke a truly powerful god and he knew who it would be. Papa Legba had abandoned his keeping of the gate; he had turned his chair around to stare into the temple. Skye knelt by the chest-high wall and cautiously raised his head to peer over the top. His nostrils were immediately assailed with a rich miasma of smells — blood, human sweat, smoke from the oil lamps and other less identifiable odours.

The substitution sacrifice, so close to that most powerful of rituals, the dread sacrifice of the "goat with no horns," had unleashed a frenzy of religious ecstasy. Two elderly women were carrying the unconscious Penelope off to one side where they would tend to her. Swarms of loas descended from the roof and sought out their favourite mounts. Nearly half the people were "possessed," rolling on the ground, or prancing through the audience with up-stretched arms and rapt, trance-like expressions. One of the young acolytes stood up and began to rip off her bloodstained gown, shredding the flimsy cloth with frantic fingers. A muscular youth, bare to the waist, slipped out of the crowd and began to dance with her.

The Rada drums spoke in a rolling tattoo like muted thunder, and the frantic activity within the temple ceased as though time had stopped. Eyes rolled heavenward as the drums beat out an imperious summons. Would the great god come to them? A sibilant whisper of indrawn breath swept through the crowd of worshippers as Baron Samedi appeared before them. As always the loa was wearing a top hat, a long black frock coat, and tattered striped pants. He also wore dark sunglasses to signify that death was blind. Adrienne bowed low in obeisance to the god, her plumed headdress almost touching the ground. Kneeling, eyes fixed on the ground, she held out the gleaming black case to the "keeper of cemeteries."

Skye vaulted over the wall and dashed toward the altar, jumping over the bodies that lay moaning and writhing on the earthen floor, avoiding an acolyte and her partner masturbating each other, and pushed aside a man who staggered into his path, his eyes glazed either with rum or a trance of possession. No one tried to stop him; their dazed minds were incapable of reacting to his sudden appearance. But an ominous growl went up when he tore the case from the god's grasp. A quick glance at Baron Samedi's face told Skye that he had never seen the man before. Undoubtedly he would be a high-ranking houngan from one of the other islands. It was impossible to see his eyes behind the dark glasses, but his deeply lined face was expressionless and he reeked of rum. As a god, he would have been stuffed with rum and food before being summoned. He offered no resistance as Skye grabbed the case from him. Out of the corner of his eye Skye saw Adrienne's hand stealthily reaching for the bloody machete lying on the altar. He was closer to it, and picked it up before she could reach it. "Snap out of it, Adrienne!" he barked. "You're in over your head." But she seemed not to hear him.

Holding the machete down at his side, he turned to face the crowd. The sacrilege he had committed against Baron Samedi had shocked some of them back into consciousness. Skye noted grimly that most of those who had regained their senses were men. Scowling, muscular men. He stole a quick sideways glance at Adrienne. The hard lines of her face were beginning to soften. Standing next to her, Baron Samedi seemed scarcely aware of his surroundings. Skye lowered the machete to the ground and began to walk toward the exit. Two men, field workers from the look of them, moved to block his path. Holding the case in both hands, he pointed it at them and they fell back, crossing themselves. Other members of the congregation also hastily crossed themselves and recoiled from the dread object, leaving Skye an unimpeded path to the exit.

"Stay under cover, Overfine!" he hissed as he saw a movement in the trees. Overfine, who had been about to leave the protection of the casuarinas to join his boss, immediately recognized the wisdom of this advice and remained where he was. There was no point in letting his friends and neighbours know he had played any part in this night's business.

* * *

"What you gonna do with that thing, Master Skye?" Overfine finally mustered the courage to ask as he parked the jeep in the driveway. "It be powerful bad medicine."

"Mistress Jocelyn loved this place more than any other in the world. She once said that when she died she wanted her ashes scattered on the ocean. That's what I am going to do. Tomorrow night." He walked around the hood of the jeep to stand beside his servant. "I want you to come with me, Overfine. So you can tell the people what has been done and that the ashes are gone. Will you do that? For her? I know it would comfort her to know that you were there."

Overfine swallowed, then straightened his shoulders. "You can count on me, Mister Skye." He looked at the case Skye was holding with an expression that was no longer fearful, but filled with tenderness. "And so can she."

"Thank you, Overfine. Tomorrow I want you to spread the word about what we are going to do. That way people will know her ashes are no longer on the island."

Chapter Four

God, the thought of his Jocelyn being made a part of that obscene ritual! Skye examined the outside of the case. It was unmarked. He twirled the dial of the combination lock that wouldn't have lasted thirty seconds against someone with a hammer, and lifted the cover. The bronze urn rested in its bed of styrofoam. Skye took a deep breath and unscrewed the top of the urn. The grey-white ash and bits of bone were undisturbed. As always, he winced at the sight of some of her teeth mixed in with the ashes. But the important thing was that her remains had not been tampered with. He had not failed her completely. What would they have done if he had not intervened? What devilish purpose did they have in mind for the urn and its contents? Skye shuddered and pushed the thought away.

In its place came memories of the traumatic days after the accident on the ski slope. Unconscious, Jocelyn had been flown to Calgary in a helicopter ambulance and placed on a life-support system in the intensive care ward. At first, he had refused to admit the possibility that she would not recover. It was not until an intensive care doctor asked if he would like a pastoral visit that he began to face up to the awful possibility. Skye had been indignant when the doctor said that he was not the one in charge of Jocelyn's case and thought of demanding to speak to the specialist who was treating her. Before he could say anything, however, he was informed that the specialist who was treating Jocelyn had a policy of never being in direct contact with the relatives of his patients.

Jocelyn's widowed father, a retired physician, flew in from Scottsdale and was greeted warmly by the intensive care staff. Here was a fellow professional who would understand the situation and the decision that had to be made. Dr. Lewis listened gravely as the neurosurgeon showed them the CAT scan of Jocelyn's brain, explaining that she had suffered a severe brain trauma. Skye had to swallow hard when the neurosurgeon, sympathetically but clinically, went on to say that her brain had swollen, closing the reservoir of spinal fluid. When he said there was no evidence of spinal fluid in her brain, and the monitor showed no sign of brain activity, Jocelyn's father looked at Skye and sadly shook his head.

"We have to let her go, son," he had said when the two of them were alone. "She's brain dead, and you and I know she could never stand to exist like that."

Unable to speak, Skye had nodded silent agreement.

Both Jocelyn and Skye had signed organ donor consents. It had been her idea. After reading some material put out by HOPE — the Human Organ Procurement and Exchange organization — she had said, "Skye, we're both healthy and we lead kind of a high-risk lifestyle, with the airplane and horses." Ironically, she hadn't mentioned skiing. They signed the forms on the back of their driver's licences that same afternoon.

She was kept alive for another forty-eight hours so that a team from Harvard could fly in to retrieve her heart. The computer network showed there was a potential recipient in Boston who was a perfect match. Local surgical teams retrieved her liver, kidneys, pancreas and corneas for patients in western Canada.

At first, Skye had been almost sickened by the thought of his adored wife being dismembered like that. But then he began to take comfort from the fact that she was helping others to lead longer and fuller lives. At least her death was not entirely in vain. As always, that thought was followed by an inner rage that the son-of-a-bitch who had killed her had gotten away with it. The Kelly power and influence had seen to that. There had never been the slightest expression of remorse or regret from the Kellys. The clan had closed ranks and took the position that whatever had happened had nothing to do with them. And now the former wife of that bastard was here on Manchineel.

A huge moth, as big as a bat, banged against the screen, waking Skye from his unhappy reverie. He picked up the case and carried it with him to the master bedroom suite where he shoved it under the bed. He knew what he would do in the morning.

* * *

Compared to the Manchineel airstrip, the runway of the Grantley Adams Airport in Barbados seemed to go on forever. Skye applied enough power to keep the 180 a few feet in the air before touching down halfway along the runway. He taxied over to the far end of the terminal where Manchineel Air was located. They knew him there; customs wouldn't be a problem and, besides, he had the necessary papers for the ashes.

Inside the office, Donald Gillespie, who flew the left-hand seat on Manchineel Air's Twin Otter, was conferring with a mechanic. After shaking hands, he asked a few desultory questions about the flying conditions between Manchineel and Barbados. Skye told him that, as usual, it was "Caribbean perfect" — unlimited visibility, high scattered cumulus clouds. Still chatting, Gillespie walked with Skye over to the "Air Crew Only" gate, where the customs officer glanced briefly at Skye and the knapsack he was carrying and waved him through.

* * *

"I know why you are here, my son. I got a call this morning." Father Donahue led the way into the cluttered livingroom of the rectory. His name was as Irish as "Paddy's pig," but the portly priest was black.

"You've heard what happened, then." Skye wasn't surprised.

Although his parish was in downtown Bridgetown, Father Donahue went over to Manchineel every Sunday to celebrate mass in the little white church. One of his Manchineel parishioners, undoubtedly a scandalized one, had called to tell him about last night's dark saturnalia.

The priest watched as Skye carefully placed the knapsack on the floor, undid the straps and lifted the black case out. "I am interested in why you came to me. Neither you nor Jocelyn are of the Catholic faith." He smiled almost mischievously. "Maybe it's because you think my ju ju is stronger than that of my Protestant brothers?"

"Something like that," admitted Skye. "Will you bless her remains, Father?"

"Of course I will, Skye. She was a lovely woman.

Come with me." The priest held out his hands for the case.

* * *

A few solitary worshippers, women with scarves wrapped around their heads, knelt in prayer in the vast nave of the old stone church. Skye, his head bent in solitary meditation, sat in a front pew. A white-robed assistant entered from a side door and lit three white candles with a taper. Father Donahue entered from another door and began to celebrate mass. The solitary worshippers, realizing that they would have the unexpected benefit of communion, quietly moved up to the front benches. The priest delivered an extemporaneous eulogy that was as moving a tribute to Jocelyn as Skye had ever heard.

After communion, of which Skye did not partake, Father Donahue asked Skye to come forward and hold the case. After reading a lengthy prayer, he raised his arms in benediction and blessed both the departed and her grieving husband.

"Thank you, Father. Now she can rest in peace," said Skye as he bade the priest goodbye.

"Bless you, my son." A frown darkened the priest's round, cheerful face. "My Manchineel brothers and sisters are going to hear from me come Sunday, I can tell you."

* * *

Jason Carmichael was on duty at the Manchineel customs desk. His eyes were bloodshot and there was a greyish cast to his black skin. What had the self-righteous customs official been up to last night? He wiped the beads of sweat from his forehead with a large red handkerchief that also effectively hid his eyes, and motioned Skye to be on his way.

* * *

The wall safe was too small to hold the case, but it would take the urn. Skye removed the bronze urn from its plastic carrying case and placed it inside the safe. He should have done that right from the start. But the villas were supposed to be inviolate. Strictly off-limits. Whistling Frog, like many of the other villas, had been designed by a renowned English architect who made them airy and open to take advantage of the constant trade winds. It made for delightful living — at the cost of security. The place was a sieve. Security wasn't supposed to be a problem on the island, especially back when the villas were designed. It hadn't mattered — until now.

With the ashes safely stowed, Skye went looking for Adrienne. If she was not too exhausted to work, he knew where to find her. She was there, standing on the reef, plucking sea urchins, the white ones with soft spines, from the rocks and placing them in a pail floating beside her. Skye climbed out of the jeep and walked out on the little jetty. A number of small boats, including his eighteen-foot Boston whaler, bobbed gently against the pilings. Looking down, he smiled at the green frog logo painted on the whaler's transom. There would be work for the little boat that night. Adrienne, anchored the floating pail and waded through the knee-high water toward him. Reaching the edge of the reef, she dove in, swam across the narrow channel, and porpoised onto the jetty.

She said nothing as she stood, dripping, beside him, seemingly fascinated by the distant, mist-shrouded horizon. The only sign of fatigue or stress was a nerve twitching under her right eye. Skye let the silence build before saying, "I thought you and I were friends, Adrienne."

"Adrienne, the lady who fishes for the hotel, and you are friends. Adrienne, the mambo, has no friends, only the gods."

"What you did last night was wrong."

"With the gods there is no right or wrong," she murmured, still staring at the horizon.

"You and I are no longer friends, Adrienne."

She turned to face him. "If we are not friends, we are enemies. Adrienne can be a dangerous enemy."

The mambo, who was also a boucor, an adept at black magic, could be a dangerous enemy indeed — to her credulous followers who believed in the power of black magic. Skye had heard of cases where strong, healthy men, learning that a curse had been placed on them, sickened and died. Adrienne herself had told him of an instance where a man had gone mad searching the jungle for a doll with a string around its neck that day-by-day was gradually drawn tighter and tighter. The hapless man had died of suffocation, unable to breathe. Skye knew that this was due to the power of suggestion. But, the thought of the angry mambo secretly collecting something from his person, a fingernail clipping, a few strands of hair, and working it into a doll fashioned in his image, was not a particularly pleasant one. Once the doll was made she could do with it as she wished — stick pins in it, break its limbs, strangle it, or condemn it to whatever fate she could devise.

"I can be dangerous too, Adrienne," said Skye. "Remember that."

She gave him another haughty stare, then turned her back on him and dove off the jetty.

* * *

With time to kill, Skye decided to drive over to the stables and check out the new horse Elizabeth Mallory was so keen on. His route took him past the tennis courts. Erin was playing singles with Gordon Rastok. Watching her lithe, athletic figure bouncing around the clay court, smashing the ball back to her opponent, it was hard to believe that once she had been in the depths of alcoholism and self-hatred. Mary Rastok was standing on the sidelines, next to a small boy and another woman. She waved at Skye to stop. Skye was fond of Mary. Her features were plain but pleasant; there was a good-natured, down-to-earth quality about her. He braked the jeep to a halt and climbed out. Walking over to join Mary, he saw that the boy had to be Patrick Kelly III — he was a spitting image of his father. No wonder he was so important to the Kelly dynasty.

Leaving her two companions behind, Mary stepped forward to greet Skye.

"The local grapevine was working well this morning. I've heard the wildest stories about last night," she said. "Our houseboy is walking around like a zombie."

"It had its moments."

"So they are true. I gather you arrived in the nick of time, like the U.S. Cavalry."

"You could say that."

"Skye, I am terribly sorry about last night. When I invited Erin to Louella's party, I didn't think that you would be there. It's been so long since you've been to Manchineel. And, well, you know. Please do accept my apologies."

"It's okay, Mary. It's not the end of the world. I admit that I was taken by surprise, but — I can't hold her responsible for her husband's actions."

"Her ex-husband, Skye. She's very much divorced from Patrick Kelly. You've no idea how difficult it was to get Erin to come — and to bring young Patrick along, too."

"Who's that woman with the boy? His nanny?"

"A bit more than that. Her name is Brenda Fewster. She's a trained social worker. She's the only reason the Kellys let Patrick come. By the way, he's a great admirer of yours. He's seen your little plane and heard how you fly it all the way from Connecticut."

For the first time Skye smiled. "When I file my flight plans, the meteorologists look at me like I'm Lindberg. Does the boy know about the connection between me and his father?"

"Are you kidding? The official line is that it never happened."

The tennis match was over. Erin and Gordon were shaking hands at the net. Skye turned away, and Mary said to his retreating back, "Remember, Skye. She didn't do it."

The words struck home. He turned to face her. "I will try, Mary. I will really try." Deep in thought, he switched on the ignition and drove off. The visit to the stables could wait for another day.

Chapter Five

S kye carefully removed the single strand of hair from
the comb and flushed it down the toilet. From now
on he would be careful not to leave anything connected
with his person where Adrienne might be able to get at
it. He let himself out of his bedroom suite and walked
through the early evening darkness to the main
building where Overfine would serve him a lonely
dinner. The bright-eyed face of a mongoose stared at
him from the dense green foliage of a "firecracker"
plant and was quickly withdrawn as he passed.

As was the custom, Overfine reeled off the menu in
his deep baritone voice. Callaloo soup — Skye's favourite
— sorbet to cleanse the palate, red snapper, which Skye
had finally convinced Agatha to serve blackened,
followed by Port-au-Prince salad and pawpaw custard for
dessert. At Skye's insistence, the staff had reluctantly
eliminated the cheese course when he was in residence.
The wine was a white California Chardonnay. Conscious

of the night's work that lay ahead, Skye was going to confine himself to one glass, but he motioned Overfine to pour another. It was Jocelyn's favourite wine — Sterling Chardonnay — and he would toast her with it.

* * *

Two hours later, they set out with Overfine driving and Skye cradling the case in his lap. The entire island seemed to be aware of their mission. Obviously, Overfine had spread the word. A gibbous moon lent its fitful light to their passage as it ducked in and out of scudding clouds. Native children, almost invisible in the dark, peered curiously and fearfully from the side of the road. Skye tensed as they approached the seawall, the place where the youth of the island congregated at night to court, sing songs, and exchange gossip. The white dresses of the young women glimmered in the moonlight. He wondered how many of them had been wearing a very different white dress last night. The thin, almost transparent, dress of an acolyte. God, was it only last night?

All of the youths jumped down from the wall as the jeep drew nearer. Overfine glanced at Skye and shifted into second, ready to smash his way through if anyone tried to stop them. Skye relaxed when the men began to pull off the woolen caps that many of them wore. They stood silently as the jeep went past, some of them crossing themselves, and all of them standing with bowed heads.

"The mistress very popular with the people, Mister Skye."

Skye nodded and tightened his grip on the case. "You'll soon be at peace, darling," he whispered.

The jetty seemed deserted, yet he had the feeling of being watched. If there was to be an attempt to steal the case, this was the most likely place. As well as being the last chance. But no one attempted to intercept them as the two men made their way to the whaler, the jetty's wooden planks moving and shifting under their feet. The planks were uneven, forcing Skye to concentrate on his footing, so as not to stumble and fall. That would have been the final indignity for Jocelyn.

The Mercury outboard purred quietly in reverse as Overfine backed the whaler out into the narrow channel and headed for the open sea. As they neared the mouth of the channel, Skye stood up and pulled on the painter to raise the bow and keep them from being drenched by spray from the waves that piled up against the reef. When they were well offshore, they turned south, heading for Tamarind Beach on the southern tip of the island. Because it was more remote than the other equally beautiful cays and beaches, and because the rock-strewn goat track petered out a half-mile from the beach, hardly anyone went there. Except for Skye and Jocelyn, whose favourite picnic spot it was. One October afternoon, the year before Jocelyn was killed, they had revelled in its isolation as they feasted on cold lobster salad, washed down with white Chardonnay, and swam nude in the gentle surf, playfully touching each other until, unable to stand it any longer, they ran laughing hand-in-hand across the beach to make love beneath the tamarind trees.

They had led a golden life, he and Jocelyn. Deeply and equally in love with each other — that equal bit was not all that common in marriages and relationships — healthy, good looking — no, Jocelyn was beautiful — and with enough financial resources to possess that greatest luxury of all — time to enjoy themselves and pursue the things that interested them.

One cloud marred their happiness and at times threatened to come between them. At the age of 19 Skye had come down with a severe case of the mumps. Some years later, at the insistence of the family doctor, he underwent tests that determined he was sterile. Not impotent, Skye smiled to himself at the thought, but sterile.

Jocelyn occasionally remarked that this had done much to shape Skye's character — that he compensated for it by flying airplanes, riding jumping horses, engaging in extreme-level skiing, and cultivating an insatiable curiosity about things. "It also," she had once added, "is probably why you are so chivalrous."

"Chivalrous? Me?"

"Yes, you. You are chivalrous, Skye. In the old-fashioned sense. You are quick to help people. Believe me, I'm not complaining. Far from it."

In the early years of their marriage Skye's infertility was not an issue but then Jocelyn began to long for a child. Skye was prepared to adopt a child, but that wasn't enough for Jocelyn. She wanted to bear her own child, and in order to do that, she was prepared to be impregnated with sperm from an anonymous donor whose credentials would be thoroughly checked by the fertility clinic. The idea horrified Skye and for years he resisted it adamantly. But he loved his wife and finally couldn't stand making her unhappy. Ironically, he had planned to tell her to go ahead on the last day of the fatal ski trip.

Spray from an errant wave splashed Skye, snapping him out of his reverie. The whaler was closing the south coast, and Frigate Island, Manchineel's closest neighbour, loomed out of the darkness. The few scattered pinpricks of light attested to the fact that it was virtually uninhabited, save for a skeleton caretaking crew. Skye sometimes thought of it as Manchineel's dark sister. The island took its name from the frigate birds who soared in from their endless oceanic wanderings to nest in the mangrove swamp on its windward coast.

The island had been purchased four years ago by the Frigate Company, a company incorporated under the laws of the Turks & Caicos, one of several Caribbean tax havens. The intent had been to turn it into an exclusive resort, like Manchineel. But the company had encountered difficulties in raising money; it was rumoured that some potential investors were scared off by the fact that the island lacked a suitable beach. It was indented with many coves and cays, but they were ringed with rock and gravel, not powder-soft sand. And it also seemed that the market wasn't ready for another expensive resort. Whatever the reason, Frigate remained undeveloped and deserted.

Once, Skye and Jocelyn had taken the whaler and a picnic lunch into Hurricane Hole, a deeply indented mangrove swamp on the leeward side. They intended to explore the island, but had been warned off by a rifle-toting guard. Adrienne had once let slip that one of the guards was a high-ranking houngan, but this one had looked much too young for that exalted office.

Jocelyn had been researching Manchineel's history, beginning with its days as a sugar plantation. She intended to publish a booklet on the subject. In the course of her research she had come across some interesting material about the neighbouring islands, including the fact that Frigate had a history of failed enterprises. Years ago some enterprising souls set up a fish packing plant on the windward side. Tumbledown plant buildings were the sole reminders of that ill-fated venture. Some local farmers tried to raise goats on the island, but even they failed to thrive on its barren soil.

Skye raised his hand and Overfine throttled back. With the motor idling, the only motion was the gentle swell of the sea. Unexpectedly, Overfine began to sing in his powerful, choir-trained voice. Skye remained seated, his head bowed, as the familiar, comforting words of "Abide With Me" rolled out across the dark sea. When it was over, he reached down and lifted the bronze urn from its case. Unscrewing the top, he stood up, the soft onshore breeze cool on his face. Exchanging places with Overfine, he tilted the urn over the stern, the ashes fanning out in a fine, grey veil. Fragments of bone made a small splash as they fell into the water. For an appalled moment Skye thought they were going to float, until they began to slip beneath the surface, the teeth sinking first. Upending the urn, he shook out the last remnants of ash, then rinsed it in the sea. Now Jocelyn's memory was safe. The urn. He hadn't thought about that. He hesitated for a moment, then filled it with water and watched it sink, throwing the top in after it.

Standing on the shore, Adrienne Jones focused the 30x spotting scope Skye had given her after she had let him watch his first voodoo ceremony, and smiled her satisfaction. She had been sure that Skye would scatter the ashes off Tamarind Beach.

Skye was about to put the motor in gear, when he caught a movement on the periphery of his vision. A native pirogue, travelling without lights, its long, low silhouette barely visible in the faint sky glow, was heading south. With four men paddling, its passage was silent and swift. It was carrying a cargo of some sort; a large shapeless hump rose above the gunwales between the two pairs of paddlers. It was covered with some material.

"I wonder what they're up to?" murmured Skye, wishing he had brought binoculars. As he and Overfine watched, the pirogue changed course onto a southeast heading.

"They be going to Frigate. Probably some of the guards reporting for duty." Overfine reached out and held Skye's hand before he could touch the throttle. "Best we wait till they be further away."

"Funny that they're paddling. I would have thought that the guards would have insisted on having at least an outboard for transportation."

"Paddles don't make no noise. Outboards do."

The pirogue disappeared around a headland but there was no doubt that it was headed for Frigate. A few minutes later, the whaler got underway. But instead of heading back up the coast, Skye pointed it south. Overfine shot Skye an uneasy, puzzled look, then stood up and grabbed the painter as they cleared the headland and smacked into the waves surging through the channel between the two islands after an uninterrupted journey from the coast of Africa, thousands of miles away. It was called Commotion Channel because of the choppy seas churned up by the sudden constriction of the waves.

Adrienne cursed softly and lowered the spotting scope. What was Skye playing at? Being thrown around in the Commotion Channel in a tiny whaler wasn't what you would call a pleasure trip. He would probably turn back soon. Just in time to catch her in the act. Shit! She shook her head at her companion and pounded a stake in the sand, lining it up with a lighthouse on Mayreau. The riding lights of an anchored yacht off the same island provided a third triangulation point. Then she sat down on the gunwale of the pirogue and checked out her diving equipment one more time.

Despite Overfine's efforts to hold the bow up, both he and Skye were soon thoroughly drenched with spray. Wiping his eyes, Skye throttled back and peered ahead. The pirogue had disappeared into the darkness of the night. Effortlessly keeping his balance as the whaler lost speed, Overfine looked over his shoulder at Skye. His look was questioning, as if asking what had made Skye go tearing off in pursuit of the native craft. Skye couldn't have told him; he had reacted instinctively, without conscious thought. Still, there had been something sinister about the pirogue as it slipped silently through the night with its mysterious cargo. He waited for a gap in the rolling waves and quickly turned the whaler around. The ride back to the shelter of Manchineel's leeward coast was much smoother, with the waves quartering their stern.

Adrienne watched the whaler's approaching lights with relief mixed with puzzlement. She couldn't figure out what Skye had been doing out in the channel. Had he been heading for Frigate? Anyway, he would be safely out of the way before the restless sea had a chance to make away with her prize. She waited until the whaler's lights disappeared behind Seabird Point, halfway up the coast, then nodded to her companion. She taped a flashlight, with its beam pointing down, to the stake; then the two women, both wearing black bathing suits, half-dragged, half-carried, the pirogue across the beach and pushed it into the small waves that curled against the shore. The companion rowed, while Adrienne strapped on her scuba equipment and buckled weights around her waist. She was sitting backward on the thwart to keep the light on the beach in view. When she was satisfied that they were the right distance from the shore, she signalled the woman, the same one who had assisted her at last night's rituals, to stop paddling. Inserting the mouthpiece, she slipped over the side.

Thirty feet down, she switched on a powerful underwater floodlight. As she continued to descend, it illuminated the sandy bottom, revealing the waving arms of an anemone clinging to a coral encrusted rock. A school of crevalle jacks, their sides burnished silver by the floodlight, darted away, then, attracted by the light, swirled back again. A sand-coloured stingray flapped past, and a barracuda with a bar jack, its tiny companion, staying close to its pectoral fin, came nosing up to the light, and followed Adrienne down until she landed softly on the bottom, tiny puffs of sand swirling around her ankles.

Adrienne wasn't particularly concerned about the barracuda. They abounded in the local waters and encountering one was an everyday experience for her. If she had her spear gun with her, she would usually kill one. Their flesh was firm and remarkably tasty. Despite their fearsome reputation, they almost never attacked humans, but seemed to be intensely curious about these alien invaders of their underwater world, often swimming alongside them for considerable distances. Still, this one was the largest specimen she had ever seen. His cylindrical, streamlined body was at least four feet long. She kept a wary eye on the sinister, silvery-green shape with its ferocious pointed jaw, as it circled around her, following the beam of the floodlight as she searched the bottom.

She reckoned Skye had been about a quarter of a mile out from the reef when he tossed the urn overboard. The ocean floor was smooth rippled sand with scattered outcroppings of coral and thick clumps of seaweed. Adrienne was confident she was in the right place, but there was no sign of the urn as she swept the area with the powerful floodlight, keeping her eye on the circling barracuda. The mask restricted her range of vision, so she had to constantly turn her head to keep him in view. It wasn't helping her search any. Suddenly the barracuda ceased circling and darted off to one side. Pectoral fins fanning the water, the little bar jack still glued to his side, evil-looking head pointing down at a 45-degree angle, he hung poised over a large clump of brown seaweed. Adrienne's heart jumped as she caught a tiny glint in the middle of the waving fronds. With strong kicks of her flippers, she glided over to it and pushed the fronds aside. Although she had never seen it before, she knew that she was looking at the cover of the urn that held Jocelyn's ashes. Despite her elation, she was almost frightened to reach for it. Its glint had attracted the barracuda and he might snap at it with his terrible teeth if she picked it up. But the giant fish had disappeared into the darkness beyond the light. It was as though his mission had been completed. Holding the bronze lid reverently in her hands, gazing at the intricate, almost cabalistic, design etched on its top, Adrienne knew that a new loa had joined the pantheon of voodoo gods. Henceforth, Lord Barracuda would be her personal god. Never again would she offend its spirit by killing one of its brethren.

Carefully placing the precious object in a net bag, Adrienne paused to think the situation through. The urn had to be somewhere in the near vicinity. It would sink more slowly than the solid cover and the slight current off Tamarind Beach ran in a southeast direction. She would shift her search a little further south and closer to the shore. Barely moving her flippers, she swam a few feet above the ocean floor. There was something caught up in a sea-fan. Adrienne plucked it out and her heart began to race wildly as she saw it was a tooth, a molar from the shape of it. Using her light, she located two more, plus a front tooth. Then she spotted a small piece of what she first thought was coral. It was slightly larger than a thumbnail, and when she picked it up she found it was solid, not porous as coral would be. There was a honeycomb of brown matter on one side of the fragment. She had sacrificed enough animals to know it was marrow. She searched the surrounding area without finding anything more. But that didn't matter. She held pieces of Jocelyn MacLeod's body in her hands. Already she could feel their power flowing through her.

After that, finding the urn itself was almost anti-climactic. It had come to rest on the far side of a miniature reef, considerably further south than she had thought it would be. Adrienne switched off the light and headed for the surface with her trophies. She was in a state of ecstasy as she began to plan the ceremony that would welcome the new god. A god who would give her power even over non-believers like Skye.

Chapter Six

Myra flicked a dishtowel at the grackle perched on the top rung of the chair next to Skye. The bird glared impudently at her out of its bright yellow eye, then flew off as she flicked the towel a second time. As soon as she returned to the kitchen it was back, greedily eyeing the marmalade dish. When Skye and Jocelyn had first visited the Caribbean they were greatly entertained by the boldness of the grackles and bananaquits who joined them at mealtimes and by the little ground doves, padding around their feet, picking up the crumbs they fed them. They soon learned, however, that the birds were a nuisance as well as a health hazard, dipping their beaks into whatever food or drink was left unguarded, even for an instant. But nothing could stop Jocelyn from sprinkling a few grains of sugar on the breakfast table for the bananaquits. Skye did the same now and two of the small black and yellow birds with their distinctive white stripe above the eye, immediately darted in and snatched up the sugar. Overfine saw this as he came out onto the patio but smiled forbearingly.

"There's someone here to see you," he told Skye.

"Oh. Who is it?" Skye craned his neck to peer into the livingroom. There was no one there.

"It's Sybil. She waiting in the kitchen."

Sybil was Agatha's predecessor as cook. Four years ago she and her young son had gone back to St. Vincent to live and look after her ailing mother. Skye had been fond of Sybil and young Andrew. Sybil had been an excellent cook and had a bright, sunny disposition. Much sunnier than the somewhat dour Agatha.

But there was no sign of that sunny disposition when Overfine showed her into the livingroom. She was obviously sick with worry. She was also obviously pregnant.

Skye shook hands warmly. Trying to put her at ease, he said jokingly, "I see you're making small bones," using the local idiom for being pregnant.

She didn't seem to hear him. Still holding his hand, she blurted, "Andrew is missing."

The welcoming smile faded from Skye's face. "How long has he been missing?"

"Three days."

"Have you talked to the police?"

"They think he run away."

"But he's only, what? Ten?"

"That's what I tole them. But they say lots of boys run away at that age." She shook her head. "But they don't know my Andrew. He's a good boy and he likes his home. You know him, Mister Skye. He wouldn't run away."

"Of course not," Skye agreed. Certainly the bright, happy little boy he knew, wouldn't. But there could be quite a difference between a six- and a ten-year-old boy. "How can I help?" he asked quietly.

Sybil's shoulders slumped with relief. "I knew you would say that, Mister Skye." Then her hand flew to her mouth and she looked at Skye with something close to horror. "I'm sorry, Mister Skye. I been so worried over my boy, I forgot the mistress had been gathered. She was a wonderful, kind lady."

"Yes, she was. Thank you." Gathered. Now there was a euphemism for the violent death Jocelyn had died. "When did you last see Andrew?"

"When he left for school Tuesday morning. He never come home."

"Has he ever disappeared before?"

"Never."

"Okay. The first thing we'll do is to hop over to Kingstown and have a word with the police."

Sybil nodded eagerly. "They bound to pay attention to you."

* * *

The Cessna's flying time to St. Vincent was twenty minutes. "Andrew sure loved this plane." Sybil's sigh echoed in Skye's headset. She was gazing down at the yachts anchored in Port Elizabeth, Bequia's beautiful harbour. "That boy thinks the world of you, Mister Skye. He always talk about you and all the things you do. If he see this plane, he come runnin'. If he can," she added somberly.

Skye was about to begin his descent but changed his mind as Sybil spoke. Instead of landing, he flew a criss-cross pattern over the island at five hundred feet. Slightly more than fourteen miles long and ten miles wide at its widest point, the pear-shaped island offered countless opportunities for someone to hide, or be hidden. People ran out from their homes to look up at the low-flying airplane, then the small hamlets gave way to jungle as they flew north, climbing steeply to clear the ridge of mountains. Skye circled Soufriere, a slumbering, but still active, volcano, at an altitude of 4,500 feet. Inside the volcano, Crater Lake was dotted with small islands of black lava and was partially obscured by the steam rising from its surface. A handful of tourists struggled up the steep path that emerged from the jungle to twist its way around enormous boulders of volcanic tuff to the rim of the crater. Apart from the tourists, there was no sign of life, although the dense jungle that crept up the volcano's flanks could have hidden an army. Dipping his wings to the climbers who had by now gained the top, two of them lying exhausted on the ground, Skye turned north, and flew low across the island's broad northern tip. Hedgehopping like this, right down on the deck, would have been an exhilarating joyride under other conditions. From time to time he glanced sideways to see how his passenger was faring. Sybil seemed unfazed, staring intently down at the ground as if expecting to spot Andrew waving up at them. But the chances of that happening were virtually nil. That wasn't the purpose of the exercise anyway. The idea was to draw attention to the Cessna so that Andrew might see it and decide to make contact. If the decision was his to make.

Skye climbed to a more respectable altitude as he flew down St. Vincent's leeward coast, where most of the resorts were located. He could see clusters of people on the beaches staring up at them as he zig-zagged back and forth across the coastline. For the first time Sybil began to show signs of queasiness and he immediately reduced the angle of his turns.

"If he's on the island and is able to see the sky, he'll know we're here," he said as he contacted the control tower. After registering a mild complaint about the way he was "beating up" the island, the tower cleared him to land. Skye and his ancient, beautifully maintained airplane were well known throughout the Caribbean and were regarded with something close to awe at every airport they visited. It was the Lindberg syndrome at work.

* * *

The ceiling fan ruffled the papers on Captain Robertson's desk, but his massive, completely bald head was beaded with sweat. Watching him tug at the too-tight collar of his tunic that dug cruelly into the folds of his neck, Skye felt like telling him to loosen up and unbutton it. But it was obvious that the police captain was a stickler for formality and protocol. His broad face had immediately taken on a guarded look when Skye introduced himself and said he was from Manchineel. People from that island were to be handled with silk gloves.

The look of wary courtesy had been replaced by disbelief when Skye said he was there to enquire about a missing boy, Andrew Hodgson. His expression cleared and he nodded understandingly when Skye went on to mention that the boy's mother had once been the cook at his villa on Manchineel.

"Very good of you to take an interest, sir," he said unctuously. "How old was the lad?"

"Ten."

"Ah." The police captain nodded again, this time sagely. "That's the age when them young lads begin to feel independent — feel their oats, so to speak. They ship out on an island schooner and work their passage to one of the bigger islands. Barbados and Jamaica mostly. Or they join a band of fishermen and end up the good Lord knows where." This last was accompanied by a pious rolling of the yellow whites of his eyes ceilingward.

"The boy's mother is positive he hasn't run away. She says theirs was a happy home and, knowing her, I believe her."

"Yes. Sybil Hodgson is a good woman."

"You know her, then?"

The policeman smiled proudly. "I know just about every living soul on the island, sir. I don't know her son, but I know of him. I hear he's a bright lad, and it's often the bright ones who are the first to strike off on their own."

"Could I see the file on him?"

"File?" Captain Robertson tugged at his collar. He was clearly discomfited. "I'm afraid there won't be a file, Mr. MacLeod." He spread his hands in an exculpatory gesture. "If we was to open a file on every child what runs away from home...." He shrugged as if anyone could see how impossible that would be.

"Then I would like to speak to the officer in charge of the case."

"Case?" The captain looked as if he were going to ask, "What case?" but he recovered quickly and said he would find out which officer had been assigned to it. Heaving his bulk up from behind the desk, he excused himself for a minute and left, closing the door behind him.

When he returned, he told Skye that Constable Tanner was conducting the investigation, but unfortunately the constable was off-duty at the moment.

"Could I have his home address? I'd like to talk to him."

Skye took out a pen and one of his business cards, the one that listed him as a financial consultant, and looked expectantly at the captain.

Robertson allowed a trace of annoyance at Skye's persistence to show on his face, but picked up a phone and asked someone for Constable Tanner's address, repeating it to Skye as it was read out to him. Skye jotted it down on the back of the card. "Thank you. Oh, there's one more thing while I'm here. Those bodies that were washed up on Manchineel. They were to be transported here."

"That's right. They were. The doctor look at them and they be buried."

"That's a bit quick, isn't it?"

"No reason not to be quick. They smell bad and come from a long way away. No business of ours."

"I see. Did the doctor say anything about the bodies? Their condition, I mean."

The police chief stared at him. "He say sharks ate them."

"He didn't mention any cuts or anything like that?"

"He just mention the bites. Shark bites."

Skye took another look at the constable's address and stood up. "I don't like to disturb Constable Tanner at home, but I don't have much time. I have to fly back to Manchineel this afternoon."

"Fly back?" Captain Robertson's eyes narrowed. "Was that you buzzing around at tree-top level? Scaring folk." The policeman looked as if he was searching his mind for some offence to charge Skye with.

"I was never below 500 feet," declared Skye. "I was hoping to spot Andrew from the air." Skye shook hands and hastily took his leave. He knew the captain would immediately get on the phone to Tanner and fill him in on the efforts being made to locate Andrew. The non-existent efforts.

Constable Tanner lived in a new subdivision of cinder block houses that was still under construction. Skye's taxi drove slowly down the unpaved street, rutted with the tracks of heavy construction machinery. Skirting the exposed manhole covers, it stopped in front of number 17. A man — Skye assumed it was Constable Tanner — was out in front, painting a picket fence. He straightened up as Skye got out of the taxi, and opened the gate. He looked uncomfortable, not meeting Skye's eyes.

"Captain Robertson told me to expect you, Mr. MacLeod." Tanner closed the gate, but didn't invite Skye inside the house. They remained standing on the narrow cement path that bisected the small patch of freshly seeded lawn.

"Then you know why I'm here." Farther down the street a tractor started up and Skye raised his voice as he continued, "I would like to know what steps have been taken to find Andrew Hodgson."

Constable Tanner looked even more uncomfortable. "The usual steps, sir. All the police officers have been given his description and told to be on the lookout for him."

"Have you circulated a photo of him?" Skye knew they hadn't. Sybil had volunteered to provide the police with a recent photo of her son, but they hadn't taken her up on it.

"No, sir. Not yet. But we will." The policeman hesitated, then blurted, almost beseechingly, "Look, sir, try to understand our position. These young kids go missing all the time. Sometimes they turn up again, but mostly they don't. They don't want to be found and, I don't like to say this, but their families don't seem to care. Or at least most of them don't. They not be like Miss Sybil that way."

"I appreciate your frankness, constable. What you're telling me is that nothing has been done and nothing will be done to find Andrew."

"That's not true, sir. Now that you're here asking questions about the boy, Captain Robertson is going to lay on a full-scale search." Unexpectedly, the policeman grinned. "Was that you flying that plane? It brought me and the missus runnin' out, wondering if it was going to crash into the house. You was sure flying low, man."

"You don't expect me to incriminate myself in front of the police, do you?" laughed Skye.

"One thing, sir."

Skye, who had been walking to the waiting taxi, turned around.

"We'll do our best to find the Hodgson boy, but I wouldn't get your hopes up, sir. He's probably off island by now."

* * *

Sybil was a remarkable woman. Her old-fashioned chattel house, built on pilings, was freshly painted, and the small patch of vegetable garden was carefully tended. Her aged mother was dozing in a comfortable chaise lounge on the porch. Skye had the taxi stop a little distance from the house so as not to wake her. According to Sybil, her mother spent most of her time sleeping. Sybil wasn't sure whether she knew her grandson was missing or not. She had asked for him once, but then had drifted off to sleep. Sybil opened the screen door as Skye tiptoed across the porch. "Don't worry about waking her. She sleeps best at this time of day. It's at night that she gets a little wakeful."

Despite Sybil being pregnant, there was no sign of a man living in the house. That didn't surprise Skye. It was the way things were often done in the islands. In the year she had spent with them at Whistling Frog, she had never once mentioned Andrew's father. She hadn't been married then and it looked as if she was still single.

She prepared lunch for him. "Just like old times, isn't it, Mister Skye?" she asked as she ladled out a bowl of callaloo soup. "Them were happy days, cooking for you and Mistress Jocelyn."

"They were, indeed." Skye took an appreciative sip of the soup, and looked around at the spotless interior. The stove and fridge were gleaming with newness. The recliner chair beside the television set also looked new. "But you seem to be doing all right for yourself."

She looked at him for a moment, then lifted her blouse to reveal a long, thin scar running under her ribcage and extending almost to her spine. "I sold a kidney. That's what bought these things. I was desperate."

"Good Lord, Sybil. Why didn't you come to me? I would have helped."

From Sybil's look of surprise, it was plain the idea of asking Skye for money had never occurred to her. "I couldn't do that, Mister Skye," she said, pulling the blouse down over her distended belly. "Besides they tole me one kidney is just as good as two."

"Even when you're pregnant?"

"I was operated on before I got pregnant. I don't feel no different than before the operation."

"Where was it done? In the States?"

"Jamaica. I was in the hospital there for three days, then I was flown back here. My family doctor took the stitches out when it was time."

"How much did they pay you?"

"Ten thousand U.S. dollars. I was a 'match' for some woman in the States."

"Do you know anything about her?" Skye's

curiosity hadn't kept him from finishing the soup. It was delicious, better even than Agatha's. Sybil removed the bowl and replaced it with a chicken pelau.

"No. 'Cept she must be rich," she replied, obviously enjoying his interest, and temporarily forgetting her troubles. "But do you know who did the operation?" She answered her own rhetorical question with a flourish. "Sir George Glessop!"

"What?" Skye was incredulous. The thought of the drink-sodden doctor cutting and slicing away at people was mind-boggling. Skye would have thought he was long past that. And yet he certainly had the necessary training and qualifications for that kind of complicated surgery. Every issue of the *Manchineel News*, the little island paper that was published once a month, contained the information that the resident doctor was no less than Sir George Glessop, FRCS (Lon.), formerly Chief of Surgery at St. Michael's.

"He came round to the ward to look at me the day after the operation."

"Did he recognize you?"

"No. He was too busy speechifying to the student doctors about the operation. He wouldn't know me anyway. Folks like him pay no attention to servants. Them students treated him like he was God himself. Since he was talking about me, I remember every word he tole them."

Intrigued, Skye asked, "What did he say?"

She paused to collect her thoughts, much like Overfine did when he was about to rattle off a menu. "First you clamp the renal artery and renal vein, 'renal' means kidney," she explained. It was clear that she had taken the trouble to learn the meaning of the medical terms. "Then he tole them to leave two inches of the ureter, that's the tube that connects the kidney to the bladder, so that it can be attached to the recipient's ureter, and then sew the residual ends of the vein and artery. It made me feel like I was a piece of machinery, but I got the ten thousand dollars."

The phone rang before Skye could respond to this remarkable account. It was Captain Robertson, requesting a photo of Andrew that he would have posted around St. Vincent and would circulate to the police forces on the other islands. A constable would come round later that afternoon to pick it up.

"I knew the police would pay attention to you, Mister Skye," said Sybil after she had hung up. She went into the bedroom and returned with a 5" x 7" photo of Andrew. He was wearing his school uniform, khaki shirt and dark brown tie.

"He's a fine looking boy." Skye handed the photograph back to her. "Do you have another print of this?"

"There's one in mother's room. I'll get it."

"With your permission, Sybil, I'm going to run an ad with this picture in all the island newspapers. I'll offer a reward, say EC$2,500, for information as to Andrew's whereabouts. If anybody knows anything, that should bring them out of the woodwork. Okay?"

"You're a good man, Mister Skye. But...." Looking troubled, Sybil broke off.

"But what?"

"I'm worried about you having your name in the papers asking about Andrew's whereabouts. No matter what the police think, I know he didn't run away. I know he'd come home if he could. He's not the only boy who's gone missing around here."

"Are you saying he's been kidnapped?"

"All I'm saying is that he didn't run away on his own."

"Hmmm. Maybe I'll use a St. Vincent post office box in that ad."

"You can use my name and this address if you like. People won't get suspicious if it's the boy's mother asking for information. But $2,500 is too much. Nobody would believe I got that much money. Five hundred is better."

* * *

Instead of flying directly to Manchineel, Skye swung to the south and turned north along the Atlantic side of Frigate on a course that took him well clear of the inhospitable island but still afforded him a good overview of it. Even so, a military-style jeep with two men on board raised a plume of dust as it headed for the non-existent beach where a ribbon of surf outlined the rocky coast. Two other men were struggling to close the door of the main building of the old fishing plant. Skye frowned and took a second look at the field stretching out from the base of a hill. Something was different from the last time he saw it. The boulders had been moved. He remembered thinking at the time that if some of them had been removed, the field would be a piece of cake for a short-take-off-and-landing aircraft. It was still not possible to land but he was sure the largest boulder had been in the dead centre of the field and not off to one side as it was now. It was a perfect set-up for a drug operation. A deserted island where no visitors were allowed, and a field that could be converted into a landing strip for STOL aircraft.

Frigate birds, with their elegant pointed wings and deeply forked tails, soared and swooped beneath him as he flew on. Frigate was one of the few nesting sites of these magnificent birds in the Caribbean. They always nested on the windward side because they needed the wind to get airborne. Skye would have loved to photograph them. Maybe Lord Fraser could arrange something. If anybody could, he could.

Crossing Manchineel's southern tip, Skye dipped his wings as he flew over Tamarind Beach. A dirt road, the colour of sand, began north of Tamarind Beach and curved through an aisle of palm trees past the fishermen's camp where the men sat outside their wooden shacks, cleaning their catch, repairing nets, or lazing about in hammocks strung between palm trees. At the sight of the approaching airplane, they dropped whatever they were doing and jumped to their feet. Some waved, while others saluted. Once again, Skye dipped his wings as he roared overhead.

The few yachts anchored off Nick's Bar were dwarfed by a new arrival — a black-hulled motor yacht that was 120 feet long. The *Caroline* was back in port. It was tied up to one of the permanent moorings the company had installed when dragging anchors began to chew up the ocean floor. The *Caroline* being in port meant more parties. Charles Pollock, her owner, was keen on parties. He was also a James of Leeds Name, which condemned him to endlessly sail the seas like a modern-day *Flying Dutchman*. He couldn't go back to England or he would lose his yacht. Skye turned out over the bay for a closer look at the ocean-going craft. Apart from a crew member cleaning the pool on the upper deck, there was no sign of life. An empty davit indicated that someone had gone ashore. Pollock was probably visiting the Frasers. He and Lord Fraser were longtime and close friends. Turning inland, Skye saw Overfine backing the jeep out of the Whistling Frog driveway. He was on his way to pick Skye up at the airstrip.

Chapter Seven

Pollock wasted no time in throwing a party. An invitation to dine on board the *Caroline* had been delivered while Skye was in St. Vincent.

No Zodiacs for the *Caroline*; her tender was a sleek Bertram power boat built in the style of a run-about with an open cockpit and "Tender to the *Caroline*" in gleaming brass letters on her transom. As he drove up to the quay, Skye saw Erin and the Rastoks lowering themselves into the boat. Louella Harper was already seated in the cockpit. Skye decided to keep on driving; he would catch a ride on the tender's next trip. When the tender was well on its way, he parked the jeep and walked out on the quay. While he waited, he was joined by the Frasers. "Did you know the real-life Caroline?" asked Skye. The yacht was named after Pollock's daughter who died of a drug overdose in a Paris slum.

"Very well," answered Lord Fraser. "As a young child she was delightful. Then when she was 15 or so she fell in with some high-born wastrels who introduced her to drugs. She had graduated to heroin by the time she died."

On its next trip, with Skye and the Frasers on board, the launch swept around the *Caroline*'s stern where Monrovia, its Liberian home port of convenience, was painted. A member of the crew, smartly turned out in a neatly pressed white uniform, waited for them on the landing platform at the bottom of the gangway. She helped Lady Fraser to step onto the platform and reached out to help Lord Fraser but he had already stepped across. Skye grinned and took the outstretched hand, earning an amused smile from her.

Charles Pollock waited for them at the top of the gangway. Save for a black Ascot knotted at the neck, Pollock was attired entirely in white — white shoes, white slacks and an embroidered white guyabera. With his olive complexion, dark eyes, sleek black hair, and designer stubble, he looked more Mediterranean than English. His mother had been an Italian countess. Pollock's age was hard to judge but Skye figured he must be close to 50.

Skye had been on board the *Caroline* once before, three years ago when he and Jocelyn were invited to dine with Princess Helen, her then lover — another foppish young Englishman — and the Frasers. A few weeks later, when the *Caroline* was once again in port, Pollock dined with them at the Whistling Frog. Now he shook hands warmly with Skye. He didn't offer condolences; after this length of time people, except for those who had known Jocelyn exceptionally well, didn't.

It quickly became apparent that their host was enraptured by Erin. He took her arm as he led his guests up a flight of stairs to the main salon where drinks were served. The walls of the salon were hung with art, including a Blue Period Picasso, a David Hockney pool painting, and an unusual Dufy watercolour. When Erin gave a little gasp of admiration, a beaming Pollock told her the provenance of each painting. How the James of Leeds people would love to get their hands on this collection, thought Skye as he listened to Pollock expound. Skye and Erin had nodded coolly when Skye had first come on board, but otherwise ignored each other.

Dinner was served informally in the fantail salon on individual clear acrylic cabinets that displayed the host's collection of dioramas of sailing ships and sea scenes. Just as they were about to sit down, they were joined by the captain. She was out of uniform and at first Skye thought she must be Pollock's wife or mistress. She smiled and shook hands with each one in turn as Pollock introduced her as Captain Marlene Morton. Their host insisted that Erin sit beside him and Skye found himself sitting next to the captain.

"There was a different captain the only other time I was on board the *Caroline*," said Skye. "That would have been three years ago."

"That was Captain Olson. He retired a year ago. That's when I signed on as captain."

She proved to be a pleasant dinner companion, responding gracefully to his compliments on the beautiful ship she commanded, and promising him a tour when their dinner was over. "But then, of course, you will already have had the tour."

"That was a long time ago. I'm ready to do it again."

They had coffee and, for everyone but Erin and the captain, liqueurs, under the stars, sitting around the plunge pool. A light, onshore breeze freshened the air. Lights glowing from the other yachts and from villas up in the hills completed the idyllic scene. Pollock lit a slim cigarillo and exhaled luxuriously. "Now you know why

I so seldom go ashore," he remarked to the company at large. Lord Fraser greeted this remark with a slightly raised eyebrow, but smiled and nodded agreeably.

Skye waited until his host had finished his cigarillo before reminding the captain of her promise to give him a tour. They all got to their feet and followed her across the deck and up a metal staircase to the bridge. A uniformed seaman stiffened to attention as they entered. Resting one hand on a computer, the captain explained how satellite navigation enabled them to pinpoint their position to within a few feet, adding, "This ship is highly automated with state-of-the-art equipment. So much so, that despite the fact that it is 120 feet long, we can run it with a crew of four plus myself." As they left the bridge, she told them the *Caroline*'s hull was insulated so the sleek yacht ran almost silently.

Even Erin, who during her years with the Kelly family had been exposed to outrageous luxury, was impressed as the tour progressed through the sybaritic bedrooms and the traditionally furnished dining salon, the only room that had paneled walls. More than once she exclaimed in admiration, further charming Pollock who remained at her side throughout.

"Maybe our guests would be interested in seeing my office," said Pollock as they returned to the main salon.

The captain shot him a surprised look before murmuring, "I'm sure they would," and led them up a flight of varnished wooden stairs. She paused outside a watertight door. Pollock said something in a language that Skye couldn't place, and the steel door swung silently open. Gallantly, he took Erin's hand to help her step over the high threshold. "This is why there is no need for me to go ashore. I can conduct business in any corner of the globe from here." He waved his hand at the vast array of communications equipment lining three walls of the spacious room. A desk the size of a drilling platform faced the outside wall, made entirely of glass. "The communications revolution has liberated us from the tyranny of offices. The London stock market will be open by now. Let's see how it's doing." He pushed a button and a computer screen sprang to life. "It's up five points. Do you wish to place any buy orders, Robert?"

"How about a sell order instead? Ten thousand Royalty Mines at five pounds or better."

"Who's your broker?"

Lord Fraser mentioned a name, and Pollock repeated the order to a voice-activated computer. "That takes care of that," he said as the computer confirmed receipt of the sell order by the broker. As they filed out of the hi-tech room, the door closed behind them with an audible thunk.

"With your permission, as chairman of the Manchineel Company, I'd like to remain in port a few days longer," Pollock said to Lord Fraser as the little group settled themselves in the fantail salon. "Despite what I said earlier, I would like to spend some time ashore."

"Granted. The *Caroline* is always welcome."

If Captain Morton was surprised by this abrupt change in plans, she didn't show it. She did, however, excuse herself, saying she had some arrangements to make.

It was obvious to everyone that it was the presence of Erin that had led Pollock to change his mind and stay in port. Mary Rastok seemed unsurprised. She had undoubtedly seen men come on to Erin like this before. Probably many times. Pollock must have spent considerable time in his mother's homeland because his blatant courting of Erin was like that of a continental suitor. Too unctuous for Skye's taste.

Louella Harper smothered a yawn and Skye immediately sprang to his feet. "I'll take you home, Louella. I'm kind of bushed myself."

The Frasers decided to leave with them, but Gordon Rastok, a supercilious smile on his face, settled back in his chair with a fresh drink.

"Charles seemed quite smitten," said Lady Fraser as the Bertram glided toward the shore. In deference to those sleeping on the other yachts in the anchorage, the engine was throttled back until it was just a faint burble.

"Small wonder," replied her husband. "Erin is a very attractive woman."

"Of course she is. But she has so much personal baggage. Those awful Kellys."

* * *

Skye lay still for a moment, his thoughts going back to the time some months after Jocelyn's death when he had driven the XK8 to Boston and checked into a hotel. The call girl was attractive and intelligent, as she should have been at one thousand dollars a night. On their third rendezvous a few weeks later, she had begun to show signs of becoming romantically interested in him. He changed agencies immediately. Staring up at the mosquito netting, still tied in a knot since he never used it, Skye grimaced as he thought of the times he had cursed himself for being disloyal to Jocelyn's memory in such a tawdry fashion. Generous and understanding as she was, she would not have approved. Still, Skye defended himself in these internal debates, it was less of a betrayal than taking up with one of the divorcees his friends were constantly trying to foist on him. No emotions were involved; the encounters were almost clinical. So clinical in fact that he had finally wearied of them. Shaking his head ruefully, Skye went into the bathroom and turned on the shower.

* * *

Overfine poured Skye a second cup of coffee while Myra cleared away the breakfast dishes. Skye leaned back in his chair and said, "I feel like some lobster for dinner tonight, Overfine."

"Good idea, boss. You want me to go down to the camp and get some?"

"No, I'll go myself. I should have a visit with Sebastian anyway."

"He be wonderful glad to see you. He ask about you every time he see me. He never forget what you did."

Skye knew that what Overfine said was true. Two winters ago, just weeks before Jocelyn was killed, she and Skye had joined in a search for a fishing boat that had gone missing in a violent storm. They were the ones who had spotted the two men, one of them Sebastian's son, clinging to what was left of their overturned boat. Exhausted by their ordeal, they were almost ready to give up and slip beneath the waves when they heard the roar of the Cessna's engine and saw it heading toward them at wave-top level. Joshua, Sebastian's son, later told Skye that when Skye dipped his wings to show he had seen them, he felt reborn.

It would be another hour before the fishermen would arrive in from the sea. Skye decided to call Sybil, although he was sure there would be no news of Andrew. If there had been, she would have let him know. Sybil tried hard to sound optimistic, but it was obvious she was on the verge of despair. There had been no response to the reward, but there had been another disappearance. A young boy, a schoolmate of Andrew's, had failed to return home after school. The distraught mother, a single parent like Sybil, had telephoned her and they, along with some neighbours, had searched for him in every place they could think of, without success. The mother was every bit as positive as Sybil had been about Andrew that her son hadn't run away.

"What is it, Mister Skye?" asked Overfine as Skye remained staring down at the phone after he had rung off.

"One of Andrew's school chums has disappeared. What the hell's going on, Overfine?"

"I doan' think it mean too much, boss. In islands boychilds often go off on their own. I did my own self when I was Andrew's age."

"Maybe so. But the world has changed since you were that age. For the worse."

* * *

The fishermen's camp was a dozen or so makeshift shacks, built from flotsam and jetsam scrounged from the sea and beach. The roofs of some of the shacks were held down with old tires. The camp was an all-male enclave. It was occupied only during certain months of the year when the fishing in the area was at its best. The men were hauling their boats above the high-water mark when Skye arrived. A number of servants, most of them maids, waited to inspect the catch. The bulk of the catch would be purchased by the commercial fish buyer, who stood off to one side. It was the custom for the villas to be given the first choice.

Sebastian saw the distinctive logo and immediately began to head across the beach toward the Whistling Frog's jeep. Skye waved him back, telling him there was plenty of time, and to finish his business first. Skye looked for Joshua, but he was nowhere to be seen. After fifteen minutes of good-natured bargaining and bantering, Sebastian came over to the jeep, stuffing a small wad of EC dollars into the pocket of his salt-stained jeans. Before Skye could ask about Joshua, Sebastian informed him, with a note of pride in his voice, that his son had given up fishing for the ministry and was attending a theological college in Barbados. "Being saved from the sea opened his eyes to the Lord."

Sebastian would be somewhere in his late fifties, and his deeply lined face and grey stubble made him look every year of it. Toughened by years of toil on the sea, his body was lean and sinewy. In his younger days, Sebastian had been a lobster fisherman. The men who scuba-dived for lobsters, often to depths of 120 feet or more, were the elite of the Manchineel fishing camp. Unlike the heavy, wooden longboats of the conventional fishermen, the sharp-prowed boats of the lobster divers were built for speed, powered by the biggest outboard engines their flamboyant owners could afford, which were always driven wide-open. These were the boats that raced out to pick up the two lost fishermen when Skye radioed in their position and Jocelyn had thrown out life preservers from the circling plane to keep them afloat until help arrived. While Sebastian could no longer dive for lobsters, he was the undisputed boss of the camp.

Sebastian was telling Skye how much it pleased him to hear once more the sound of Skye's airplane in the air. "Joshua always say that when you found him, it fill the whole sky."

Another man, who had been waiting for Sebastian to finish welcoming Skye, came over to them with hand outstretched. It was Warren, Joshua's fishing partner who, along with Joshua, had been clinging to some broken planks from their boat when Skye found them. As if this was a signal, the other men lined up to shake Skye's hand. Some were middle-aged, others arrogant with youth, all of them with crushing handshakes. Having paid their respects, they went off, to leave

Sebastian and Skye alone to talk.

"I see that Frigate Island is as inhospitable as ever," said Skye. "They didn't like it when I flew a little close yesterday."

Sebastian's face darkened. The fishermen bitterly resented the island being placed off-limits. Until the Frigate Company had taken over, they had had the complete run of the island, often camping there for weeks at a time as they fished for sea bream and porgies off Hurricane Hole.

"You must know Frigate pretty well," said Skye. "From the days when you were allowed to stay there."

"I know ever' inch of dat island. They had no call to kick us off."

"Why do you think they did that?"

"Because they don' want nobody snooping around, seeing what they're up to."

"What do you think they're up to?"

Sebastian shook his head. "I dunno for sure. But something they doan' want nobody to know about. Sometimes when we out fishing at night we see boats without lights heading for there."

"I saw one of those the other night."

"And sometimes we hear planes flying low without lights. It be hard to tell but sometimes I think they land on Frigate."

"Sounds like the drug trade to me."

"That's what we think. But it be an evil place. Full of booby traps. See Matthew over there?" He pointed to a burly young man, clad only in khaki shorts, seated on a sawed-off log, making a lobster snare from long strips of bamboo and wire. A livid purple scar circled his right leg above the ankle.

"Matthew went ashore one night and hadn't gone more than a few feet when he got hisself caught in a leg trap. They let him suffer for a whole day before they let him go. They sent a message back with him that this is what happens to people who go where they not allowed."

"Charming!" That put paid to any ideas Skye might have had about making a nocturnal visit to Frigate. He went over to the holding tank and purchased several one-and-a-half pound lobsters. Holding a newspaper-wrapped package, from which their delicate antennae waved disconsolately in the unfriendly air, he said goodbye to Sebastian, and asked to be remembered to Joshua.

"He say a prayer for you every day."

"I need all the help I can get," Skye replied lightheartedly as he began to move away.

"Skye." The tone of Sebastian's voice made Skye stop and turn around. "Baron Samedi be an angry god."

So Sebastian knew about the dust-up at the voodoo ceremony. No surprises there. The whole island would have heard about it.

"I know," Skye replied. "The keeper of the cemeteries is a Petro loa." There was a brief silence while both men pondered this uncomfortable fact. Petro gods were born in the slave quarters, created out of the cruelty and degradation of slavery. Because of the harsh conditions under which they were spawned, they were much more malevolent and violent than the gods the slaves had brought with them from Africa.

Finally Skye said, "I'll watch my back."

Sebastian nodded and Skye left.

Chapter Eight

With the long afternoon stretching before him, Skye decided it would be a good time to try out Elizabeth Mallory's new horse. He changed into jeans and roper boots and drove the short distance to the stables.

"You're just in time," Elizabeth called out as Skye pulled up in front of the tack room. "I was about to ride him myself when I go out with this group from the hotel." Six novice riders, of various shapes and sizes, stood beside their patient mounts, gingerly holding the reins and cracking jokes to relieve the tension. There was no doubt about which horse was Elizabeth's new acquisition. The ex-racehorse, a handsome bay — Skye's expert eye judged him to be sixteen hands two inches — stood out from the rest. Elizabeth's Rastafarian groom, with whom she lived in a dilapidated little house up in the hills, was holding his bridle. His habitual surly expression deepened as he handed the reins over to Skye without a word. Skye nodded curtly, lengthened the stirrups, tightened the girth, patted the gelding on the neck, and sprang onto his back in one fluid motion. Gathering up the reins, he asked the groom what the horse's name was. Without looking up, the Rastafarian muttered, "Sun Dancer," and slouched off, his bare heels scuffing up little puffs of dust.

"'Sun Dancer'? I wonder if that makes you a descendant of Northern Dancer, the great little Canadian horse who won the Kentucky Derby. If so, they certainly bred some size into you." The horse's left ear flicked back at the sound of Skye's voice. Skye let him walk for a while, then eased him into a collected trot on the narrow dirt shoulder of the road. Posting easily to the horse's smooth gait, Skye smiled with satisfaction as Sun Dancer flexed his neck and settled into the snaffle bit. His smile broadened as they came to a level field and a slight touch of his heel put Sun Dancer into a ground-covering canter. Elizabeth was right. The horse, with his smooth gaits and beautiful manners, was a treasure. For a racehorse, his mouth was extraordinarily soft; unlike most racehorses who required a mouthful of hardware to control them, he responded perfectly to a single snaffle.

Dogs barked and chickens squawked as they clattered past the little wooden house where Elizabeth lived with her Rastafarian lover. As usual, the back yard was littered with junk. Skye wondered why the Company let them get away with it. Possibly because the location was so remote. Even more surprising was why Elizabeth chose to live like this. In their rides together, Skye had learned something of her life. She had been brought up in Devon under what obviously were privileged circumstances, complete with horses and sailboats. When she was 18 she had run off to the continent with an Irish horse trainer. She endured his wild drinking bouts for six months, then made her way to Nice where she signed on as crew on a charter yacht that cruised the Mediterranean. As best as Skye could gather, she had done that for a number of years, switching boats and skipper-lovers from time to time. Then she had joined forces with the owner of a thirty-six-foot ketch that had proven to be too small for successful Mediterranean chartering, where people tended to travel in groups. He had decided to try his luck in the Caribbean, and, after a storm-tossed Atlantic crossing that took four weeks, they made Manchineel as their first landfall.

As luck would have it, the Company had been thinking about enhancing the amenities of the island by offering day charters. Elizabeth used her well-bred charm to convince the directors that she and the swarthy, bearded captain should be given a chance. They lasted one season. People liked Elizabeth but were put off by the taciturn captain. When they were told that the arrangement would not be renewed, Elizabeth decided to part company with her lover and persuaded the Company to let her start up a riding stable. In this she was successful; the stables were well-run and she maintained a string of horses to suit every level of expertise, from plodding plugs for the novices to ones like Sun Dancer for the few experts who occasionally showed up.

While Skye mused about the woman he had come to think of as a somewhat tattered English rose, Sun Dancer's long strides carried them far up the Atlantic coast. Beaufort was just over the next hill. He decided to pay the Frasers a visit. Dismounting in front of Beaufort's massive gate, he spoke to Ralston, Beaufort's butler, on the intercom and the gate swung open. Lord Fraser, two

Scottish deerhounds on a leash, waited in the courtyard to greet him as he clattered down the driveway, Sun Dancer's shod hooves occasionally striking sparks from the cobblestones.

"What a magnificent animal!" exclaimed Fraser as Skye dismounted. "Don't tell me it's one of Elizabeth's?"

"It's her latest acquisition." Skye loosened the girth and handed the reins over to a servant. He knew there was no need to tell the man what to do; the horse would be properly cooled down and rubbed before being turned into a corral. "She claims she's only going to let expert riders ride him and I hope she sticks to it. He's too good to be ruined."

"Maybe you should purchase him."

"I don't spend enough time here to justify owning a horse. But because of him, I'm certainly going to do a lot more riding than I planned on. I haven't been riding for a while and it's wonderful to smell horse sweat again."

The two friends chatted easily as they climbed the stone steps that led to the villa's imposing foyer. Zulu, Lord Fraser's pet cheetah, clicked its way across the marble floor, sniffed, in its dog-like fashion, Skye's outstretched hand and emitted its chirping purr as he stroked it behind the ears. Lady Fraser put down the magazine she was reading and rose to greet him, saying that they would be having tea in the garden and inviting him to stay.

"I talked with Charles this morning," said Lord Fraser when they were seated around a table in the shade of a tamarind tree. "He's taking Erin and the Rastoks for a cruise this afternoon. Of course the real attraction is Erin. With old Charles it's hard to tell whether it's her looks or her celebrity that appeals to him. Probably both. He's an interesting man," he went on after a thoughtful sip of tea. "He comes from an old established family. Successful merchants — never managed to get a title — but they owned a lot of property, some of it prime real estate in and around London. He's had some tragedy in his life — his daughter dying the way she did, that nearly finished him — and his wife divorced him to marry a peer, although I don't think he regarded that as a tragedy. Despite all, he was leading a very satisfactory life until he got tangled up in that James Name business. As the cash calls kept coming in he had to sell off properties that had been in the family for generations to meet them. He knew that the *Caroline* would be the next to go. So he smuggled those valuable paintings on board and sailed away."

"I wonder how he can afford to run a yacht like that?"

"A numbered Swiss bank account, I expect. Charles is no fool, and when he realized how serious the situation was, I'm sure he would have squirrelled his cash and securities away where the syndicate couldn't get at them. Still, he can't go back to England and I know that bothers him terribly."

"I once toyed with the idea of becoming a Name myself," Skye remarked. "The return was incredibly attractive at the time."

"But you didn't?"

"No. I couldn't accept the idea of unlimited liability. Names were required to pledge their entire personal wealth, right down to the last cuff link."

"There are thousands of investors today who wish they had paid more attention to that little detail." Lord Fraser got up from his lawn chair as Skye declined a second cup of tea, saying he must be on his way.

As they passed through the Great Room, Skye glanced down at the glossy magazine Lady Fraser had been reading: *High Society*, a monthly publication devoted to the comings and goings of the international set, with particular emphasis on the titled aristocracy of England. Much to the dismay of the royal family, salacious stories about Princess Helen and her "flavour of the year" lovers frequently adorned its pages. But the face that looked up from the cover was far more sinister. It was Lord Lassiter, a notorious rakehell, who had gambled away his inherited fortune and, one fearful night, had bludgeoned his estranged wife to death.

The favourite theory at Scotland Yard was that he had planned to stuff his wife's body into a waterproof plastic bag and place it in the trunk of an inconspicuous Ford sedan he had stolen. The car had been stolen in London and abandoned in a back street in Scarborough, not far from the home of a close friend of Lassiter's, whom the police believed a desperate Lassiter had called on in the early morning hours. The friend denied seeing Lassiter, but the police were sure that her denial was just part of the universal cover-up they were confronted with. Their investigation uncovered the fact that Lassiter, ostensibly because of concern over his Aston Martin, had made exhaustive enquiries at his garage about how cars were broken into and hot-wired.

The front seat of the Ford was bloodstained, and the blood samples were a DNA match with Lady Lassiter. According to the police theory, Lassiter's original intent had been to drive back to his apartment, a short distance away in fashionable Belgravia, clean himself up, and meet four friends who were attending the theatre for a pre-arranged late supper at his club. This was to be his alibi.

In the early hours of the morning, so Scotland Yard theorized, he planned to drive down to the coast in the stolen car, load his wife's body onto a boat he had rented under an assumed name, carry it out into the English Channel, weight it down with chains and dump it overboard. But he had failed to realize how much blood there would be. His wife dropped to her knees with the first blow of the metal pipe and he kept hitting her. As long as her heart kept pumping, every blow sent blood spurting everywhere, splattering the walls, the floor, and even the ceiling of the bedroom, and all over her killer. Covered with blood, and unnerved by the horror of what he had done, Lassiter made a half-hearted attempt to make it look like the work of an intruder by smashing a leaded glass panel and reaching through it to unlock the front door. Then he fled, and disappeared off the face of the earth. The police investigation also turned up the fact that on the night in question, Lassiter had been completely sober.

"You must have known him." Skye picked up the magazine and flipped through the pages.

Lord Fraser made a grimace of distaste. "He was more or less in the same set. Saw him at the occasional social function, although he spent most of his time in the gambling clubs with his ne'er-do-well friends. Never could stand the fellow myself."

"It's amazing the way he just vanished into thin air. That's why the press won't let go of the story. Do you suppose he's still alive?"

"Not a chance. The only course open to a gentleman in his position is to fall on his sword. My own theory is that he took a boat out into the Channel and drowned himself."

"I'd like to borrow the magazine when you've finished with it. The Lassiter story is fascinating in a gruesome sort of way."

Lord Fraser glanced at his wife, who nodded. "Take it with you when you go. No, that would be a bit awkward since you're on horseback. I'll have one of the boys run it over for you."

* * *

Back at the stables, Skye handed Sun Dancer over to the dreadlocked groom and assured Elizabeth that the gelding was even better than he had expected. Instead of going directly home, he drove up to the top of the hill overlooking the harbour. The *Caroline* wasn't there. Pollock was probably going to serve his guests a moonlit dinner at sea.

* * *

After finishing his lobster dinner, Skye carried his coffee into the livingroom and settled down to read the article on Lord Lassiter. Like nearly everyone in the English-speaking world, he was familiar with the basic facts of the case. Even after five years, the fate of the murderous English lord was the subject of much debate in certain circles. Most of those who continued to follow the case favoured Lord Fraser's theory that Lassiter had committed suicide, but others clung to the more romantic notion that he was living under an assumed name, with his appearance altered by plastic surgery, somewhere in South America. The article in the magazine was an in-depth treatment, or at least the author had attempted to make it so. She had travelled to London to interview Lassiter's friends and associates, but had been stonewalled for the most part. Even those who consented to see her were reluctant to talk. Some were clearly frightened. The author of the article, however, managed to learn that the dead Lady Lassiter had been widely disliked. A close friend of Lassiter's, whose wealth and title made caution unnecessary, told the interviewer, "If she'd been my wife, I'd have bashed her head in years before old Larry got around to it."

The writer also learned that Lassiter's circle had immediately closed ranks around him. The police were convinced that he had called several of his friends on the telephone and might even have visited one or more of them on that fateful night, but none of them would admit anything. The police searched everywhere for the missing peer, including country houses and stately homes. Rumours as to Lassiter's whereabouts abounded, each one more fanciful than the rest. The most colourful one had him driving to his closest friend's country estate where he shot himself and was fed to the tigers in the private zoo. The police, attempting to learn the ways of the high born, tried to infiltrate the clubs they frequented. This greatly amused the toffs, who treated the police with icy contempt, or openly mocked them. Frustrated and confused, the police eventually scaled down the investigation, but the Lassiter file remained very much open.

Skye made a mental note to stop in at the Manchineel Company office in the morning to make a photocopy of the article before returning it to the Frasers.

Later that night, Skye sat out by the pool for a look at the stars, which seemed closer and brighter in the tropics than anywhere else. From far out at sea came the faint, but unmistakable, whine of a turbo prop. Skye walked to the end of the pool and looked in the direction of the sound, but there was no sign of any lights. It was very unusual for a small airplane to be in the air after dark. The airports on all the smaller islands shut down for the night. Probably a drug run from Colombia, thought Skye as the sound receded in the distance.

Chapter Nine

"**W**here's Myra?" asked Skye, surprised by the unusual sight of Overfine doing the dusting.

"She had to go to the clinic. She won't be long."

"What's the matter with her? Is she sick?"

"No. Leastways not so far as I know. Word come round for her to report to the clinic to be tested. The doctor is afraid there might be an epidemic of some kind."

"Strange." Skye decided he would walk to the Company office and look in at the clinic on his way. Picking up the *High Society* magazine, he set off. Along the way, he encountered a group of young black women coming in the opposite direction. All of them had a band-aid on the inside of their arms at the elbow and all of them looked frightened, and returned his greeting in a subdued manner. Myra, dressed in her maid's uniform, was standing outside the clinic's entrance, talking to Penelope. As he drew closer, Skye saw that both of the young women had band-aids on their arms. He quickly cut short Myra's apologies for being away from the job, assuring her that it was perfectly all right and not to worry. The two teenaged girls began to walk away as he pushed open the door of the clinic.

Edwina, looking very professional in her nurse's uniform, was alone in the outer office. "Something wrong, Skye?"

"No. I feel fine. I was just curious as to what this testing was all about."

"Sir George is concerned about a possible outbreak of tuberculosis. He didn't like the look of a couple of girls he saw in the village, so he ordered a random sampling of the population to see if there was any cause for concern."

Edwina looked around to make sure the door to Sir George's office was closed. "I think it's unlikely that there's an epidemic on Manchineel. There's been no report of it from the other islands, as one would expect. But there's no doubt Sir George was correct in taking precautions. Anyway, we should know within the hour when the results are in."

Skye took comfort from Edwina's relaxed attitude, but what if she was wrong and Sir George was right? An epidemic of TB sweeping through the population of the island was a grim prospect. He paused at the door and looked back at the nurse. "Thank heavens these days tuberculosis is very treatable."

* * *

As usual, the Manchineel Company office hummed with unhurried efficiency. Telephones rang with muted peals, fax machines spewed out their messages, and Skye was greeted with friendly smiles on all sides as he walked over to the copier. Also as usual, the chairman's large office was empty. Lord Fraser was anything but a "hands-on" executive; he was content to leave the day-to-day administration to the staff. Skye made his copy, blew a kiss in the general direction of the attractive social director who, as always, was on the phone. She waved him into her office and shoved *The Daily Telegraph*, opened at the editorial page, across the desk. The lead editorial was a stinging rebuke to Princess Helen for indulging in yet another affair with a man young enough to be her son at her luxurious Caribbean hideaway. It is this sort of conduct, the editorial thundered, that brings the Royal Family into disrepute and makes even the most loyal subject wonder whether the monarchy is still a viable institution. The editorial ended by sharply criticizing Downing-Harris, "a young man who has brought honour to this country in the show ring," for acting the part of a gigolo. Covering the mouthpiece, the social director said, "I hear he's leaving," and resumed her conversation. Skye pursed his lips in a gesture of surprise and left. He wanted to ask Henry Armbruster about the airplane he had heard late last night.

"Bound to be a drug run," the airport manager agreed during a break in the radio traffic. "As you say, it probably originated in Colombia. They usually stay so far out to sea to avoid the radar that you can't hear them, but occasionally, if the winds are against them or they're running out of time, they'll come closer to shore. They carry extra fuel bladders, so it's anyone's guess where they'll land. Could be anywhere on the eastern seaboard."

"I hear The Highness's playmate is leaving?"

"He's going out on a charter flight at ten o'clock." The radio crackled into life and Armbruster began to fiddle with the dials. Turning away, Skye saw Adrienne running up the road from the sea. She had been fishing, for she was wearing a swimsuit and carried a spear gun. The look on her face was murderous. Skye hesitated, then stepped onto the roadway to intercept her. Despite what she had done, he couldn't stand by and let her get into trouble.

"Yo, Adrienne. What's up?"

Panting slightly, either from exertion or emotion, she glared at him. "They took blood from my daughter. Without asking me. They just took it."

"It didn't do her any harm. I saw Penelope and she looked just fine." That seemed to calm her down somewhat, and Skye went on, "They had a good reason to do it. They need to find out if there's some kind of epidemic on the island. They don't think there is, but they have to be sure. That's why they tested a whole bunch of girls, not just Penelope. They needed a large sample."

"I'll give them a large sample," Adrienne snarled as she started off for the clinic.

Skye stepped in front of her. "Not with that spear gun, you're not. You could get yourself into serious trouble, and I'm not going to let that happen. Give it to me. You can collect it from Henry afterwards."

"You like Adrienne, don't you, Skye?" Adrienne's furious snarl turned to a sultry purr as she handed over the spear gun. "You can't help yourself."

Later that morning, Skye placed a call to the clinic. Edwina told him that the tests were all negative and the scare was over.

* * *

Late that afternoon, Skye was doing laps in the pool when Lord Fraser rushed out from the house, holding aloft two sheets of paper which Skye recognized as the checklist of birds he had prepared on his last visit. Fraser's face was beaded with sweat and peppered with insect bites, but his expression was triumphant.

"I've finished it!" he announced. "I've ticked off

every blasted one. It's taken me two years and I had to spend hours in the bloody swamp, but I finally saw a mangrove cuckoo and that did it."

"Congratulations!" Skye climbed out of the pool and shook Fraser's hand. "You're only the second person, apart from myself, who's pulled that off. And she was a lifelong birder. Where did you see the cuckoo?"

"Well, it was in the swamp, of course," Fraser replied, referring to the little swamp across the road from Banyan that was preserved as a bird sanctuary. "At the north end, just before the bridge. He flew in from nowhere, landed on a branch and stayed there until I got tired of looking at him."

"I'll check it out. Let me congratulate you once again, Robert. That's a real accomplishment." Wiping his hands on a beach towel, Skye took the much-creased and folded list from the elated lord. There was a check mark beside each entry and a notation of where each of the fifty-eight species had been spotted. "This definitely calls for champagne!"

"Capital idea! Let me wash up first."

"Very clever, the way you do that," said Lord Fraser as Skye eased the cork out of the bottle of Tattinger.

"The secret is to hold the cork and twist the bottle." Skye filled both glasses and raised his in a toast.

"Speaking of matters ornithological," he went on as they were seated companionably by the side of the pool, sipping champagne and nibbling on the hors d'oeuvres Agatha had magically produced, "there's a frigate bird nesting site on Frigate Island. It's in a mangrove swamp on the windward side. I read somewhere that there are only four nesting sites in the entire Caribbean; conditions have to be just right." Skye paused for emphasis. "It would be a real coup for me if I could photograph that nesting site. I could write an article for *National Geographic* if the photographs were good enough."

"The people on Frigate are not a very friendly lot."

"Don't I know it. I wouldn't think of attempting it without permission. That's where I thought you might be able to help me."

"Me? What can I do?"

"You carry a lot of weight in these parts, my noble friend. More than I suspect you know. You're the chairman of the Manchineel Company, you have one of the most prestigious titles in England, and everyone admires and respects you. If you spoke to the head of the Frigate Company as one chairman to another, I think they'd go along. I would, of course, agree to be escorted by guards and any other conditions they might want to impose."

"Sounds like a reasonable request to me. The only problem is I don't know who runs that company. I suppose I could make some enquiries through the law firm we use in Bermuda. I'll do my best for you."

That settled, they sipped champagne as Fraser reminisced about when and where he had spotted each bird.

"You know that Downing-Harris has left?" Skye asked when the subject of the island's bird life had been exhausted.

"Yes. Bad business, that."

"Do you think it was his decision?"

"I know it wasn't. The Palace finally put its foot down. They can feel the winds of change rattling the windows."

"It's kind of funny, his leaving on the very day of her big party."

"Don't think for a moment that it was pure coincidence. Where do you think the tabloids get some of their stuff? There is always the occasional guest who is not above abusing her hospitality by sending an incriminating photograph to them. Say a picture of the tipsy Princess clinging to her beanpole of a lover. They're an ill-matched pair at the best of times."

"Speaking of matched pairs, how is your friend Pollock making out with the fair Erin?"

Fraser eyed him speculatively. "They're not a pair. Nor in my view are they ever likely to be." He made as if to say something else, thought better of it, put his empty glass down with great care, using both hands, and got to his feet.

* * *

Princess Helen always gave one party during her annual stay on Manchineel. It was held on the extensive grounds of her villa, Serenity, and was very much a command performance to which invitations were eagerly sought. It was a smallish affair; for the most part, invitations were confined to homeowners; renters were sometimes included, but only if they were celebrities or had been coming to the island for a number of years. Marquee tents had been set up on the lawn and bonfires lit on the beach, the finest stretch of sand on the island. It was always cordoned off from the public when she was in residence. There was a certain irony to this since she swam only in her pool. She had given up swimming in the ocean after nearly drowning in Casuarina Bay when the undertow swept her out to sea. Her bodyguards had watched helplessly from the shore while a windsurfer went to her aid.

The Highness was wasting no time in finding a replacement for the banished Downing-Harris. Skye shook with suppressed laughter at the spectacle of Princess Helen vamping poor Charles Pollock. Caught unawares by this unexpected turn of events, Pollock's expression was a comical mixture of shrewd calculation and alarm. His body language was revealing — his face smiled down at his unlovely companion while the rest of him leaned away from her.

Smiling to himself, Skye looked away, and saw Erin also enjoying the scene. Her lips were twitching and her eyes were dancing with mischievous delight. They exchanged amused glances and Skye, still smiling and not taking his eyes off her, walked across the lawn toward her.

"Friends?" she asked, holding out her hand.

Wordlessly, without conscious thought, he took her hand and drew her toward him. Her green eyes were wide with surprise as their lips met.

"I guess we are. Friends, I mean," she said with a shaky little laugh as they drew apart.

Skye started to apologize, but she laid her finger across his lips. "Don't say anything. I'm glad you did that. Very glad."

Gravely, without smiling, they looked into each other's eyes, recognizing and acknowledging what was happening between them. A waiter appeared beside Skye with a vodka tonic. Politely, Skye turned it down, asking for a Virgin Caesar instead. After drinking champagne with Lord Fraser for a good part of the afternoon, he wanted to watch his intake. Could it have been the Tattinger that had propelled him across the lawn to Erin? If so, it had only allowed him to do what he subconsciously longed to do.

Mary Rastok walked past with a muttered aside, "Remember Skye, she's my best friend."

The rest of the party passed in a kind of daze for Skye. He and Erin stayed close together, briefly touching each other whenever it was not too obvious. Fortunately for them, everyone's attention was focused on their increasingly amorous hostess and the hapless Pollock.

"What do you think he'll do?" Skye asked Lord Fraser at one point as Princess Helen squished her doughy breasts against Pollock's arm.

"Pollock? Oh, he'll bite the bullet and go for it, as you Americans say. This will open doors that up to now have been closed to him. Especially if he can ever arrange his affairs so he can go back to England." Fraser chuckled as the thought struck him, "He can close his eyes and think of England."

Erin laughed delightedly — a clear, tinkling laugh that sent a shiver of excitement up Skye's spine.

As always at Serenity, dinner was served at eight o'clock sharp. The cook brooked no delay. Skye and Erin were summoned to Princess Helen's table where an anxious-looking Pollock was already seated on her right. As they sat down, Louella Harper was saying that she would never swim in the ocean again.

"Why?" asked Skye. "Because of the bodies on the beach? That attack took place hundreds of miles away." There was no point in going into his own doubts about it being the work of sharks.

"You mean you haven't heard? About the Haitian refugees? It was on the six o'clock television news."

"I haven't been watching television lately," said Skye. "What was it? More of their unseaworthy boats sinking and people drowning?"

"It was horrible." Louella shuddered. "Their bodies were washed up on shore in the Bahamas. Some of them were young children. They had been attacked by sharks, and were horribly mutilated."

Skye frowned. Was it possible the feeding habits of sharks in the Caribbean were undergoing a sea change? No pun intended. Maybe some component of their food chain had disappeared. If that turned out to be the case, it would be a disaster for the entire Caribbean.

"I gave up bathing in the sea years ago," Princess Helen said complacently. "You won't find sharks in a swimming pool." Patting Pollock's hand, she asked coquettishly, "Speaking of the sea, when are you going to take me out on that yacht of yours?"

"It's at your service, ma'am."

"Lovely. We'll have lunch on board tomorrow."

Pollock waved his hand in an expansive gesture. "You're all invited. We'll make it a party."

The others at the table looked at one another, then smiled and nodded acceptance.

"Splendid. Be on the main wharf at eleven."

There was no further talk of Haitian refugees. As the conversation moved on to more agreeable subjects, Skye was startled to feel Erin's hand resting lightly on his thigh. She was staring straight ahead with a demure smile on her face. It was the same cool and mannered sexuality that Grace Kelly had portrayed so unforgettably in *Rear Window*.

Princess Helen frowned when the butler, with an apologetic glance at her, bent over to whisper something in Lord Fraser's ear. "You know how I detest being interrupted at the table, Robert."

"Indeed I do, ma'am. But this is a call I simply must take. It will be of interest to you and everyone present."

"Very well. But it better be good." Coming up with the idiomatic phrase restored her good humour and she smiled benignly at her guests before favouring Pollock with her attention. Within a few minutes Fraser returned to whisper in her ear. She smiled and nodded, and he tapped a glass to attract the attention of the other tables, although this was scarcely necessary since all eyes were already on him.

"Ladies and gentlemen, I have just been informed that our beloved Prime Minister is being flown in an air ambulance to Boca Raton, Florida, where there is a private clinic that specializes in heart transplants. I was unable to confirm that this means a match has been found, but I believe that must be the case. We must all pray that this is so because I have been told that without a new heart the Prime Minister has but a few days to live."

An excited buzz of conversation followed this announcement. The easygoing and pleasure-loving Prime Minister was popular in the islands, nowhere more so than on Manchineel, which thrived under his hands-off policy.

"That will cost a pretty penny," said Louella Harper. "My operation cost two hundred thousand dollars and it was only a kidney."

"Marcellus Thomas doesn't have that kind of money," said the Princess. "Where can it be coming from?"

"Politicians in the PM's position always seem to have generous supporters who are only too happy to help them in times of emergency," Lord Fraser replied.

As eleven o'clock approached, Skye and Erin and a number of the other guests went down the hall to the small, little-used study. Television does not play a large role in island life and TV sets tend to be located in out-of-the-way places. When the news came on, the washed-up bodies on the shore of Great Exuma in the Bahamas were the lead-off story. "The investigation continues into the mysterious deaths of thirteen young men, women and children." The television reporter was standing on a beach against a background of palm trees. "Few details have been released so far, but this much is known. The victims are from Haiti and are said to have left that island more than a week ago. The police believe that they drowned when their boat sank and that sharks then fed on their bodies. This is known to have happened after a recent air crash off the coast of Dominica."

Erin flinched when the picture of two young girls lying side-by-side flashed on the screen. The hideous wounds on their bodies were open and gaping. "This is worse than what they showed earlier. It's more of a close-up."

The news item ended and Skye switched off the set. As the others drifted out of the room, he said to Erin, "No sharks did that. Those wounds look like surgical incisions to me."

"But you could see where they had been chewed and bitten."

"Oh, something has been feeding on them all right. But not sharks. Maybe barracudas or some smaller fish. Nibbling and tearing at the edges of the cuts. After the cuts had been made. Sharks tear off great hunks."

"What are you saying, Skye? What do you think happened to those poor people?"

"It could be a number of things. It might have been straight butchery. The poor devils could have been captured by pirates who tortured them and then threw the remains overboard. It could also have been something to do with voodoo, which seems to be a growing force these days. Or," he paused as if the thought was too monstrous to contemplate, "they could have been killed for their body parts."

"Do you really believe that, Skye?"

"I'm beginning to. There's a tremendous demand for human organs, and Haitian refugees would be an ideal source. When they set out in their homemade boats nobody expects to ever see them again. The same thing with the kids living on the streets of the big South American cities."

The guests were beginning to leave. "I'll get a key from Mary and tell her not to wait up," said Erin.

"Great," Skye, somewhat taken aback by her directness, managed to say.

Pollock tried to leave with the Frasers but the Princess pouted and insisted that he stay for a nightcap. "Think of England, old boy," Lord Fraser whispered wickedly as he left. Skye and Erin doubled over with gleeful laughter as soon as they were safely outside. They joined the parade of jeeps streaming past the gatehouse, then Skye turned off and drove down a side road that led to the Aisle of Palms. They didn't speak until he parked between two palm trees at the edge of the beach. A waning moon hung low over the water. The sky around it was clear of stars as if to showcase its remote, silvery beauty. Erin slid across the seat and into his arms. They kissed, softly at first, then with growing passion. The firmness of her breast pressed against his arm and her lips parted, inviting him to enter. Half-turning in his seat, he held her so she could feel his arousal. Her hand reached down and stroked him through the light cotton of his slacks. When they finally broke apart, he looked around the interior of the jeep, and said wryly, "Since we're no longer in high school, I'm not sure how much we can achieve in these cramped quarters."

Her fingers still caressing his erection, Erin said, "Oh, I think there's a lot we can achieve." Slowly, her eyes fixed on his, she unzipped his pants and slid her hand inside his undershorts. He groaned aloud as her cool fingers touched his pulsing penis. His low groans turned to a gasp as she took him in her mouth. Without stopping the slow rise and fall of her head, she raised herself on the seat and lifted her skirt above her hips.

Her lace-trimmed panties gleamed silkily in the moonlight. Skye tugged at them, stripping them down her legs until they were lying on the floorboards. She made a little sound deep in her throat as he touched her wetness. Lifting her head, she whispered, "I'm not on the pill or anything."

"That's okay," he whispered back. "I've had a vasectomy." She looked surprised, then told him to get underneath her.

He moved across the seat until he was clear of the steering wheel and she straddled him, crying out as she impaled herself on his erection. "Oh, God, Skye, it feels so good!" she whispered as she began to ride him. Leaning forward, he kissed her breasts; her pink nipples coming to delicious life at the touch of his tongue. He came to orgasm before she did, but remained hard inside her as she pumped herself to a back-arching climax.

She rested her head on his shoulder and whispered, "I guess we are friends, aren't we?"

"Lovers and friends," Skye corrected her.

"'Lovers and friends.' I like that. That's what we'll be."

She snuggled against him for a contented moment, then sat up. "Let's go for a swim."

"Perfect."

Hand in hand, they raced across the sand and dove naked into the gentle waves. Surfacing, they played and splashed each other in the silver swatch of the moon.

"That was magical," Erin sighed as they emerged from the sea and walked along the beach to let the night breeze dry them off.

She shivered suddenly. "I have the feeling we're being watched, Skye. I'm probably just imagining it, but ..."

"Christ, I hope not." Skye turned to look at the thick clumps of sea grapes that grew right down to the edge of the beach. The moon cast long shadows in their midst, providing perfect places of concealment. Something scuttled away as Skye walked across the beach, but it was only ghost crabs racing back to their burrows. Skye peered intently into the dense growth, but it was hopeless.

Standing in the shadow of the jeep, they dressed hurriedly, using Skye's shirt to wipe away the last remaining drops of water. Skye turned on the ignition, then paused for a moment and said, "I wouldn't have believed I could feel like this ever again. Thank you for being you," before driving off.

Rounding a corner, they nearly collided with the medical clinic's jeep, easily recognized by the red cross on the door. In the glare of the headlights they saw Edwina driving and Sir George sitting beside her.

"Where could they be going at this hour?" asked Erin. "It's one-thirty."

"Maybe somebody's had a heart attack. We'll find out in the morning."

* * *

Lying prone on the sand behind a screen of sea grapes, Adrienne watched as Skye and Erin drove off. The American bitch had sensed her presence. She didn't know whether to be flattered or annoyed about that. So much for all the talk about Skye and the Kelly woman not being able to stand each other. She stood up, brushed the sand off her clothes, and began the long trek to her chattel house high up in the hills. She was one of the few blacks allowed to live outside Sterling Hall. The Company didn't dare mess with Adrienne.

Penelope was still out. Adrienne glanced in her daughter's bedroom and shook her head. Penelope would be out there somewhere in the night, rubbing herself against that Knowles boy. He was a labourer with the maintenance crew and would never amount to anything, but all Penelope could see was the bulge in his pants. Adrienne had made it clear to her daughter that if she got herself pregnant, she was on her own.

Two tethered goats bleated at her as she crossed the hard-packed yard to her temple. Round in shape, it was constructed with cinder blocks, and had a conical roof of galvanized metal. Inside the temple, she lit five black candles arranged on the altar, uncorked a bottle of rum and sprinkled a few drops around the base of the peristyle, drew a pentagram by dribbling maize on the earthen floor, took a deep pull of the rum bottle, and began to dance. Genuflecting before the bronze urn in its place of honour on the altar, she picked it up and danced with it, putting it down from time to time to take another swig of rum and to rub her crotch through the black jeans. Prostrating herself before the altar, she opened the urn and took out the fragment of bone and Jocelyn's teeth. Holding them in her cupped hands, she begged Lord Barracuda to descend and mount her.

It was the crowing of a cock that brought her back to consciousness. Dazed, she raised her head and looked around. The candles had burned down and guttered out. She was lying on her stomach and gradually became aware of a throbbing ache in her shoulders. Her arms were down by her sides with the palms of her hands facing upwards. When she moved them she saw the backs of her hands were covered with scratches. Her knees were scraped and raw, and there were scratch marks on the floor. She had been swimming! Her *loa* had come!

The bright sunlight made her eyes burn and her head pound as she walked unsteadily to the outdoor privy. Then she crossed the yard to her house and went directly to Penelope's bedroom. The bed was still neatly made up. It was the first time Penelope had stayed out all night. She would have a word with that young lady! Then she saw the note on the dresser. Thanks to the island school, Penelope could write properly. The note read: "Mama, I am going away for a while. Don't try to find me. I will come home when it's time. Your daughter, Penelope."

Adrienne opened Penelope's closet. Her few things were gone. But it was strange that she hadn't taken her stuffed panda; it was propped up against her pillow on the bed. She had doted on the little black and white animal ever since she had been given it as a child of four. Maybe it was to show that she was a grown woman and had left childish things behind. Penelope would be all right; with her looks and figure she wouldn't have any trouble getting a job as a waitress in one of the fancy restaurants over in Barbados. She had been talking about doing that. When Adrienne had mentioned the Knowles kid, Penelope had said that wouldn't stop her, she was outgrowing him.

Head aching, worry about Penelope niggling at her, but in a state of religious exaltation from the *loa*'s visitation, Adrienne tottered to her room and collapsed on the bed.

Chapter Ten

Pollock and Captain Morton stood at the head of the gangway to greet Princess Helen as she stepped onto the deck. She had sent Serenity's butler on ahead to assist with the lunch and he was waiting for her with a gin and tonic. She gave Pollock a conspiratorial smile as she accepted it. Skye and Erin followed her. Pollock greeted Erin graciously, a glint in his eyes acknowledging the humour of the situation. Within minutes they were underway. Pollock announced that they would sail to Tobago Cays and would have a picnic lunch ashore. "Philippe has been preparing something wonderful for you. I believe, Ma'am, that you are fond of pheasant in gin?"

As usual, the Cays were crowded with sleek sailing yachts, elegant white swans resting on the water. The *Caroline* slowed to a crawl as she edged her way through the first rank of anchored boats. The crews of some of the boats jumped to their feet and stood by the rails, ready to fend off the black-hulled boat that loomed over them. Skye flinched and sucked in his breath as they bore down on an anchored sloop, almost scraping its side as they slid past. The sloop's skipper shook his fist and cries of "stinkpot" went up on all sides. Skye and Erin exchanged quizzical glances as the engines went into reverse and the *Caroline*'s forward motion stopped.

Pollock was up on the bridge conferring with Captain Morton. He then ran nimbly down the stairs and spoke to his guests assembled in the main salon, telling them that because of the crowded conditions in the anchorage, they would be taken ashore with their lunch and the *Caroline* would put out to sea, returning for them when it was time to go back to Manchineel.

"I must say I wasn't too impressed with the good captain's seamanship," Skye muttered as he and Erin stood on the beach watching the *Caroline* manoeuvring through the line-up of yachts. "She damn nearly ran that little sloop down."

"We weren't exactly welcomed with open arms, were we? Charles did the right thing to send her away, and out of everybody's hair."

"She seems to be doing okay now," said Skye as the *Caroline* slipped past the last yacht and headed for the open sea.

A cork popped and champagne foamed onto the sand. "That's a terrible waste," Lord Fraser said to the butler. "Show him how to do it, Skye."

Skye obliged, and opened another bottle with a soft hiss and no spillage, explaining his technique to the butler who nodded and opened the next bottle in the same fashion. Skye and Erin changed into their swimsuits in the shelter of some sea grapes. As they walked across the beach, a sunbather looked up and said, "Haven't you heard about the sharks?"

Skye grinned down at him and kept on going. "Suit yourself," the man grunted and rolled over on his stomach.

"Do you notice anything different?" asked Skye as he and Erin floated side by side.

"No. What is it?"

"There's hardly anybody in the water. Only four others besides us. Normally everyone would go for a swim before lunch."

"It's the shark scare. Are you sure there's nothing to it?" Erin cast a sidelong look at the shore.

"I don't have enough hard data to be sure one way or another. But if there are sharks, I think they're likely to be human. Anyway it's time to go in."

As Pollock had promised, the lunch was a gourmet triumph, washed down with Dom Perignon. Spreading a spoonful of caviar on a biscuit, Skye remarked, "James of Leeds would have a fit if they could see this. For someone who's a Name, old Charles lives mighty high on the hog."

Erin made a face when he offered her the canapé. "It's all yours. I wonder how he does it? Charles, I mean. Running that yacht alone must cost a fortune."

"According to Robert, he saw what was happening in time to prepare for it. Selling off properties and moving money offshore to Switzerland. He got away with the *Caroline* and all those paintings too." He broke off to stare at the northern horizon. "That's interesting," he murmured, shading his eyes against the sun.

"What is?"

"That airplane. Do you see it? It's low, just above the horizon."

"What's so interesting about it?"

"It's a float plane. A Twin Otter. You almost never see float planes in the Caribbean. The islands are so close together there's no need."

He lowered his hands as the low-flying aircraft disappeared from view behind a hump of land. He didn't say it out loud, but the thought occurred to him that a Twin Otter equipped with floats and retractable wheels so that it could land on both water and land would be mighty useful in the drug trade. Furthermore, it had STOL capability.

"That was wonderful, Charles," Erin sighed and put down her spoon, giving him a smile that made hope flare up in his eyes, only to flicker out as his dumpy consort held out her glass for a refill. Erin turned to Skye. "We never did find out who was sick last night. I'm ashamed to say it went right out of my mind until this minute."

"I did try earlier this morning. I called the clinic but all I got was a voice-mail message that it was closed."

"What made you think anyone was sick," asked Princess Helen. "I certainly haven't heard about it."

"It's just that we saw Edwina and Sir George driving somewhere late last night."

"Maybe they were just out for a drive," Pollock suggested. "It was a lovely night," he added, forcing a smile as the Princess reached out and squeezed his arm.

"The mind boggles at the thought," laughed Skye.

Captain Morton's timing was impeccable. The *Caroline* hove into view just as the guests had had a chance to rest and digest their food. The anchorage was still crowded, but this time she managed to slide through without calling down the wrath of the other crews.

* * *

An assembly of jeeps awaited their arrival at the dock. Inspector Foxcroft helped Princess Helen into the passenger seat, then drew Skye aside. "Penelope Jones seems to have gone missing."

"Adrienne's daughter? When?"

"Oh, it's early days yet. She didn't show up for work this morning, and her things are gone. She also left a note. Adrienne seems to think that she went to Barbados to look for work in a restaurant. But I don't believe it."

"Why not?"

"The boy she runs around with says he saw her at eight o'clock last night. How can anyone get to Barbados, or even off the island, at that time of night?"

Skye frowned. "You have a point. How is Adrienne taking it?"

"She looks like hell. You don't suppose she could have done something to Penelope in one of the orgies of hers, and is covering up with this story that the girl is missing?"

"Not a chance. Adrienne is very proud of her daughter. Apart from involving her in that voodoo business, she's always been a good mother. Raised the girl all by herself."

"Do you have any idea who the father is?"

Skye shook his head. "Not the slightest. I'm not sure that anybody does, apart from Adrienne herself."

"I was just thinking the girl might have gone to be with her father."

Against Skye shook his head. "That won't fly. To the best of my knowledge there never has been any contact between Penelope and her father, whoever he might be. It's always been just Adrienne and Penelope."

Walking over to the jeep where Overfine waited, Skye decided that he would seek out Adrienne and see if there was anything he could do. He would never forgive her for what she had tried to do to Jocelyn's ashes, but they had been friends for a long time and he had gained quite a bit from that friendship. Beneath the excesses of voodoo lay some universal truths as its followers sought to accommodate themselves to a world over which they had no control.

As they turned into Whistling Frog's driveway, Skye saw that he wouldn't have to go looking for Adrienne. She was standing by the front door. Agatha would never have let her in the house. Foxcroft was right; she looked God-awful.

"You know," said Adrienne.

"I just heard. Come into the house and we'll talk." Skye wondered about the scratches and bruises on her arms, but there was no point in asking.

Agatha frowned her disapproval as Skye led the mambo into the villa. Partly to placate his stern cook, he walked through the livingroom and out onto the patio.

"Why are you so concerned, Adrienne? It's not unusual for girls her age to leave home and strike out on their own."

Adrienne shook her head stubbornly and told him about the toy panda.

Skye was unconvinced. "Maybe she decided it was time to leave her childhood things behind."

"I thought that too, at first. But I think she left it because I would know she would never go without it."

"You mean to tell you she had been abducted? Why would ..." Embarrassed by his naiveté, Skye clamped his lips shut. A girl with Penelope's spectacular figure would be literally worth her weight in gold in the white slave trade.

Reading his thoughts, Adrienne nodded grave agreement, and sighed with relief. Despite what had happened between them, Skye was going to help her.

Remembering Foxcroft's theory, Skye tried another tack. "Maybe she ran off to be with her father."

"Penelope don't know who her father is."

That settled that. "What would you like me to do,

Adrienne?"

"Help me find her. Like you're helping Sybil find her boy."

"I haven't been of much help there, I'm afraid," Skye demurred, wondering how much Adrienne knew about that incident. "What I can do, is to find out whether Penelope had applied to any of the top restaurants in Barbados. We should at least eliminate that possibility." He got to his feet. "I'll get on it right away. One more thing," he paused for emphasis. "I'll help you, Adrienne, but I want you to promise that you will never put one of your spells on me."

Unexpectedly, she crossed herself. "I promise." In one of those startling transformations of which she was capable, she had shed her haggard appearance and stood before him in all her challenging sexuality. Then she was gone, climbing effortlessly over the wall at the end of the garden.

Going back inside, Skye smiled to himself as he found the kitchen deserted. Agatha, doubtless filled with righteous indignation, had retired to her quarters. Maybe she would vent her displeasure by ruining tonight's dinner. Then Skye remembered he would be dining at Beaufort. Chuckling to himself, he picked up the phone and called Serenity. As part of his job, Foxcroft maintained close connections with the Barbados police. The inspector readily agreed to contact the chief and have the restaurants checked out to see if Penelope had shown up at any of them. "It shouldn't take long. They're all pretty much in the same area."

Skye thanked him and before ringing off, mentioned that Penelope had no idea who her father was.

"Right. Then if we don't find her in Barbados, it looks as if ..."

"Exactly," replied Skye as he rang off.

Chapter Eleven

"There's a certain protocol to attending a Beaufort social event," Skye informed Erin as they drove toward Lord Fraser's baronial villa on the rocky, surf-battered Atlantic side. By Caribbean standards, it was an inhospitable location, and the Frasers had the northeast sector of the island all to themselves. It must remind them of Scotland, thought Skye as he negotiated a steep turn in the narrow track that passed for a road. A hundred feet below, the Atlantic boomed and seethed whitely against the black rocks.

Continuing north, the cliff shelved down to form a rocky ledge which was as close as Beaufort came to having a beach. The roar of the surf diminished to a sibilant murmur as the incoming combers curled up the long incline. It was at this point that one could first hear the skirl of bagpipes welcoming the guests. Ralston, Beaufort's butler, incongruously attired in a Fraser tartan kilt with a checkered glengarry jammed on his woolly grey head, was playing a lively Scottish reel. As soon as he saw Skye's jeep he switched, with much groaning and wheezing of the pipes, into the "Skye Boat Song." Knowing what to expect, Skye brought the jeep to a halt and shut off the engine. The slow, lilting tune, commemorating the indomitable Flora MacDonald leading Bonnie Prince Charlie to safety "over the sea to Skye" after his crushing defeat at Culloden, never failed to thrill him, sending an atavistic tingle up his spine.

When the last notes died away, Erin whispered, "That's the song of your clan, isn't it?"

"Yes. Although I never thought much about it until I began coming to Manchineel and Lord Fraser made such a big thing about my Scottish heritage." He waved his thanks to Ralston, but made no attempt to start the jeep. Sheena, Lord Fraser's pet chimp, was coming, in her rolling chimpanzee fashion, across the driveway, bearing a silver tray with two glasses of champagne. She also was wearing a kilt with the Fraser tartan and had a glengarry tilted rakishly over one ear. Smacking her lips softly, she held the tray up to the jeep's open window and Skye took the glasses from her.

"I had to take both glasses or Sheena would have been offended. And we don't want that, I can assure you."

"You can drink both of them. Good health."

"It's curious," Skye mused as he sipped the champagne, "the penchant some of these British aristocrats have for keeping exotic animals. I was reading about Lord Lassiter ..."

"That horrible man."

"A monster, I agree. Anyway, one of the wildest stories about him is that he shot himself on the estate of a friend, a belted earl no less, and his body was fed to the tigers in the earl's private zoo."

Sheena, a look of intense concentration on her simian face, came back to collect the empty glasses. Knowing he would be somewhere nearby to control the ape, Skye looked around for Logan, Beaufort's enigmatic head groundskeeper. The taciturn Logan — if he had a first name, nobody knew what it was — kept very much to himself and almost never left the confines of the Beaufort estate. He was quite good-looking in a sullen sort of way, but his surly demeanour made people give him a wide berth.

It was easy to locate Logan. All Skye had to do was to follow the chimp going back with the empty glasses. Logan was waiting for her under a breadfruit tree, with glasses and champagne for the arriving guests. It was a menial, almost demeaning task, but Logan was going about it with his usual inscrutability. Skye waved at him as he reached for the ignition, but Logan pretended not to see the friendly gesture. The driveway was lined on both sides with Norfolk Island pines. The symmetrical evergreen trees, floodlit from below, lent a suitably northern, untropical, look to the imposing pile of stone that was Beaufort. The kilted nobleman, flanked by his brace of Scottish deerhounds, stood at the top of the broad staircase to welcome his guests. From the number of jeeps in the parking area, Skye figured that he and Erin must be among the last to arrive.

Lord Fraser smiled his approval when Erin held out the back of her hands for the giant hounds to sniff. They wagged their tails majestically as she patted their shaggy coats.

"Oh, dear. Ralston is being very naughty," Fraser murmured, as the distant piper struck up another tune. "That will be Her Royal Highness arriving and the rascal's playing 'The Blue Bonnets are Back Over the Border.'"

Skye chuckled, "Not exactly the most loyal tune in the world, is it?"

"Not to the English." Then His Lordship brightened. "She'll never recognize it, anyway."

"Let me guess," Erin said as they strolled arm-in-arm through the great entrance hall where the other guests were assembled, waiting to pay homage to the Princess before dispersing into the garden and the villa's two drawing rooms. "That tune has something to do with Bonnie Prince Charlie and the Highland Uprising, doesn't it?"

"How about that," exclaimed Skye. "An American who actually knows something about Scottish history! I thought I was the only one outside of a university who did."

"You've just heard everything I know." She paused as Zulu the cheetah, its non-retractable claws clicking on the marble floor, made its calm, unhurried way among the guests. It wore a choke collar with no leash but Skye spotted a gardener, who worked under Logan, keeping an eye on it.

Erin made a clicking sound with her tongue and the animal came over to her, pressing its blunt, uncatlike snout into her cupped hand and giving its chirping purr as she rubbed it behind the ears.

"You Jane, but me not Tarzan," murmured an impressed Skye.

Still stroking the purring cat, Erin looked up at him. "It's funny you should say that. When I was a young girl I really related to Jane. My grandfather — the most interesting and charming man I've ever known — had a private zoo on his estate at Newport Beach, including no less than five of these fellows. Grandfather had the theory that you needed at least that many before they would breed. He figured the males needed competition.

He must have been right because he managed to breed them when nobody else could. I spent all my school vacations there, and I guess I was sort of a juvenile Jane Porter, swinging through the trees with a pet chimpanzee and playing with lion cubs and monkeys. There was even a vine where you could swing over a creek stocked with crocodiles and alligators."

Somewhat overwhelmed with this flow of information, Skye selected one piece to respond to. "I'm amazed you remember Jane's last name was Porter. That would make a great trivia question."

"Grandfather had all the Tarzan books in that incredible library of his. I devoured them and, like I say, I fantasized about being Jane."

A commotion under the archway framing the entrance made everyone glance in that direction. Her lady-in-waiting was dabbing a furious Princess Helen's face with a Kleenex while Lady Fraser wrung her hands and made inarticulate, apologetic noises. Charles Pollock was struggling, without too much success, to keep a straight face.

"That wretched ape of yours threw champagne at me!" The Princess's normally plummy voice was strident with fury and was clearly audible to everyone present. Those guests who were at a safe distance exchanged delighted smiles, while those closer to her murmured "How awful!" "Are you quite all right, Your Royal Highness?" and similar sycophantic phrases. Followed by her lady-in-waiting and an agitated Lady Fraser, the Princess swept across the floor to a washroom. Lord Fraser was considerably less upset by the incident than his wife. There was a gleam of amusement in his eyes as he came over to where Skye and Erin were standing and hooked a finger under the cheetah's collar. "Somehow I don't think Her Royal Highness is in the mood for any more animal acts tonight," he said, beckoning the gardener to lead the cat away. "Sheena has never acted up like that before," he added. "I'll just go and have a word with Logan to find out what really happened."

Sir George Glessop stationed himself outside the washroom door. "I want to make sure that animal didn't bite or scratch her," he told Skye and Erin. "If he broke the skin, she'll have to have a tetanus shot."

"I'm glad it's you who'll be telling her that, and not me," said Skye.

But when the Princess, freshly made up by her lady-in-waiting, emerged from the washroom, she brushed by the doctor and called imperiously for a drink. But Glessop didn't give up that easily. As Skye watched, the surgeon looked at her from every angle and turned away only when he was satisfied that she bore no bite or scratch mark. The old guy hasn't lost it altogether, thought Skye. That was a pretty professional performance. He was even more impressed when Glessop asked for soda with a dash of lime instead of his usual large whisky.

"I have to operate tomorrow," he said importantly. Edwina Stewart heard him and came over to tell him that his flight was all arranged. "I talked to Manchineel Air this afternoon and they have received permission to take off at 6:30 in the morning." The nurse smiled somewhat apologetically at Skye. "I realize the early take-off might disturb those of you who live near the airstrip, but this is a special case."

"No problem." Skye waved her concern away. The Company had decreed that no flight could leave before 7:30 a.m., but the noise of the planes taking off never bothered Skye since he always slept with the windows closed and the air-conditioning on.

"I was talking to a patient of yours a few days ago.

Over in St. Vincent," Skye said casually to Glessop.

"Oh." The doctor was instantly wary. His bloodshot eyes — one day's abstinence could never clear those eyes — narrowed behind his gold-rimmed glasses. "Who was that?"

"Her name is Sybil. That wouldn't mean anything to you, but she was the cook at Whistling Frog when we first came here. But she, of course, remembers you. You operated on her in Jamaica about six or seven months ago."

"I trust she has made a complete recovery?"

"She's fine physically. But her son has gone missing. The police think that he's run away, but she doesn't believe that. I'm trying to help her. I'm running an ad in the *Gleaner* with his picture."

"How old is her son?"

"Ten. His name is Andrew. Andrew Hodgson."

Glessop's forehead was damp with perspiration. He dabbed at it with a handkerchief. "Let's continue this discussion outside." Skye followed him out into the fragrant garden. "I want you to understand that the harvesting of human organs for transplantation is perfectly legal in this part of the world. I am breaking no laws." Glessop paused to take his glass of soda from the waiter who had followed them out with their drinks. "On the contrary, I am rendering a service to humanity. Just as you and your dear wife did when you donated her organs."

"That was somewhat different." Glessop's pompous attitude irritated Skye. "That was a case of harvesting organs from someone who was brain dead. But in Sybil's case, a perfectly healthy person was selling an organ for profit. From what I learned about transplantation at the time of Jocelyn's death, that would be illegal in both Canada and the United States."

"And in the U.K.," agreed Glessop bitterly. "Many so-called 'civilized' countries have seen fit to pass laws making such a transaction illegal. Our misguided Parliament passed the Human Organ Transplant Act to prohibit commercial dealings in human organs and the transplanting of organs between persons not genetically related. The sanctimonious bastards!" Indignation purpled Glessop's veined cheeks as he paused for breath. He had reeled off the wording of the act as if he knew it by heart. The reason for his familiarity with the act became apparent as he continued, this time with a little smile that was almost reminiscent. "I was attached to a private hospital in London where people from India and Turkey came to sell their kidneys. Word of that got about and caused an uproar that persuaded our gutless politicians to enact that ridiculous law. I chose to defy it and continued performing the operation. I felt it was for the higher good. Eventually, I paid the price."

The higher good, and the higher money, thought Skye sardonically. That private hospital must have been a gold mine. But there was no denying the underlying sincerity in Glessop's voice. The man obviously believed that what he was doing was right. So this was the scandal that finally had knocked him off his perch in the medical hierarchy.

Glessop seemed unwilling to let go of the subject. He continued talking, almost as if delivering a well-rehearsed lecture. "It is worth noting," he was saying, "that legislation had to be passed to make the transplantation of human organs a crime. In other words, there was nothing intrinsically criminal in the act itself."

"Some people might think it was morally wrong to sell one's organs," interjected Skye, his interest fully engaged.

"In heaven's name, why? Everyone benefits from the transaction. The donors receive a payment that enables them to improve their living conditions, send their children to university, or just put food on the table. The recipients receive the most precious gift of all — life itself. Can you imagine the agony and suspense that a patient goes through — wondering if a kidney, or a liver or a heart will become available before it's too late? I've known cases where the patient died the very day a match was found. The queue is getting longer all the time. Nowadays, it frequently takes a year or eighteen months, or even longer, before someone's turn comes up. And the supply of organs is falling off." Glessop looked at his drink with distaste. He handed it to a passing waiter and asked him to add a small jigger of whisky. He was obviously enjoying his role as an authoritative lecturer.

"I find that hard to believe," said Skye. "With all the publicity on the subject, you would think more and more people would be donating their organs."

"There are two reasons for that." The waiter returned with Glessop's drink. It was dark brown. Knowing who it was for, the bartender had poured Glessop's usual triple. The surgeon hesitated, then took it from the tray. Before he could raise it to his lips Edwina took it from him and emptied it into a nearby heliconia plant. "The woman you are operating on tomorrow is a friend of mine, Sir George," she chided him.

"Is that so, my dear? You never told me. With you there to help me, she will be in good hands." Glessop positively glowed with the thought of playing so important a role in Edwina's eyes. She might be the nurse, but he was the surgeon on whose skill her friend's life would depend. "Skye and I were just enjoying a fascinating discussion on the sale of human organs."

"Can anyone join in?" Erin had kept her distance while the two men were deep in conversation, but now she followed Edwina over.

"Of course." Skye smiled at her and took her hand. She squeezed his lightly in return. "Sir George was saying that the supply of organs was decreasing and he was about to tell us why."

"As I said, there are two reasons. The most significant source for organs has always been the high-risk group — young males between the ages of 15 and 26. They are the ones who tend to get in accidents that result in head injuries and render them brain dead. But with the advent of air bags and less emphasis among the young on the consumption of alcohol, there has been a remarkable reduction in fatal head injuries in that group. Particularly in North America. The second reason, which, I fear, reflects no credit on my profession, is that some prospective donors are being frightened off because they feel the attending physicians might be tempted to let them die so that their organs can be harvested, perhaps for some high-paying recipient."

"What are your views on the ethics of people selling their organs for money?" Skye asked Erin, intrigued by what her answer would be.

Years of exposure to the Kelly family had taught Erin what the politically correct response to virtually every situation should be. "Doesn't it exploit the poor and give medical priority to the wealthy simply because they have the ability to pay?"

"Spoken like a true Kelly," Skye murmured. "Yet don't I recall something about your father-in-law getting a new kidney some years ago? Did he wait in line?"

"Ex-father-in-law, please. And no, he didn't. Wait in line, I mean. He had the operation in some private clinic in Florida. It was all done within a matter of days." She gave Skye a speculative look. "Not many people know about that."

"As to the poor being exploited," Glessop was intent on pursuing the subject, "surely people's organs belong to them, just like any other personal property. If you're dealing with adults of normal intelligence, they can make decisions about their own priorities. What about the miner who descends into a dangerous gas-prone coal mine in order to feed his family? Or a chemical worker who continues to work in a plant that he knows is unsafe because there are no other jobs available?"

"It still strikes me as a new type of Darwinism," said Erin. "Survival of the richest."

Edwina's eyes blazed. "That's easy for you to say. But the woman Dr. Glessop will be operating on tomorrow is selling her kidney to raise money so her husband can go to the States for an eye operation. If he doesn't have the operation, he will be blind within the year."

Erin bit her lip. It was not the first time the difference between those to whom money was never a problem and those who had to scramble to survive had been brought home to her. She had the good sense to realize that it was only too easy for the wealthy to take the moral high ground on issues that would never intrude into their own comfortable lives.

"I keep hearing that the operation will be performed tomorrow," Skye interjected before Erin could respond to Edwina's biting attack, although it didn't look as if she intended to. "But from here to Jamaica is one hell of a long flight, especially in a light twin like the Super Baron. Will you be able to operate after flying all day?"

"The operation will be in Grenada. St. George's University Medical School has a tertiary care hospital that's every bit as good as the one in Jamaica." Glessop was staring resentfully at the heliconia.

Skye was relieved, for the sake of Glessop's patient, if nothing else. Grenada, which anchored the southern end of the Grenadines, was only a few minutes away by air.

Waiters began to bustle about, arranging place settings on the tables. It was another cloudless Caribbean night, the velvet sky bejewelled with softly glittering stars, and dinner would be served outdoors on the terrace. Lady Fraser came out from the villa to collect Erin. Princess Helen wished to have a visit with her.

"I probably shouldn't have spoken so sharply to her," Edwina said uncomfortably. "After all, she's an important guest, and I'm just an employee."

"She won't take it that way." Skye assured her. "She's not that kind of person. But if that had been her dragon of an ex-mother-in-law, you'd probably be out on your ear, as valuable to the Company as you are. The power that family has is incredible. And they enjoy using it."

From somewhere up in the hills came the distant sound of a solitary drum. As always it caused Sheena to react. From her enclosure at the foot of the garden came the sound of her anxious hooting. Nick, vacuous pale blonde on his arm, came up to Glessop and began to talk to him about a reception the doctor was going to hold to mark the installation of some new equipment in the clinic. The Company would pick up the tab, naturally. Stifling a sneeze, Skye led Edwina out of range of the restaurateur's overpowering perfume.

Edwina frowned in the direction of the drumming. "I hear from some patients at the clinic that there's something very big brewing in the voodoo world. Something to do with the appearance of a powerful new *loa*." She paused and listened to the chimp's hooting. "If I were Lord Fraser, I'd keep a close eye on that ape of his. I think I should warn him."

"You mean because she could be a substitute 'goat with no horns'?"

"It's a thought that has occurred to me."

"Sheena would put up one hell of a fight. Chimps are extraordinarily powerful."

"You forget these people are Carouns, descendants of one of the most war-like tribes in Africa. They're good workers, but I'm beginning to think it was a mistake to bring them to Manchineel."

"They would also have Logan to deal with," Skye pointed out.

"Ah, yes. Logan," the nurse replied enigmatically.

"By the way, you and the good doctor were out pretty late last night. Erin and I thought somebody must be sick."

"Oh? That was you in the jeep, then. Sir George needed some fresh air, but he wasn't in any shape to walk, so I took him for a drive with the windows down. It always seems to help."

As they talked, Edwina kept her eye on Glessop. When she saw Nick and his blond companion wandering away, she excused herself and hurried over to join him. It seemed the good doctor was in for a sober evening, whether he liked it or not.

Unexpectedly, the distant drumming ceased. "Thank heavens for that." Louella Harper, awash in layers of chiffon, floated up. "Those drums make my skin crawl." Linking her arm with Skye's, she said. "The Highness is very taken with Erin. I guess they have something in common because they're both so much in the public eye. They're having a great time exchanging horror stories about the press. Anyway, by royal command we're all to sit together."

As they joined the stream of guests moving toward the tables, Louella cleared her throat nervously and looked up at Skye. "Annette, that's my new cook, had some extraordinary tale about a voodoo ceremony and dear Jocelyn's ashes. The story is all over the island. Is there any truth to it, Skye?"

"No harm done," replied Skye abruptly, effectively cutting off any further discussion.

As soon as they were seated, Princess Helen wanted to have the latest word on the PM. Sir George cleared his throat. "The news is not encouraging, I'm afraid. He's starting to hallucinate, which is a bad sign. It means his system is turning toxic. The clinic is standing by, ready to operate the minute a matching heart shows up. But I can't hold out much hope of that. His being B-negative cuts down the chances drastically." Sir George took a sip from his glass, realized too late it was water, and hastily put it down.

"Robert was quoting you the other night to the effect that there's the best chance of a match if there's a family relationship between the donor and the recipient," said Erin. "Is that really true?"

"Absolutely. If you're talking about a heart, as we are in this case, you must have a blood type match, but there also are something like eighty tissue matches that are very important. The chances of tissue matchings are much greater if there's a blood connection. That's why kidney transplantations between siblings are so successful. Obviously, a familial connection is not absolutely essential, but it does help."

"Interesting. I hadn't realized that before." Erin picked up her salad fork.

By the time dessert was served, Princess Helen was well into her cups. Scowling at her host who was seated across from her, she muttered, "That insolent rogue, Logan, deliberately put that ape of yours up to throwing champagne at me."

Lord Fraser looked shocked. "Logan would never dare to do that, ma'am," he protested. "Apes are unpredictable and chimps are the worst of the lot. They're the most ..."

"Robert," interrupted the Princess, "I'm not in the mood for a lecture on animal behaviour. Have someone fetch Logan so I can question him."

"That would not be advisable, ma'am, if I may say so." Fraser was visibly upset. "He will have retired by now, in any event. He rises very early in the morning."

"So?"

Fraser patted his mouth with a napkin and got to his feet. "I will fetch him myself, ma'am."

If Logan had been wakened from sleep, he gave no sign of it. His face was set in its usual sullen expression, and he looked at the inebriated Princess with thinly veiled contempt. "Her Royal Highness is very upset over that incident with the champagne. As we all are." Lord Fraser was doing his diplomatic best to placate the irate Princess. "She feels that you might have put Sheena up to it. I tried to explain that chimps, even ones as well trained as Sheena, are unpredictable. I'm right about that, aren't I?"

"That's right. If Sheena doesn't ... don't ... like a person she has her own ways of showing it. Just the other day, she crapped into her hand and threw it at one of the gardeners. Hit him square in the face, she did. Maybe Her Royal Highness got off lightly," he added, after Louella had stopped choking and spluttering.

"Why you insolent cur!" A furious Princess Helen dashed her full glass of red wine in Logan's face. Logan didn't flinch or blink. He stood stock still while the wine ran down his face and onto his shirt. "Well, I guess that evens things up," murmured Skye.

Despite herself, Princess Helen grinned. Lord Fraser exhaled a sigh of relief, touched Logan on the arm and walked away with him. When he returned, the party was beginning to break up. He drew Skye to one side. "All this excitement with The Highness nearly drove it out of my mind, but I've arranged for you to visit Frigate. You'll be contacted by someone called Baker."

"Fantastic. I really appreciate that, Robert. How did you manage to arrange it so quickly?"

"It turned out that the law firm I use in Bermuda is associated with the Turks & Caicos firm that acts for the Frigate people. The arrangements were made through them."

Skye smiled to himself as he mentally catalogued the photographic equipment he would take — the Nikon with a motor drive, two zoom lenses, and a tripod. Definitely a tripod — the photos would have to be razor sharp if he expected *National Geographic* to accept them. He was still smiling as he went to collect Erin.

* * *

"Logan's not exactly your average humble servant, is he?"

"Not much tugging of the old forelock there," Skye agreed, slowing down to follow Louella's jeep through the gate.

"I wonder what made Sheena throw the champagne at Princess Helen?"

"We'll never know. Like Robert said, chimps are unpredictable as hell. Maybe she didn't like the Princess's perfume, or the smell of gin on her breath. Or maybe Logan put her up to it. I wouldn't put it past him."

"Logan is what, in my college days, we would have called a hunk."

"Yeah. I guess you could call him handsome in a dark, Heathcliffian way."

"Women who marry dark, Heathcliffian men usually end up in shelters for battered wives."

"Did that happen to you?"

"No. I wasn't a battered wife. Patrick did hit me once. Early on in our marriage. But he was so horrified by what he had done that it never happened again. He's not a bad person, just terribly weak. But that didn't prevent him from continuing a lifestyle that no woman should be asked to put up with."

"Is that what led you to drink?" Put so directly it sounded harsh, but Skye sensed that Erin preferred to confront her problems head-on.

"Partly, I guess. But what finally tipped me over the edge was the Kelly clan, and that ogre of a mother-in-law. I came to despise everything they did, and everything they stood for, and they felt the same way about me. The only one I have any use for is the old man himself. We got along right from the start. He even made a pass at me."

"You're joking!"

"It's the truth. He tried it on with every girl Patrick brought home. And I gather he succeeded more often than not. When he saw I wasn't interested, he laughed it off, and we became good friends." She paused, "Patrick and I are friends, too. He's as much a victim of that family as I am."

Skye made an inarticulate sound in this throat, and she took a deep breath. "I know you may not want to hear this, but that accident took a heavy toll on him as well. It's the O.J. syndrome at work. He was never convicted but everybody knows he was guilty. Worse, they know he ran away and left your wife to die. He was going to run for the Senate on the Democratic ticket but the party bosses backed off."

"Couldn't the Kelly clan fix that?"

"They tried. God, how they tried. Patrick Senior called in every marker he had, and promised to contribute millions to the campaign, but the party wouldn't touch Patrick with a barge pole. They knew they would lose if they let him run. Now the family is pinning all their hopes on my Patrick. I can't let them turn him into the kind of man his father is."

"In all of this, I haven't heard one word about remorse."

"Oh, he was remorseful, all right. But with him it's hard to tell whether he was feeling remorse for what he had done, or self-pity for what it had done to him."

She looked out the side window as they passed by the stables. The horses were motionless statues in the starlight. A barn owl, called the jumbie bird by the superstitious natives, ghostly white in the glare of the headlights, flew up from the side of the road. "I can see I've upset you, Skye. I'm sorry, but I wanted you to understand why Patrick didn't stop. He had no choice. All his life the family has covered for him and bailed him out of scrapes. That's how he reacts to everything. He's a man-child. I'm not trying to make excuses for him; running away like that was a cowardly, despicable act, but that's the way he's programmed."

Skye was jolted with a realization that he no longer gave a damn about Patrick Kelly. Let him go to hell in his own way. He, Skye, had wasted enough time brooding about the worthless son-of-a-bitch. He could almost feel the tension leaving his shoulders as another piece of baggage fell away.

Erin looked sideways at him as he drove past Banyan without turning in. She nodded happily when he said, "Let's make love. This time I came prepared." He continued, "There's an air mattress in the back. We'll head for the beach."

Lying in Skye's arms after a leisurely and satisfying session of lovemaking, Erin looked up at him and asked, "I guess you and Jocelyn didn't want children?"

"Huh? Oh, you mean the vasectomy? That was just a convenient shorthand. It wasn't exactly the time to go into a long, detailed explanation. The fact is I came down with the mumps when I was 19. Complications arose that left me sterile. Thankfully not impotent, as you may have noticed."

"With pleasure," Erin gave his penis a playful tweak. "Does it bother you?"

"There are times when I feel incomplete. Does it bother you?"

"Not in the slightest. You're the most complete man I've ever known."

Chapter Twelve

The *Advocate* was always flown over from Barbados on the first flight of the day. Overfine brought it out to Skye with his second cup of coffee. There was a brief follow-up item on the mutilated bodies of the Haitian refugees that had been washed up on shore in the Bahamas. Oddly, there was no attempt to link that incident with that of the three bodies that had come ashore on Manchineel. Now that he thought about it, there had been no mention in the local papers about the Manchineel bodies after the first excited accounts. The Company's fine Italian hand, no doubt.

The lead story was that James of Leeds had experienced another financial blow. The loss of £2.3 billion had actually been incurred three years previously, since it took that long for the insurance syndicates to total up the financial results. It was the fourth year of massive losses for the centuries-old insurer.

Skye read the lengthy article with avid interest and a

frisson of apprehension over how close he had come to being one of the James Names himself. That had been at a time when the Names were enjoying annual returns of 60 percent or more. Then came a series of disasters — oil spills, industrial pollution, chemical plant explosions, asbestos health claims, earthquakes and other catastrophes. Hundreds of the Names, individual investors with unlimited personal liability, had already been bankrupted, and the article said that hundreds more would be unable to survive the next round of cash calls. One source was quoted as saying the amount of money now being demanded of the Names was "usually only obtained with a mask, a gun and a get-away car." Countless marriages had been wrecked, and the article claimed that the financial debacle had been the direct cause of at least fifty suicides.

Skye winced in sympathy at the thought of those poor devils, all of whom had once been wealthy, waiting for the next blow to fall. It had been that unlimited personal liability that had finally made him decide not to invest. The possibility of losing everything he and Jocelyn possessed was just not an acceptable risk. But it hadn't deterred thousands of other investors, lured by years of handsome returns. As his economics professor would have said, they had failed to do scenario planning and had relied purely on statistical evidence.

Skye's musings were cut short by the ringing of a telephone. Overfine carried the phone out to him, telling him that a Mr. Baker was on the line.

"I understand you are interested in our frigate bird rookery, Mr. MacLeod."

"Very."

"I will be more than happy to show it to you."

"Wonderful. When?"

"What about this morning? I could come over and pick you up at the dock. Say half-an-hour?"

"Excellent. That will give me time to assemble my gear."

* * *

The black cigarette boat rumbled into reverse and gently nudged the fenders of truck tires nailed to the dock. Skye caught the painter and looped it around a cleat, then bent down to give the passenger, whom Skye took to be Baker, a hand as he clambered up the ladder. Baker, middle-aged with an incipient pot, was wearing the usual business attire in the islands — long pants and long-sleeved white shirt open at the neck. He shook hands and handed Skye a business card. It was embossed with the name of the company and a small logo of a frigate bird in the upper left-hand corner and, underneath the company name, the words: Roger Baker, Sales Representative.

Wondering what there was for sale on Frigate Island, Skye thanked him again for his kindness. He decided not to mention the time he and Jocelyn had been chased off the island. He didn't want anything to jeopardize his chance of photographing the rookery.

"Your reputation as an investor is well known to us, Mr. MacLeod."

"Skye, please." So there was going to be a sales pitch.

"Thank you. I'm Roger." Baker grunted as the cigarette boat slammed into a wave. The waves seemed to be higher than normal. Clinging to his seat as they continued their crashing progress, Baker leaned over and shouted in Skye's ear, "When this boat hits them, it's the waves that move aside." Then he shrugged and smiled apologetically as conversation became impossible. The turmoil abruptly ceased as they entered the mouth of Hurricane Hole. The driver eased back on the throttle and it was almost eerily quiet as they glided down the long inlet, lined on both sides with sheer volcanic rock. At the base of the cliffs, a dense growth of mangroves crowded out into the water. Except at the far end, where the cliff dropped sheer and straight to a narrow rock shelf. Herons flapped clumsily into flight as the boat went past. The bow wave died away to a ripple as they approached the jetty where a military-type jeep waited for them.

"In my opinion, this is the best natural harbour in the entire Caribbean," declared Baker. "The entrance is both wide and long. The harbour itself is surrounded on three sides by cliffs. Makes a great sanctuary from storms. Best of all — it's deep, one hundred feet at the base of the cliffs."

"That's how it got its name. Boats took refuge here from tropical storms for years. But I gather that's no longer allowed?"

Baker frowned as they settled themselves in the jeep, "I know that we are criticized for keeping strangers off the island. But I am sure you will understand the need to protect our property. In this part of the world it is very difficult to eject squatters once they have settled in. In Manchineel, the Company has tried for years without success to remove the fishermen's camp."

"You have a point," Skye conceded.

Like the operator of the cigarette boat, the driver of the jeep appeared to be unarmed. Skye was to be shown a sanitized, non-threatening island. And he could count on his guides to steer clear of any booby traps.

As the jeep ground in low gear up the narrow switch-back track that had been bulldozed into the cliff face, Baker said, "I realize you are here for the birds.

But, as I mentioned before, your reputation as a successful investor is well known. Maybe I could give you a brief tour of our beautiful island so you can see for yourself its potential as a resort."

Investing in a resort, in the Caribbean or anywhere else, was the last thing Skye would think of doing. But he wasn't about to turn down a chance to find out more about this mysterious and forbidding island. "That would be very interesting, so long as we leave plenty of time for the birds."

"Of course," Baker agreed and launched into what was obviously a well-rehearsed spiel. "Our research indicates that the time has finally arrived for this island to be developed. The big tourist islands, Barbados, Jamaica and the like, are touristed-out. More and more, sophisticated travellers are seeking a different Caribbean experience, one that is well away from the crowded tourist haunts. Manchineel is no competition; there are only a few building lots left and, in any case, it can accommodate only a small number of people. Our plans call for much higher density, but without losing the unique Caribbean ambience that people will pay for."

"I'm interested to hear that your plans are so far advanced." Skye grabbed the handhold on the dash as, with a final lurch, the jeep gained the level ground at the top of the cliff. "I was under the impression that development had been indefinitely delayed."

Baker sighed gustily. "It's a matter of obtaining the necessary financing. That's something you might be able to help us with. With all your contacts. But let's not talk about that now. Just enjoy the view."

Baker stood up as the jeep jerked to a halt and pointed to the north. "Just take a look at that!"

Skye had to admit the view was breathtakingly beautiful. Manchineel dominated the foreground, but other islands could be seen beyond it, receding in a gentle curving arc into the blue distance. Skye's gaze travelled down to the base of the cliff. The dark cobalt blue colour of the water revealed a precipitous drop into the depths. There was no beach, just a narrow band of black volcanic rock.

Seeing the skeptical look on Skye's face, Baker said, "This would be a perfect place for scuba diving."

"No doubt. But from the air, the island looks to be completely rock-bound."

"Sand can always be imported," replied Baker as they bumped their way across a field of tough brown grass.

And be swept away by the next tropical storm, thought Skye, but he merely nodded noncommittally. Whoever had purchased the island with the idea of turning it into a resort was either deluding themselves or had very deep pockets.

They came to the top of the hill where a well-worn, rutted track led down to the dilapidated buildings of the abandoned fish-packing plant. The buildings faced the field with the boulders. "Those, of course, will have to go," said Baker. "The land is perfectly level where those buildings are, and I can see tennis courts and a communal swimming pool there.

"There's no point in taking the time to look at them," Baker added as they drove on. "At the moment we use them to store our equipment and vehicles."

Skye nodded. He could see the tracks of vehicles criss-crossing the sparse grass. Some of them were very wide, at least eighteen inches, like those of a backhoe. That would explain the nomadic boulders. They were heading south and Baker was saying how a low rise to their right would make a perfect site for a hotel.

Hotel. So that was what Baker had in mind when

he talked about density. There goes the peace and tranquillity of neighbouring Manchineel. The thought made Skye tense until he told himself that there was little chance of Frigate Island being developed any time in the near future. Baker's sales talk lacked conviction, as though he realized that himself. It was probably the effect he wanted — trafficking in drugs was much more lucrative than running a resort.

A movement in a roadside bush caught Skye's attention. He motioned the driver to stop and peered into the scraggly foliage. "A white-eyed vireo," he pronounced with satisfaction. "This is pretty far south for that little fellow."

"You are the one who compiled the checklist of birds for Manchineel, aren't you?" Baker asked as they drove one.

"Yes. And I would be more than happy to do the same for Frigate."

"Wonderful. I'll get back to you on it." Baker paused. "You've been very patient, and I know you're anxious to see the nesting site. I have taken the liberty of arranging a picnic lunch. The question is, would you like to have it before or after you take your pictures?"

"You really are very kind. The light is ideal now so, if you don't mind, I'd like to visit the rookery first."

The ground was getting progressively boggier as they went. The jeep finally came to a halt in front of what appeared to be an impenetrable wall of mangroves.

"We'll have to walk the last bit," said Baker as they climbed out of the jeep. Skye wondered how anyone could be expected to penetrate that dense and swampy growth but then he saw that Baker was leading them to an opening that had been hacked into the trees. Beyond the opening, planks had been nailed across the arched roots to make a precarious path over the ooze of the swamp. Overhead, more than a hundred adult birds, including many white-breasted females, soared high above the sea, uttering a curious whistling, muttering sound that the birds made only when near the colony.

"Spectacular," murmured Skye as they emerged into a clearing and he had his first view of the rookery. Male frigate birds, the sacs under their beaks inflated like bright red balloons, squatted on crudely constructed nesting platforms, cackling hoarsely to attract a mate. Large nestlings bumbled about on other nests, begging for food with open beaks. There were splashes of white guano everywhere.

Setting up the tripod, Skye began to shoot, the motor drive whirring as he took one exposure after another. In rapid succession, he went through three rolls of film. Reloading, he gave Baker a thumbs-up. Then he hastily looked through the viewfinder again as he spotted a male bird standing on the edge of its platform nest, stretching its legs and furiously flapping its wings in its struggle to get airborne.

"That's why they always nest on the windward side. They need the wind to take off."

"Interesting." Baker was clearly enjoying Skye's enthusiasm.

A brown booby, flying low above the water, suddenly plunge-dived into the sea. Seeing this, a frigate bird immediately folded its wings and dove straight down to be in position when the booby surfaced with its prize. As soon as the booby took off, the frigate bird was after it, the booby twisting and turning in a frantic, but vain, attempt to evade its pursuer. It was no match for the larger, faster frigate bird and, realizing there was no other escape for it, the hapless booby disgorged the fish and flew away. The frigate bird caught the piscine ransom in mid-air and carried it off to its nest.

"Now there's an executive for you," Baker remarked admiringly. "Get someone else to do all the work while you reap the spoils."

"More piratical than executive," smiled Skye. "But I suppose it could be much the same thing."

A school of flying fish suddenly broke free of the water and launched into their gliding flight. A low-flying frigate bird immediately set off in aerial pursuit and plucked one of them out of the air.

"I've heard of them doing that, but I've never seen it before," said Skye. "This place is a naturalist's paradise!" He turned to face Baker. "If your people develop this island, they must take steps to protect this site."

"I'm sure they will. Have you seen enough? Good. Let's go grab some lunch."

Back in the jeep, they drove to where lunch had been set out on a folding table, presided over by a rough-looking customer in dungarees. A bottle of wine was cooling in what Skye saw was a metal wastepaper basket. A faded beach umbrella had been rigged to provide some shade.

"Say, that looks great! Excuse me for a moment while I pump ship." Before Baker, who was already sitting down, could say anything, Skye headed for the cover of some gnarled trees almost leafless with age. A few yards further in was a withered-looking poinsettia. He walked behind it and unzipped his jeans. Zipping up his crotch after relieving himself, he heard a faint chipping sound, like the call of a tiny bird. Curious to identify the species, he took a few steps further into the vegetation and peered in the direction of the sound. It wasn't a bird, it was the sound of the revolving blades of a ventilator set into the ground. Skye beat a hasty retreat, the sound fading into nothingness as he went. The dungaree-clad guard was coming after him, but turned back when he saw Skye returning.

The lunch was pretty basic, thick ham and overcooked beef sandwiches, but Skye enjoyed it. Baker was proving to be good company; he was both a good talker and, even rarer, a good listener.

"This has been a great day, Roger. Thank you very much," said Skye as the cigarette boat headed back out through Hurricane Hole.

"You're very welcome. I enjoyed it myself. What you said about those birds was really interesting." Then they smacked into the waves outside the inlet and conversation ceased until they reached the other side of Commotion Channel.

Skye broke into a smile when he saw Erin, mind-blowing in bum-hugging shorts and sleeveless top, waiting for them on the dock.

Baker whistled under his breath. "That's Erin Kelly. She's a lot better looking than her pictures. Is she waiting for you?"

"Yep."

"You're quite a guy, Skye MacLeod. Quite a guy."

"You've had a great time, haven't you? I can tell," said Erin as they watched the departing cigarette boat. Baker, who had seemed almost starstruck on meeting Erin, was sitting in the front cockpit beside the driver. As the boat picked up speed, he turned and waved. The two figures on the dock waved back and then headed for the Banyan jeep.

"My God, Erin, you look good enough to eat!"

"Maybe later," she said and smiled.

"Let's have a drink and I'll tell you about my day," Skye said as he parked the jeep in front of Nick's Bar. Ignoring the passers-by, he leaned across and kissed her soundly on the lips.

Skye's account of his day had to wait. Nick himself

was in the bar, a rare occurrence, and came over to sit with them. To him there was no mystery about Penelope's disappearance. She wanted to get off the island and away from her mother. She was getting fed up with Adrienne's mumbo-jumbo. It hadn't looked that way to Skye the night of the goat sacrifice, but he didn't interrupt as Nick went on to say that he had offered Penelope a job in the restaurant, but she wanted to find something in Barbados.

If that's where she had gone, Skye would soon know. Foxcroft should have had a report from the Barbados police by now. Skye said something noncommittal and Nick heaved himself to his feet and went off to chat up some of the other customers.

Skye told Erin about Foxcroft's enquiries. "It makes sense," he went on, "It's natural for an attractive girl her age to want to expand her horizons. I must say, however, that she seemed pretty wrapped up in the voodoo ceremony when I saw her — I'm sure she was in a trance. Either that or she's one hell of an actress."

"Maybe that's why she wants to break away. Maybe she was frightened of the hold it was getting over her." Skye nodded thoughtful agreement and Erin said, "Okay, now tell me about your day."

Skye described his tour of the secretive island, dwelling mostly on the rookery, and omitting the part about the ventilator. He had no intention of sticking his nose into the drug trade. That was the US Coast Guard's business, not his.

"I can hardly wait to see the photos."

"That's going to take a little time. I'm sending them to the States to be processed."

Their drinks — a Red Stripe beer for him and iced tea for her — were finished. She shook her head when he asked if she would like another one. "I guess it's my turn to tell you about my day." A cloud seemed to pass over Erin's face as she spoke. "The Kellys are on the warpath."

"Somehow that doesn't surprise me. What happened?"

"I had a phone call from the old man. He placed the call but it would be the Dragonlady who made him do it. You and I being involved with each other is driving them up the wall."

"Brenda?"

"Yes. Keeping the family informed is part of her job. They think you are trying to get at Patrick through me." She twisted around in her chair to face Skye. "I sometimes wonder about that myself."

"Don't. I'm involved with you despite your ex-husband, not because of him."

"I believe you, but the Kellys never will. Paranoia doesn't begin to describe how they react when they think the family is threatened. And there's no limit to what they'll do to remove that threat." Erin shivered. "They're so powerful, Skye, it's scary."

"Well, I'm not scared. What about you? Do you want to break it off?"

Mutely, Erin shook her head, and Skye, in an attempt to lighten the mood, said, "Apart from me, Brenda would have to give them a glowing report on how well you are doing. No doubt the Kellys will be pleased to hear that." Skye's lifted eyebrow was ironic.

"What would please the Kellys to hear about me is that I'm dead."

They sat in silence for a few moments, then Erin said Mary would like him to come for dinner that evening. "The cook wants to go to church, so could you come early? Around six."

Chapter Thirteen

Before leaving for the Rastoks, Skye checked with Foxcroft. The inspector told him that the Barbados police had contacted all the up-scale restaurants on the island and no one answering Penelope's description had approached them for a job.

* * *

Skye wasn't the Rastok's only guest. Charles Pollock was there as well, no doubt in return for his hospitality aboard the *Caroline*. Settling into a chair with a drink in his hand, Skye as he usually did at this time of day checked the horizon below the setting sun. Almost always there was a small band of cloud just above the horizon, but tonight the sky was clear.

"We are in for a rare treat. It looks as if we might see a green flash," he informed his companions. "Keep your eyes on the horizon as the sun sets."

"What's a green flash?" asked Erin.

"Just keep looking and maybe you'll see. Try not to blink or you might miss it."

The sun, in its tropic fashion, slipped rapidly behind the horizon, like a penny dropping into a slot. As its rim disappeared from sight, there was a flash of intense emerald green, drawing murmurs of wonder from the spectators.

"I've heard of the green flash, but I've never seen one before," said Mary Rastok. "Thank you, Skye, for sharing it with us. Do you know what causes it?"

"He'll know." Erin shot Skye an amused look, folded her arms, and settled back in her deck chair.

"It's due to the refraction of light," Skye explained. "When the sun is setting, its rays have to pass through a great thickness of atmosphere. Blue and violet light are very scattered, that's why the sky is blue, and relatively little comes directly to our eyes. The orange and yellow portions of the spectrum are absorbed by water vapour, especially over an ocean. So the light that reaches our eyes is largely a mixture of red and green. This light is bent — refracted — as it passes through the atmosphere. Because red light bends more than green, it disappears below the horizon before the green does. For a brief moment, the only light reaching us is the green portion of the spectrum. The green flash only occurs when the temperature and atmospheric clarity are just right, which seems to happen most often in the tropics."

"Fascinating," Mary murmured while her husband stared at Skye as if incredulous that anyone would stuff his head with such useless information that had nothing to do with golf or tennis. Skye returned the look with an amused smile. Seeing the green flash always gave him a lift.

As the darkness thickened, Mary Rastok said, "There's your gecko, Erin." The little lizard of the night, with its pale, flesh-coloured body and huge dark eyes, appeared on the wall over Erin's head, clinging effortlessly to the stucco with its velcro feet. Then it ran down the wall, hopped onto the arm of Erin's chair and jumped onto the stem of her wine glass. The glass contained fruit punch, but that wasn't what the gecko was after. A small bead of condensation had formed on the stem of the glass and this the tiny reptile lapped up eagerly. Then it was gone, scampering up the wall to begin the nightly hunt for its insect prey.

"In all my time in the islands, I have never seen that before," murmured Skye.

"It's become a nightly ritual," said Erin.

The butler came out to summon them to the dinner that the cook had prepared before going to the evangelical prayer service. Midway through the meal, the phone rang. It was Lord Fraser with the news that a match had been found and the PM was being operated on as they spoke. "Does The Highness know?" Skye asked.

"Yes. I've just finished speaking with her. She was elated. It'll be on the eleven o'clock news. You should watch it."

The meal was interrupted once again. Pollock's pager buzzed as the butler was serving dessert. Pollock switched it off with a murmured apology, and said he would have to contact the *Caroline* immediately. Mary led him over to her husband's den, which had no books but lots of trophies, and shut the door so he could talk in private.

"That was Captain Morton," he said as he returned. "Apparently an underwater volcano is beginning to act up somewhere south of Kick'em Jenny. There's no immediate danger, but if it continues to erupt the sea will start to act up."

"It already has." Skye told them about his trip across Commotion Channel where the waves were bigger than he had ever seen them there.

"Kick'em Jenny," said Erin. "That's an odd name. Where is it?"

"It's a large rock all by itself out in the sea north of Grenada," Skye told her. "Currents swirl around its base and kick up a wicked sea, which is how it got its name. Like everything else in the Lesser Antilles, it's of volcanic origin. We're in a subduction zone where the North and South American plates push beneath the Caribbean plate. When that happens, rocks at the edge of the plates melt into magma which blips its way up, something like a lava lamp."

Erin gave him that amused half-smile again, and Skye made a deprecating gesture. "I know I sometimes tell people more than they really care to know. It's a bad habit of mine."

"Not at all," Mary protested. "I find it fascinating."

Erin smiled fondly at him and reached out to squeeze his hand. "You're just like my grandfather — walking encyclopedias."

Charles had remained standing. "I must get back to my ship. But let me say again, the volcano doesn't pose a threat. At least not to those on land."

Skye stayed at the Rastoks until it was time for the news. The announcer was black and spoke in the clipped accents of the BBC. The Prime Minister was still undergoing heart transplant surgery and the station would broadcast bulletins on his condition as the reports came in. The next item was the volcanic activity north of Grenada. It was being monitored closely and the station would also provide updates on that situation.

"It's like a miracle," Mary murmured as she switched off the set. "The Prime Minister, I mean. The poor man is on his deathbed and a match shows up at the last possible minute."

"When you think about it, it's awesome what can be done with organ transplants these days," agreed Skye. "A person is condemned to certain death and then a few hours later gets a brand new lease on life." He got up to leave, and thanked the Rastoks for dinner and the evening.

"Thank you for the green flash," Mary replied. "I feel almost as though a blessing has been conferred on me."

As the butler opened the front door for them, Erin glanced up at Skye in the brightly lit vestibule. "You can see a green flash every time you look in the mirror," he told her.

She smiled and lifted her face for a kiss. "Will I see you tomorrow?"

"Of course. I'll call you in the morning."

* * *

Skye's clock radio wakened him in time to catch the early morning news. The PM had survived the operation and was now in intensive care. The station would update reports on his condition throughout the day. It looked like the old boy was going to make it. If the news continued to be good, champagne corks would be popping all over the island. The volcano was still erupting, and small craft advisories had been issued. If the submarine upheaval continued, they would be upgraded to warnings.

Immediately after breakfast, Skye went out to sit in the gazebo and began to work his way through a stack of company annual reports. Most of the companies were ones in which he had invested and the rest were on his list of potential investments. Dissecting the financial statements of Century Minerals Inc., he decided to take his profit and bail out of the shares. The mine that had caused the shares to run up so satisfactorily had reached full capacity and the revenues had plateaued. He was making a mental note to call his broker before the market closed when Overfine came out with the portable phone. It was Sybil calling from St. Vincent to tell Skye that Andrew had returned home.

"That's great!" enthused Skye. "What happened to him?"

"He just run away. He was hiding out in the hills. He was being bullied at school. Last night he came back when he got tired of living on bananas and sugar cane."

"He's all right, then?"

"Yes. 'Cept he should get a good hidin'. But I'se so glad to see him, I won't."

"Sybil's boy is back," he said as he handed the phone to Overfine.

Beaming, Overfine said, "That be great news. Praise the Lord."

Impulsively, Skye asked for the phone back and dialled Banyan. "Come fly with me in my flying machine," he said when Erin came on the line.

"When?"

"Right now. I have to go to St. Vincent and I thought you might like to come along for the ride. We can have lunch over there."

"Lunch? It's already 11:30."

"That's okay. St. Vincent is only forty miles away. We'll be there in twenty minutes flying time. I'll pick you up."

Overfine drove them both to the airport and went over to have a chat with Jason Carmichael. Overfine didn't much care for the humourless Carmichael, but figured it never did any harm to be on good terms with a customs officer.

"I've been meaning to ask you," said Erin. "How

did Overfine get his name?"

"Ask him how he's feeling this morning."

Erin waited until Overfine had finished buttering-up Jason, then casually asked him how he was.

"Overfine, Mistress Erin." He flashed her a beaming smile. "Just Overfine!"

"That's a wonderful way to be," Erin smiled. Overfine was still beaming as he watched the Cessna's take-off. He raised a hand in salute as it lifted off the runway and began its climb out over the sea.

Flying conditions were ideal, but the sea was getting increasingly angry as the underwater disturbance continued. Normally it would be dotted with yachts, but today only a few of the largest motored along on bare poles. From this height, Skye could see the spray flying out from their bows as they breasted the white caps.

They had barely reached their cruising altitude of 1500 feet when Skye began to receive landing instructions from the St. Vincent tower.

They lunched in the cool dimness of the Cobblestone Inn, built with cobblestones brought from England as ballast in the sailing ships.

"My appointment's not until three-thirty," Skye said as they sipped their coffee. "Want to do a little shopping?"

"Love to."

They browsed through the arcade of shops for the next hour, then Skye climbed into a taxi and set off for Sybil's place. Andrew should be arriving home from school before too long. If he was in school. Telling the taxi to wait, Skye walked up the short path to the front door.

Sybil didn't seem surprised to see him. He explained that he had some business on the island and had popped around for a visit. "Come in. Come in," she said with her sunny smile. "I'll make some tea."

Sybil hummed as she filled the kettle, and Skye knew his concerns were unfounded. "Is Andrew at school?"

"Yes. I walked him over this morning and had a talk with the principal. He be home soon and he be ver' happy to see you, Mister Skye."

Skye was refusing a second cup of tea when the front door opened and an apprehensive-looking Andrew stuck his head in. He gazed at Skye as if expecting a lecture, and it wasn't until Skye smiled and held out his hand that he relaxed.

The boy had grown quite a bit taller in the years since Skye had last seen him, but his build was slight and his shoulders were narrow. When he spoke, his voice was free of any trace of the local patois. A perfect target for a school bully.

Sensing from his mother's smiling face that he had been forgiven, Andrew chatted pleasantly with Skye, asking about the airplane and saying how sorry he was about Mistress Jocelyn.

Skye considered asking whether he had seen the Cessna when he flew low over the island. Best to leave well enough alone. Getting to his feet, he shook hands with them both, asked after the grandmother who was asleep in her bedroom, and walked out to the waiting taxi.

* * *

"How did your meeting go?" Erin asked as Skye walked into the lobby of the Cobblestone Inn. Three parcels piled on the table beside her showed that her shopping had been a success.

"Very well, indeed," Skye smiled. "Better than I expected, in fact." He picked up her parcels. "I've got a taxi waiting to take us to the airport."

* * *

"Have you ever flown an airplane?" asked Skye, as he throttled back and trimmed the Cessna for level flight.

"Me?" Erin looked startled. "No. Never."

"It's easier than you think. Just put your hands on the control column ..."

Gingerly, she did as she was told.

"Don't over-control," Skye said calmly as the nose shot skyward. "Push the column forward. That's it. Now pull it back a little. Try to keep it on the horizon. Let the airplane do the flying. That's what it's designed to do."

After some jockeying up and down, the Cessna levelled out and Erin's death grip relaxed somewhat. He showed her where to place her feet on the rudders and said, "Now we'll try a turn. Just move the column slightly to the left and apply a little pressure on the left rudder. Easy. Try and watch the horizon. Keep the nose on it. Good. Now straighten out. Nothing to it, is there?"

Erin gave a shaky laugh, but kept her eyes riveted on the horizon. They were heading east out over the sea, so Skye had her turn to the right, back toward the long curve of islands.

Skye had been astonished to discover that this was Erin's first visit to the Caribbean. Her travels had mostly taken her to Europe, which was consistent with her finishing school background. As a child, she had accompanied her beloved grandfather on several trips to East Africa, invariably returning with some exotic new specimens for his animal collection.

"You had a wonderful childhood," Skye remarked after she told him about the African safaris.

"I'll always be grateful for that. But it didn't last. Grandfather died when I was 15, and my parents were killed in an auto accident just before I graduated from

Smith. Daddy was an alcoholic, although he would never admit it. He and Mother had pretty well run through the money Grandfather left them by the time they were killed. What little was left in the estate was wiped out in a lawsuit over the accident. The insurance company denied liability on the ground that Daddy had been drinking."

So you had neither the financial resources nor the family support to stand up to the Kellys, Skye thought to himself.

He glanced at his watch and said "We have time to do a little sightseeing. Let's take a look at Grenada."

Erin tensed as they hit a patch of rough air, but they were out of it before she had time to do anything. "I can't get over how casually you can flit from island to island."

Skye patted the top of the instrument panel. "We have a magic carpet at our disposal."

Erin had flown many thousands of miles on the Kelly private jet; but it had never gone where she wanted to go, only where the family wanted. Skye's little airplane, with its pretty red and white colour scheme, was a much better "magic carpet."

"I'll drive and you look." Skye took over the controls as they came abreast of St. George's, the capital of Grenada.

He flew in a lazy circle to show Erin the colourful jumble of colonial buildings climbing up the amphitheatre of hills. The sun of endless summers had bleached both stone and paint into muted pastels.

"It's like a picture postcard." Erin was snapping pictures with her compact Nikon.

Skye flew over the port crowded with cruise ships. "That's one of the best harbours in the Caribbean. It's the crater of a volcano with one wall fallen in to make the entrance."

"You're a remarkably well-informed person."

Skye laughed. "I read a lot. And I admit to being incurably curious. The Caribbean is rewarding to study. It's a small area and its history is so recent that you can really get a handle on what makes it tick."

"That's where Sir George removed Edwina's friend's kidney," Skye remarked as they flew over a number of long, low brick buildings on both sides of the road. "It's the St. George's University Medical School. Students who can't get into medical schools in the States come down here to study. If they can afford the hefty fees, that is. After two or three years down here, they go back home to complete their degrees."

"His nurse sure put me in my place. I still cringe at the thought of coming on all self-righteous when the poor woman was selling her kidney so her husband wouldn't go blind."

Skye thought it best to concentrate on flying the airplane, and after a few minutes Erin said, "I'm afraid my mind boggles at the thought of Glessop performing an operation. The man's a lush. God knows I can sympathize with that, but the fact remains."

"I agree the thought does give one pause. He was a topnotch surgeon, and I've had doctors tell me that the human body is very easy to work with. It's the right size for one thing, lots of room to cut and splice. The tricky part comes after the surgery. Keeping the donor alive, and the donated organ functioning until it reaches the recipient."

"Do you suppose they did the transplant there? Put it in the sick person, I mean."

"No. The kidney would have been bought by someone in the States and it would have been flown directly there."

"I'm going to fill out an organ donor card. I'm

ashamed to say I hadn't thought of it until I met you."

He looked at his watch and said, "We better head back. We have to be on the ground in Manchineel before six o'clock, while it's still light. You take over. For level flight, try to keep the top of the panel four inches below the horizon." He placed his hand on top of the panel. "That's an easy way to tell. A hand equals four inches."

"As in measuring the height of a horse," she murmured.

"Exactly."

He told her to make a right-hand turn. "We're flying east, so we have to fly at an altitude that doesn't have an even number. Remember 'odd balls fly east.'"

Erin gave him an uneasy glance as they continued to head straight toward a bank of white cumulus clouds that frequently formed in the late afternoon. Smiling, he pointed out three dials — the altimeter that showed the altitude, the vertical speed indicator, and the bank indicator that would tell whether they were flying level.

Then the gauzy whiteness engulfed them.

"It's like skiing the moguls in a whiteout," Erin said with a shaky laugh as air currents in the cloud bounced them up and down.

"I know what you mean, but here you've got instruments to help you orient yourself. You must always trust your instruments even when your instincts tell you not to believe them." With a slight sense of shock Skye realized he had not immediately thought of Jocelyn at the mention of skiing.

When they broke out of the clouds and into a clear patch, he took over the controls and began to instruct her on radio procedure. One dial was set at a frequency of 121.5 — "that's the emergency frequency and every aircraft is required to constantly monitor it. Now turn the other dial to the Manchineel frequency, 130.5. We've been flying east for some time and now I'm going to change course for Manchineel, which is west of us, so what's the first thing I should do?"

"Go to an even altitude."

"Good. I'll descend to two thousand feet." After a few minutes, he said, "It's time to report in. Press the key and tell Manchineel it's Cessna 180 November 115 Charlie, inbound ninety degrees."

Erin gave a small smile of triumph when Henry Armbruster matter-of-factly acknowledged their call, cleared them to land, and gave them an advisory. Conditions were ideal with a light, steady wind blowing almost straight down the runway. "Let's grease this one in," Sky grinned, dipping his wings over Whistling Frog to let Overfine know they were back. Erin followed him on the controls as he put on 10 degrees of flap, adjusted the propeller pitch to full fine and the fuel mixture to full rich. "Those are the settings for take-off and they're set that way in case we have to go round," he told her.

When he could see the V's painted on the end of the runway, he dumped the flaps and cut the throttle. Just as the wheels touched down, the stall warning horn began to sound.

"What was that?" asked Erin, never taking her eyes off the runway.

"That's the sign of a perfect landing, when the stall warning goes off just as you touch down."

In the sudden silence after he switched off the engine, she asked, "Do you know what I'm going to do as soon as I go back to the States?"

"Learn to fly. If you like, I'll get you started while you're here."

"Fabulous!" Unbuckling her safety belt, she leaned across and kissed him.

"If I pulled off a landing like that, I'd be smiling

for a week." Armbruster came over to help Skye tie down the airplane.

"Conditions were perfect." Skye smiled up at the immaculate blue sky. "What's the latest on the PM?"

"He is still in intensive care, but he's making good progress. The doctors expect him to make a full recovery."

"What about Adrienne's daughter? Any word on her?"

Armbruster shook his head. "Not a word."

* * *

On the way to drop Erin off at Banyan, they saw the *Caroline* putting out to sea.

"The Flying Dutchman sails again," Skye murmured.

"That's sure a different lifestyle. Endlessly sailing the ocean like that."

"It beats bankruptcy," Skye replied as they turned into the Banyan driveway. "I expect he's sailing north to get away from that volcano." As Erin reached for the door handle, he said "Let's go up again in the morning. Why don't we make it a picnic. I'll have Agatha pack a lunch."

* * *

The ground lizard with the extraordinarily long toes sprawled on the hot cement flagstone on the path leading to Skye's sleeping quarters. It was blissfully soaking up the last rays before the sun began its swift descent into the sea. If it was the same one as two years ago, it had certainly prospered, for it had almost doubled in size. Unblinkingly, it watched Skye approach and seemed inclined to dispute his right of passage. Finally, it reluctantly waddled off the path and crawled under a chenille plant from where it glared balefully up at him. Jocelyn and Skye had spent that last Christmas on the island, and she had decorated a small Norfolk Island pine with the long, trailing red flowers of the chenille plant to make an impromptu Caribbean Christmas tree.

Chapter Fourteen

"Oh, God, Skye, life can be wonderful!" Erin lay on her back, staring up at the cloudless blue sky.

Propped up on one elbow, Skye smiled down at her golden perfection. "You look like a painting by Matisse," he told her. "With more than a touch of the Vargas girl."

She stretched like an indolent cat and sat up, pulling the picnic hamper toward her. "This is one of the times when I wish I could have a drink. A glass of wine would add the perfect touch." She laughed at the look on his face and laid a finger against his lips. "I said I wish I could drink. I know I can't. Besides, we don't have any wine."

"Maybe we should put on our swimsuits," she added as she opened the lid of the hamper. "I know this place is pretty remote, but somehow ..."

"Dress for dinner?" Skye interrupted with a laugh. "Sure, why not?" He stood up to put on his swim trunks and looked around. Sabine Rock was not so much remote as it was inaccessible. It climbed precipitously for three hundred feet out of the sea, its sheer walls offering no toehold for even the most determined of shrubs and plants. It was long and flat enough for a small plane such as the Cessna to land safely, although Skye only attempted it when, as was the case today, the trade winds were blowing steadily. He and Jocelyn had flown out here several times to picnic and make love, a thought that made him wince inwardly. Still, if he were to avoid every place in the Caribbean where he and Jocelyn had made love, he would have to range pretty far afield.

Sabine Rock lay one hundred miles to the south and slightly west of Manchineel. On the way down Skye had kept a casual lookout for the *Caroline*, flying at a higher altitude than was warranted by the short hop, and constantly checking the horizon. But there was no sign of the black-hulled ship.

As always, the lunch Agatha had prepared was delicious. She had smiled as she handed him the hamper. "It's good to see you happy again, Mister Skye." So the formidable Agatha approved. Skye finished the last of the peach melba and, with a sigh of contentment, lay back on the blanket and air-filled mattress they had brought.

"That boat is coming awfully close to the shore," said Erin. "Won't it run aground?"

"Huh?" Skye, who had almost dozed off, sat up. A power boat, Skye judged it to be in the forty-foot class, was heading directly for the island as if to smash itself against the monolithic rock. "They know what they're doing." Skye pointed down to where the water near the shore was dark blue. "They're going to use the channel. Otherwise they'd have to go miles out to sea to avoid the reef. See all that green water farther out? That's all reef."

As it entered the narrow channel, the launch

throttled back, its bow wave subsiding. "It's not very often you see a small boat painted black in these parts," said Skye. "It absorbs too much heat."

He walked over to where the Cessna was parked in the sparse shelter of a scraggly, wind-sculpted sea grape, and returned with a pair of Leitz binoculars. To Erin's surprise he dropped down and crawled over to the edge of the cliff on his hands and knees. Grinning back at her over his shoulder, he said, "Whoever they are, they would never think of anyone being up here. No point in telling them otherwise."

"What do you make of that?" he asked, handing the glasses over to Erin who had crawled up beside him. Adjusting the focus, Erin counted seven young teenagers in the open cockpit. Two of them were girls and rest were male. One girl and two of the boys were black and the others looked like South Americans. "I see some kids being taken on an outing of some sort," she said, giving the binoculars back to Skye.

"Maybe, but I kind of think not." His eyes narrowed as he saw the cabin windows were tinted so that nobody could see inside. "Those kids are too quiet. If they were on some kind of a joy ride they'd be all over the boat, raising hell. But they're just sitting there, looking ... scared. That's it — they're frightened!"

"Let me see. You're right. They do look frightened. My God, Skye, there are two babies! Look, they're on the floor. At the feet of the two girls. Unless they're dolls. You look."

"Those aren't dolls. One of them is crying. Its face is all screwed up."

Skye lowered the binoculars and they watched in silence as the launch reached the end of the channel and headed for the open sea, the bow rising as its speed picked up.

"You think they're connected with the body parts trade, don't you? There's a sort of 'the game's afoot' look about you, as Sherlock Holmes would say."

"Shakespeare."

"What?"

"Shakespeare said it first. *Henry V*, 'I see you stand like greyhounds in the slips, straining upon the start. The game's afoot!'"

Erin stared at him. "You never cease to amaze me, Skye. And," she added softly, "I hope you never will."

He laughed and kissed her, nuzzling the smooth, sun-warmed hollow of her neck. "I have suspicions, that's all. Nothing concrete. Just a feeling in my gut that something big is going down." He looked out to sea where the motor boat was rapidly receding in the distance. "To answer your question, yes, it's possible that boatload would be part of it. I just don't know."

Erin began to put away the remains of their picnic lunch. "Do you mind if we delay our take-off until 4:30?" asked Skye. "That will give us plenty of time to land at Manchineel before the light goes."

Erin slipped a strap of her bathing suit off one smooth shoulder. "I think we can find a way to fill in the time somehow."

* * *

Bathed in the warm afterglow of love-making, they lay side by side on the blanket, fingers touching. Erin glanced at her watch. "We still have an hour to go. Why don't we go exploring? Is there some way of getting down to the beach?"

"It's a scramble, but there's a sort of path on the Atlantic side. The natives pasture a few goats up here in the wet season when there's some grass."

"You call that a path?" Erin stared in disbelief at the

barely discernible trail that traversed the cliff in steep, vertiginous pitches. True, the cliff on the Atlantic side was not as sheer as on the Caribbean where the reef was, and some scattered rocky outcrops offered firm footing but, in addition to being steep, the path itself was no wider than a man's foot.

"We don't have to go down it. There's nothing much to see. Just a small pebble beach at the bottom."

"You've been down it, then?"

"Once."

Jocelyn would have been with him. "Let's go," said Erin, cautiously stepping onto the path. Fortunately, they were both wearing sandals with rubberized soles. Not daring to look down, Erin leaned toward the cliff face as they edged their way along the path and over the rocks. Following right behind her, Skye admired the way her one-piece bathing suit did wonderful things for her slender, beautifully proportioned body. Everything about her was perfectly to scale. Skye's years of showing horses had made him into a keen judge of conformation, whether equine or human, and this lady had conformation to burn. Jocelyn had been built on a more generous scale, but, once again, everything was in perfect proportion.

"Almost there." Skye told her to rest for a moment on the broad, rocky platform of an outcrop. Moments later, they were standing on a strip of beach covered with small, rounded pebbles.

Skye's attention was fixed on a round object in the water, bobbing gently in the wavelets lapping against the shore. His sandals crunched on the pebbles as he walked across the narrow beach and waded into the water.

"It's a skull," he said, holding it out so Erin could see it. "From its small size, I'd say the person was young."

Oddly enough, the object he was holding in his hands evoked neither fear nor revulsion on Erin's part. Scoured by the sea, it looked like a sculpture, a piece of art. Gazing down at it dispassionately, she asked, "What are you going to do about it?"

"Nothing. There's no point in reporting it to the police. The good Captain Robertson would just shrug it off."

Maybe he should give it to Adrienne. It would make a wonderful prop for her voodoo rites. Skye couldn't help but smile at himself. Here he was, furious at the outrageous thing she had planned to do with Jocelyn's ashes, and yet thinking of doing her a favour. Shaking his head, he placed the skull at the base of the cliff, well above the high water mark.

Erin half-expected him to murmur "Alas! poor Yorick," as he straightened up. Instead he gazed out to sea, a grave, preoccupied look on his face. Then he led the way over to the path. "It'll be much easier going up than it was coming down."

* * *

Sitting in the left-hand seat, Erin was flying the airplane while Skye scanned the ocean, still dotted with boats, although they were all power launches or large sailboats with furled sails. He winced when a pocket of turbulence jammed the binoculars into his eyes. He told her to turn onto a course of 275E; he had spotted a boat that seemed to be keeping well clear of the others.

"That's it all right. But there's nobody in the cockpit."

"What does that mean? Could they have dumped them overboard?"

"Like the old slave ships? No. They'll be inside

the cabin to keep them out of sight out here in the open water."

Skye took over the controls as they approached Manchineel. This was rush hour as the little inter-island airplanes raced to finish their rounds while there was still light. On the tarmac, Overfine was helping Andy Foster load luggage into a Twin Otter. Foster had been away for a couple of days on a charter flight to the Virgins. When Skye asked if he had seen the *Caroline*, he said that he had spotted her steaming south, abreast of Soufrière on Saint Lucia.

"When was this?"

"About an hour ago."

"Do you think he's headed back here?" asked Erin as they climbed into the back of Whistling Frog's jeep.

"He could well be. On the other hand, he could be just cruising aimlessly about."

Skye asked her to join him for dinner, but she begged off, saying that she wanted to spend some time with Patrick. "I'm feeling a little guilty about him, as a matter of fact. It's so wonderful being with you, that I've been neglecting him."

"Which the worthy Ms. Fewster would have duly noted?"

Erin sighed. "And passed on to the Family."

* * *

There was an item in the paper about the Names. It was on the front page under the headline that said James of Leeds was pressing the Names for cash. As always, Skye read the story with a tingling of nerves at his own close call and empathy for the poor devils who were staring ruin in the face. James' chairman said it was facing a serious cash shortfall and needed to take drastic action in order to be able to pass a crucial Department of Industry solvency test due within six months. If it failed the test, the central fund and all the syndicates would collapse. The article speculated that the British government, already rocked by the failure of several large financial institutions, could not afford to let this happen and might be prepared to pass legislation to assist James in enforcing its claims.

If the government intervened, the Names, at least those within its jurisdiction, were doomed. Skye put down the paper and went out on the patio for a solitary dinner under the stars. He was buttering a slice of Agatha's coconut bread when he realized Adrienne was in the garden, somewhere beyond the reach of the lights. He recognized her fragrance in the still night air. He should, since he and Jocelyn had brought it to her from Jamaica. When Adrienne had learned that they were planning a trip to Jamaica, she had begged Skye — she tended to steer clear of Jocelyn — to bring her back a bottle of the white witch of Rosehall's perfume. They had intended to visit the notorious plantation, owned by a young widow who was skilled in obeah magic and whose three husbands had all died in mysterious circumstances, in any case, so it was a simple matter to fulfil Adrienne's request. Adrienne had been ecstatic when Skye presented her not with a bottle, but with a case of the stuff.

Without moving from his chair, Skye called out to her, asking her to join him. The mambo materialized out of the shadows, a questioning look on her face. Sensing her hesitation, Skye stood up and held a chair for her. Reassured, she stepped onto the patio with queenly grace. A whistling frog, bleeping away under a flowering hibiscus, fell silent and did not resume its harsh serenade. Overfine, coming out to clear away the entree dishes, halted in the open doorway, his jaw actually dropping and the breath going out of him in a loud whoosh of astonishment. Adrienne ignored him, and Skye gave him a look that set him in motion again. Adrienne declined Skye's offer to join him in coffee and dessert, saying instead that she would like a glass of dark rum.

"I remember that perfume," said Skye, suppressing a sneeze. "It is ... ah, very distinctive." When Adrienne made no reply, he went on, "I take it you haven't heard from Penelope?"

She shook her head and they stared at each other in silence. Penelope and her mother got along very well together. In some ways they were like sisters. Penelope may have wanted to leave the island but she wouldn't want her mother to worry about her. As if reading Skye's thoughts, Adrienne said, "She know I wouldn't stop her from going to Barbados. She wouldn't leave without telling me to my face."

"I know."

"She be worth a lot of money to some people."

"Don't let yourself think like that, Adrienne. She'll turn up."

Adrienne gave him a look that said she knew better, and abruptly changed the subject. "You bin sleepin' with that Kelly woman."

"Adrienne —"

"Her man killed Mistress Jocelyn."

"I like you, Adrienne, but there are times when ..." Skye's exasperated retort was interrupted by the sound of engine coughing and "dieseling" into silence in the front yard. Skye got up to greet the new arrivals, whoever they might be. It was the Frasers; His Lordship was having some difficulty extricating his long legs from under the steering wheel. "Hello, dear boy," he said breezily as he finally got his feet planted on the asphalt driveway. "We haven't seen much of you in the past little while, so we thought we'd drop in for a brief visit. Hope you don't mind, and that we're not interrupting anything."

"Not at all. I'm delighted to see you both!"

Skye led them inside, a quick glance at the patio telling him that Adrienne had disappeared. Lady Fraser's nose wrinkled as she sniffed the air. "Is that a new aftershave lotion, Skye? Or do you have a visitor?"

Skye laughed. "That's Adrienne. Jocelyn and I brought her that perfume from Jamaica. It is reputed to have been used by the witch of Rosehall, which explains why she wanted it. She stopped by for a few minutes, but she seems to have left."

Lady Fraser settled into a patio chair with an elegant rustle of skirts. With her grey hair pulled back and her calm, almost unlined face, she was the picture of assured patrician grace.

"Rum thing, her daughter taking off like that," said Lord Fraser, accepting a glass of port from Overfine.

"Adrienne is convinced Penelope didn't leave of her own free will."

"Really? I suppose it's only natural for a mother to feel that way."

"Adrienne isn't exactly your average mother," Skye said dryly.

"Quite," Lord Fraser acknowledged with a chuckle. "Now for some good news. I had Sir George call the clinic in Boca Raton and talk directly with the surgeon who operated on the Prime Minister. He's doing famously. The surgeon said it was the best heart match-up he had ever encountered. Practically every one of those tissue matches that Sir George talks about were positive. According to the surgeon, it's almost as if the donor was related to the Prime Minister. And it's a young person's heart so Marcellus could be with us for a good long time."

From out of the darkness came an inhuman howl, blood curdling in its primordial anguish. The hairs were standing out on the back of Skye's neck as he and his guests stared at each other.

"You don't suppose Sheena has escaped, do you Robert?" Lady Fraser asked when the unearthly wail died away.

"No ape made that sound," her husband replied, "I've never heard anything like it."

"What do you suppose it was?" Despite the warmth of the night, Lady Fraser shivered.

Skye had an idea what it was but he needed another piece of information before he could be sure.

"I think we can assume it was human," Skye told her. "In fact I think it was Adrienne. She likes to frighten people from time to time. It gives her a feeling of power."

"I expect you're right." Lady Fraser visibly relaxed. "Such an extraordinary creature. You know her quite well, don't you, Skye?"

"I guess you could say we are friends. Although there are times when she ticks me off."

Overfine came out with a tray of drinks, cognac for the men and sherry for Lady Fraser. He bent over as he handed Skye his drink and whispered, "That yell be Adrienne."

After some agreeable conversation, Lord Fraser put down his empty snifter and got to his feet. "Why don't you and Erin join us for lunch tomorrow?"

"Sounds great. We've been planning to go for a ride together, so that's what we'll do."

Chapter Fifteen

E xcept for the lobster fishermen whose boats were
pulled up on the beach, the fishing camp was
deserted. The yellow tail bonitos were running off
Carriacou and, despite the heavy seas, the fishing fleet
had sailed over there to reap the harvest. They would
sleep on the beach and would stay there until the run
was over, or the sea continued to make up, forcing them
to leave. Skye's question would have to wait. Climbing
back into the jeep, he told Overfine to drive to Banyan.
Erin had done a good job of outfitting herself for the
ride; she was wearing slacks with a pair of socks pulled
over them and low-heeled shoes.

When Skye and Erin arrived at the stables Elizabeth
Mallory and her groom were unloading a two-horse
trailer. The two animals were totally dissimilar — the one
standing on the ground and shaking itself vigorously was
a common-looking cold blood with a pronounced
Roman nose, while the chestnut who was acting up as

Elizabeth tried to back him out of the trailer was a thoroughbred, most likely an ex-racehorse. Standing to one side of the trailer Skye took a firm grip of the horse's tail and pulled. Beset at both ends, the horse snorted and backed down the ramp. Holding onto the halter shank, Elizabeth followed him out.

"Getting ready for the spring break?" asked Skye, patting the horse's soft muzzle. Elizabeth nodded. The spring break was her busiest time, when she needed every horse she could lay her hands on. She had to have the right mix, plugs for the novice, and more spirited mounts for the experienced rider. After the school break, her business gradually tapered off until by the summer months it dwindled to practically nothing. "But the horses still have to eat," she had once remarked wryly.

"You're busy with the new horses," Skye said to Elizabeth. "I'll saddle Sun Dancer myself. Which one should Erin ride?"

"How much riding have you done?" Elizabeth asked Erin. The new thoroughbred was proving to be a handful. She shortened her grip on the halter shank as he tossed his head and tried to rear.

"I had riding lessons at school, but I haven't been out much in years." Erin stepped back as the horse's hindquarters swung in her direction.

"Belle should be perfect. Besides, she and Sun Dancer are friends."

"Check," Skye agreed. The little dun-coloured mare stepped right out and never put a foot wrong.

"You can find a hard hat that will fit her in the tack room," Elizabeth said as she led the restive horse away.

* * *

"They must have had good instructors at that school," Skye said as Erin posted alongside him in perfect rhythm with Belle's fast-paced trot.

"We did quite a bit of it, actually." Erin patted Belle's neck.

"Want to try a canter?"

"After you."

Skye glanced sideways as the eager horses broke into a smooth canter. He quickly saw there was no need to worry about Erin. Caramel-blond hair bouncing beneath her black riding cap, she sat firmly in the saddle, moving easily with the horse's rocking gait.

"I guess it's like riding a bicycle," she laughed gaily, "you never forget how."

Good as she was, Skye knew that if they overdid it, she would have sore muscles in the morning. Shortly before they reached Elizabeth's place, he pulled up and the horses, blowing contentedly, fell into a walk.

Erin stared in disbelief when Skye told her that the dilapidated shack and rubble-strewn yard was where Elizabeth lived with her dreadlocked lover.

"I don't understand it myself," Skye shrugged. "But there it is."

A few hundred yards past Elizabeth's rundown abode, he veered left and led the way down to the base of the hill. "Not many people, except the locals, know about this place," he said, pointing to the little cemetery located a short distance out on the flats.

"It dates back to the time when the island was a sugar plantation. The company would love to get rid of it but the people won't let the bodies be disturbed."

"Is it still used?" asked Erin. "As a burial ground, I mean."

"God, no. The company makes sure that the body of anyone who dies is sent back to their native island for burial."

"It's so beautifully maintained."

Skye nodded. The low white fence was freshly painted, the grass was mowed, the plots were weeded, and some of the graves were decorated with flowers. "It's always like this," he said as they moved on, angling up the hill to the road.

Without dismounting, he leaned down and pressed the intercom button at Beaufort's entrance. Ralston answered and, after Skye identified himself, the gate swung open.

"The Highness is here," Skye muttered as he saw the two jeeps parked in the cobblestone yard.

"I like her," said Erin as she slid down from the saddle. She took a few unsteady steps before regaining her balance. Skye pretended not to notice.

Lunch was to be served in the gazebo. Princess Helen was already seated there, smiling benignly as she tucked into her second gin and tonic. Lord Fraser, who doted on the animal, had Zulu at his side as he walked across the grass to greet the new arrivals. The cheetah immediately went up to Erin, holding up its blunt muzzle to be patted.

"My grandfather bred these beauties," Erin murmured, smiling as the cheetah chirped its pleasure.

"Really?" Lord Fraser was impressed. "I must hear about that. All about it." He paused, then said, "I want Logan to be in on it too. He's very keen on animals. But he won't be available until after lunch, so maybe you can tell us about it with our coffee. I must say I'm absolutely riveted."

Looking around and not seeing him, Skye asked about Foxcroft.

"He and a fellow officer are having lunch in the main house," Fraser told him.

Lunch was a very pleasant affair. In the company of people she liked, the Princess was genial and relaxed.

She drank too much, but, then, she always did. As Ralston served coffee to the two Americans and tea to the others, Lord Fraser asked him to find Logan and have him join them.

Logan bowed to Princess Helen, an exaggeratedly low bow that had more than a trace of mockery in it, and accepted a cup of tea. "Ms. Kelly's grandfather succeeded in breeding cheetahs," Lord Fraser said as Logan sat down. "I've asked her to tell us how he did it."

The inscrutable Logan actually looked interested. Balancing a cup of tea in one hand, he reached down with the other to scratch Zulu behind the ears, and looked enquiringly across at Erin.

"It began on the plains of Serengeti," she said. "I was there on safari with grandfather and we saw three male cheetahs fighting each other. They really went at it until one managed to drive the other two off. The victor immediately mated with a female who was waiting on the sidelines. I remember grandfather exclaiming, 'That's it! The males need competition to get aroused.' He arranged to have two males shipped to the States to join the pair he had there that had never bred. A few months later, the female gave birth."

"Your grandfather must have been Jason Harding," Logan murmured.

"That's right, but how could you possibly know that?" asked a puzzled Erin.

"He's quite well known in zoological ..." Lord Fraser coughed and Logan's lips clamped shut.

Princess Helen hiccuped suddenly and got unsteadily to her feet, muttering that she had to visit the loo. Before anyone could catch her, she tottered backwards and fell on the recumbent Zulu.

Reflexively, the startled animal struck out with both hind feet, carving two parallel gashes in the leg of the ill-smelling person who had suddenly attacked him. "Get him away!" the Princess screamed in terror and agony.

Logan cursed and grabbed the cheetah by the hind legs, intending to pull him away. Zulu whirled and fastened his teeth in his trainer's upper arm. Clenching his teeth against the pain, Logan got hold of the leash as Zulu, his muzzle covered with blood, wiggled his hindquarter out from under the Princess and stood on all four feet. Confused, he remained perfectly still as if waiting to be told what to do. Sheena began a frenzied hooting from her enclosure at the bottom of the garden.

Holding his arm in a vain attempt to staunch the flow of blood, Logan glared down at the wounded Princess sobbing with pain and fright. "You always were a spoiled, drunken brat and you always will be."

"We've got to get them to the clinic," said Skye "And we need towels and blankets."

"I'll get them," said Lady Fraser, lifting her skirt around her hips as she began to run toward the house.

"I'll go with her," Erin said as Lord Fraser took her place supporting the Princess. Skye told her to call Glessop and alert him. "Make sure Edwina is there as well," he called out as she sped away. "There's no telling what kind of shape Sir George will be in and tell Foxcroft and the other bodyguard to get down here."

Some bodyguard. Foxcroft was in for the mother of all rockets when Scotland Yard heard about this fiasco.

Foxcroft would know this too, but he didn't let it distract him as he briskly took charge. The royal jeep was equipped with a first aid kit and he expertly bandaged the Princess's wound. She seemed to be drifting in and out of consciousness. Wrapping her in a blanket, he picked her up and told his subordinate to run ahead and get the jeep started.

Skye asked Logan if he could walk. The groundskeeper nodded mutely, holding a towel pressed against his wound.

"Come on, we'll get you to the clinic," Skye said, telling the hovering Ralston to get the keys to the Beaufort jeep. Holding the passenger door open, he told Logan to get in, saying it would be easier for him riding in the front. "That towel is soaked through." He took the bloodstained one from Logan and handed him a fresh towel. The blood-soaked one he threw in the back of the jeep.

* * *

"The first thing is to clean these wounds," said Glessop, gazing down at his two patients.

Once again, Skye was impressed with the surgeon's professionalism. When the need arose, he seemed capable of rising to the occasion.

"We'll start with a saline solution," Glessop said to Edwina who silently handed him a white enamel bowl and strips of gauze. Taking them from her, he said, "I'll attend to Her Royal Highness and you look after Logan."

His hands trembled slightly as he placed the bowl on the table, but they were steady enough as he began to swab out the cuts. The Princess, who seemed to have calmed down now that she was receiving medical care, bit her lip as he scrubbed away at her wounds, but didn't cry out.

"Are you going to stitch the cuts?" asked Skye, concerned that Glessop would botch the job. He had helped Logan into the clinic and stayed on, since no one seemed to mind.

Glessop shook his head. "You don't suture wounds like this. You want them to drain outside, not inside.

After the wound is as clean as we can get it, we'll pack it with antibiotics."

"Won't there be a scar?" asked the Princess in a faint whisper.

"Yes, there will be. But there are lots of plastic surgeons in London who can take care of that little problem."

When he finished swabbing her cuts with the saline solution, he packed them with gauze held in place with steri-strips. On the next examining table, Edwina was following the same procedure with Logan.

Closing the curtain between the two patients, Glessop said to Skye with a gleeful smile, "I'm going to give them a tetanus shot, and since it will be in a rather private part of the royal anatomy, I'll ask you to step outside."

* * *

"They'll be fine," Skye told those in the waiting room. Inspector Foxcroft exchanged glances with Detective Goodwin. This could be the end of their careers. Their instructions were to use their discretion and stay out of Her Royal Highness's way when they were satisfied the situation was secure. Manchineel was regarded as low risk, and what could be more harmless than having lunch at Lord Fraser's villa? But that wouldn't help them now.

Skye asked the inspector if he could have a word with him and the detective followed him outside. "Do you know who's in charge of the Lord Lassiter case?" asked Skye.

"Chief Inspector Harradine." The officer peered intently as Skye. "Why do you ask, sir?" As if to make up for what he saw as a dereliction of duty, Foxcroft had reverted to a rigid formality.

Skye reached into the Beaufort jeep and took out the

blood-soaked towel. "It's probably a wild goose chase, but I suggest you send this to the Chief Inspector and have him run a DNA test. I assume he'll have something of Lassiter's that this can be compared with?"

"Bound to, sir. They will have collected any number of things in the course of the investigation." He paused, then said dubiously, "Logan doesn't look anything like Lord Lassiter."

"I realized that." Skye thought back to the arrogant, yet petulant face on the cover of the *High Society* magazine he had borrowed from Fiona. It certainly bore no resemblance to Logan. "But there is such a thing as plastic surgery. Anyway, the chances are nothing will come of it. It's just a hunch on my part. Still, there's nothing to lose. But there's one thing I am sure of: Logan is not the humble groundskeeper he pretends to be."

"Right, sir," the detective replied briskly as he took the towel, holding it between his thumb and forefinger. His report of today's disaster would go down much better with his superiors when he told then he was sending a possible clue to the whereabouts of Lord Lassiter. If it led to an arrest of the world's most sought-after fugitive, and a successful conclusion to the celebrated case, he would be a bloody hero! Maybe he would make chief inspector after all.

* * *

Erin was still at Beaufort with Lady Fraser when Skye drove the jeep back.

"Thank God for that," Lady Fraser breathed when Skye told them that Princess Helen and Logan would be okay. "But there will be the most dreadful fuss."

Skye declined the offer of tea, saying he had to get the horses back to the stables. "I can pony Belle," he said to Erin, "if you don't feel like riding."

"I'll ride."

"Fiona was right about there going to be a fuss," Erin said as they rode through Beaufort's main gate. "The press will descend on this like a plaque of locusts. That poor soul seems to stumble from one public relations disaster to the next."

"'Stumble' is the word," Skye replied dryly. "She's not what you would call a model of decorum and discretion."

As they rode, the horses stepping out companionably side by side, Skye was uncomfortably aware that in his enthusiasm over his theory that Logan might be the evil Lassiter, he had put his good friend, Robert Fraser, in jeopardy. If Logan was indeed Lassiter, Robert could be charged with harbouring a fugitive from justice. A notorious one at that. It was just the sort of thing an aristocrat like Fraser would do. Beneath their veneer, they seemed to have a careless contempt for the lesser orders. Robert must have known Lassiter a great deal better than he let on. But the chances of Logan being Lassiter were remote to nil, so he was worrying himself unnecessarily. Skye put Sun Dancer into a trot and Belle immediately followed suit.

When they arrived at the stables, Elizabeth was unloading two more horses. Both of them were thoroughbreds, and one of them, a chestnut gelding, was snorting and rolling his eyes as Elizabeth led him over to a railed enclosure that would separate him from the rest of the horses. "I'll talk to you in a minute," she called over her shoulder. "I want to hear what happened."

"I'm glad it's not more serious," she said when Skye finished telling her about the cheetah incident. "Some of the rumours that were floating around had both of them at death's door."

As they talked, Skye watched the chestnut gelding, racing back and forth behind the rails, wheeling around just before he crashed into them. Looking around the paddock, he said "You've got some pretty spirited horseflesh here. Aren't you afraid of overmatching the riders?"

"Normally I'd agree. But not this year. A member of the U.S. International Jumping Team is coming here with his girlfriend. They're staying at Cormorant Bay. The only way the team coach would let him come was if he promised to ride for at least two hours every day. His girlfriend is an expert rider as well, and they wanted thoroughbreds with lots of spirit."

"Looks like they got their wish," muttered Skye, instinctively stepping back, as the chestnut again charged up to the rail.

* * *

Overfine had driven the jeep to the stables and left it there for Skye. On the way to drop Erin off at Banyan, Skye swung around by the waterfront. There was no sign of the *Caroline*.

"How about a flying lesson in the morning?" he asked as he parked in front of the Banyan.

"Super."

Skye climbed out and held the door for her. The slam of the doors brought Mary running out of the house, anxious to know about The Highness. Walking back from the Company office with her mail, she had seen the procession of jeeps turning into the clinic's driveway. Like Elizabeth Mallory, she was relieved that it wasn't as serious as the rumours had it.

"There goes our celebrated privacy," she sighed. "By tomorrow we'll be inundated with reporters."

Skye was about to kiss Erin goodbye but checked

himself when he saw young Patrick peering out from the doorway. "I'll call you tonight," he said as he climbed back into the jeep.

Chapter Sixteen

"There's the fishing fleet. I'll take over." Skye pushed the control column forward and dove down on the wooden pirogues that were spread out in a wide circle on the water. They were riding up and down in the surge of the sea, but they had managed to get their nets out.

"It's amazing that they can fish in all those waves," said Erin.

"They'll stick it out as long as they can. The fish they're catching will bring a fancy price. Those boats are incredibly seaworthy and so are the men."

As if to prove Skye's point, the men stood up in their wildly rocking boats and waved at the diving plane.

"I know why those men worship you," Erin said. "Louella Harper told me. I also know about the mercy flight you made with Penelope."

Skye's face darkened at the mention of Penelope. Regaining altitude over Carriacou, he handed the controls over to Erin and told her to head northeast. Twenty minutes later, he said, "There's the *Caroline*." Raising the binoculars to his eyes, he saw that she was travelling at reduced speed and pitching and rolling heavily. "Looks like she's heading for Manchineel. Charles will no doubt be rushing back to comfort the wounded Princess Helen."

"I just don't understand him. You'd think that now that he's out in the open sea and with the volcano as an excuse, he'd steer well clear of her."

Skye laughed, the sound rattling in her earphones. "I'm sure that's what he would like to do, but he knows that she may be his ticket back to England. Let's say hello." Taking the controls back, he put the Cessna into a shallow dive. Erin waved as they swept past the yacht. Flaring up in a climbing turn, Skye flew parallel to the *Caroline*'s port side. Charles Pollock stood on the flying bridge, clinging to the railing and waving one hand at the low-flying airplane. Skye was enjoying himself. Wrapping the 180 around in a tight turn, he made another pass at the ship, this time flying directly over her superstructure.

"Okay. Take us home," he said, handing the controls back to Erin.

"That was fun," Erin said, as, feeling like a pro, she advanced the throttle and put the airplane into a steady climb. "Here we are, in absolutely smooth air while down below they're being tossed all over the place."

"You can do the landing," Skye said as they closed in on Manchineel. "I'll talk you in."

Doing exactly as she was told, Erin was both thrilled and more than a little scared to find herself lined up with the runway. She cast an appealing look at Skye, but he merely smiled and said, "You're doing fine."

When he retarded the throttle and told her to pull the stick back, she did it a shade too abruptly and they hit and bounced. "Keep the stick in your lap." he said urgently. She nodded and the tailwheel banged down on the runway and they came to a stop.

After tying down the airplane, they walked across the tarmac to the terminal. Normally the airport dozed in the sun during the midday lull in the air traffic. Today, however, it bustled with activity as the media flocked in on chartered aircraft to cover Princess Helen's latest escapade. Skye smiled to himself as he saw the long line of journalists, bedecked with cameras and tape recorders, fuming with impatience as the officious Jason methodically examined each piece of luggage.

Brenda Fewster came forward to greet them as they entered the open-air terminal. Erin ran forward, "What is it, Brenda? Is Patrick all right?"

"He's fine, Erin. The cook is giving him lunch. I had a phone call from Mrs. Kelly. She wants me to talk to you two."

"Why don't you join us for lunch?" Skye suggested.

She looked a little startled, then nodded acceptance. "I walked over so I'll ride with you."

A taxi, a jeep with Nick's Tours painted on the sides — one of two the Company permitted to operate — turned into the parking area to pick up more journalists as Skye and his passengers drove off. "Nick's Plaza," the street where virtually all the commercial activity on the island took place, was crowded. Jeeps were drawn up outside Nick's general store, customers streamed in and out of the two boutiques, one of which he owned, or sat outside on the boardwalk, having coffee and ice cream. On the other side of the street, passengers from a chartered yacht were treating their hangovers with some hair of the dog in Nick's Bar. Knowing Erin would be recognized instantly, Skye looked for anyone who might be a journalist. But they were all either people he recognized as belonging on the island or others who were obviously vacationing tourists from chartered yachts or on day tours. Chances were that the reporters who had passed through Jason's gruelling inspections would be camped out at Serenity, Princess Helen's villa. Erin was wearing fashionably outsize sunglasses, which helped.

Skye parked in a space beside the market where the fishermen sold lobsters.

"What's this all about, Brenda?" Erin demanded as soon as they were seated.

"I'm just the messenger, that's all," Brenda protested.

"She told you to warn Skye off, didn't she? Because the Family is worried he might persuade me to break the 'code of silence' the attorneys talked about, and go public."

Throughout this exchange, Skye sat relaxed in his chair, smiling pleasantly. Erin gave him a puzzled glance, then hesitantly returned his smile, and began to eat her salad. She was puzzled even more when, after the lunch was finished, Skye suggested he and Brenda have a little chat. She pulled him to one side and whispered, "You don't seem to be taking this very seriously. But it is serious. You don't seem to realize how powerful the Kellys are."

Smiling, he tapped her gently on the nose. "I know exactly how powerful they are. Probably better than anyone outside the Family itself. What is it that they say? 'Don't worry your pretty little head about it.'"

Seeing her exasperated look, he laughed and kissed her firmly on the mouth. Turning to Brenda, he said, "Let's have our little chat."

He led past the crowded tables to the railing where they could look out over the harbour and the moored yachts. "You're more than a social worker, aren't you?" he asked pleasantly.

"I am a qualified social worker, but I also have my

private investigator's licence." As she spoke her voice took a sharper edge.

"I wouldn't have expected anything less from the Family."

"You're a pretty cool customer, Skye," calling him by his first name for the first time. "But you don't know what you're up against. The Kellys are very concerned about you having an affair with their daughter-in-law."

"Ex-daughter-in-law."

"She's still part of the Family as far as the public is concerned."

"So?"

"So you're to stop seeing Erin. As of now."

"And if I don't?"

"You're a wealthy man. Not by Kelly standards, of course, but still wealthy. The first thing that would likely happen is that you'd be ruined. Stone broke."

The smile that Skye turned on her was almost friendly. "You told me how you make your living. Now I'll tell you how I make mine. Research. Research into potential investments. I'm good at it. And ever since my wife was killed I've researched the Kelly empire. Thoroughly."

"I heard you were poking into things that were none of your business. But, so what?"

Skye laughed. "Are you trying to sound like a hard-boiled private eye? I'll tell you 'so what.' You know Senator Grafson?"

"I wouldn't say I know him. He visits Mr. Kelly at the compound from time to time."

"He's a very powerful senator. He's the chairman of the Ways and Means Committee. Have you heard of the Astro Project?"

"No."

"That doesn't surprise me." Skye paused. "Tell Mr.

Kelly that I mentioned those two names in the same breath. I think it'll attract his attention. And tell him to pray for my continued good health."

"What is this? Blackmail?"

"No — countermail."

* * *

"How did it go?" Erin's expression was half-fearful, half-hopeful as they sat in the jeep watching a subdued-looking Brenda Fewster walk in Banyan's front door.

"I think I spiked their guns."

"How could you possibly do that?"

"Your ex-father-in-law holds himself out as a great patriot, doesn't he?"

"It's his proudest boast. Always has been."

"Exactly. So he wouldn't want people to know that he doesn't always act in the best interests of his beloved country, would he?"

"My God, Skye, I hope you know what you're doing."

"That old pirate knows how these things work. I think we'll be all right." Shaking her head, she opened the jeep's door and climbed out. "I'm going to take Patrick snorkelling."

"Good. I think I'll pay my respects to The Highness. See how she's making out."

* * *

There were at least twenty reporters camped out in front of Serenity's massive iron gate. Inspector Foxcroft was telling the impatient crowd that Her Royal Highness was resting and could on no account be disturbed, so they might as well go away. Spotting Skye's jeep, he waved it forward and Skye eased it through the grumbling journalists who reluctantly moved aside. Detective Goodwin came up to help Foxcroft keep the reporters from rushing in when the gate opened. When it swung shut behind Skye's jeep, the frustrated reporters began to talk about leaving. There was no overnight accommodation available and they had to be off the island before nightfall.

Foxcroft rode up to the villa with Skye. "Her Royal Highness will be glad to see you, as always. But she is not in a good mood."

"How come?"

"The Palace has ordered her home."

"She can't do that!"

When Foxcroft stared at him, Skye grinned sheepishly. "I know that sounds funny, but I'll explain it later."

Serenity's butler gently closed the bedroom door behind him and informed Skye that Her Royal Highness would be delighted to see him, but asked him to kindly wait for a few minutes while she completed a long distance call to the Palace. In the brief interval when the door had been open, her voice, sharpened into stridency, was clearly audible. Whatever it was she was being asked to do was clearly not to her liking.

She was still seething when Skye was ushered into her presence. The drapes were pulled and the room was in semi-darkness, lit only by a bedside lamp. "They want me to return to London," she said, fiercely stubbing out a cigarette. A maid appeared, seemingly out of nowhere, and silently replaced the ashtray. "But I told them not to be so damn stupid. My beloved brother-in-law claims it's so I can have proper medical treatment, but I know damn well it's so they can lock me away in some institution for a 'cure.' Fuck them!"

"Glessop seems to know what he's doing," Skye remarked mildly.

"I told them if they were so concerned about my health, they could bloody well send over a Harley Street physician to look after me."

"Are they going to do that?"

"I don't know. But it's the scandal they're worried about, not the state of my health. It'll give the anti-monarchy bastards another reason to bitch."

"The paparazzi are at the gate as we speak."

"I know. But it won't do them any good. I'm not venturing out of this room." She waggled a glass of vodka tonic, making the ice tinkle. "Would you like a drink?"

Skye shook his head. "No thanks. I just dropped in for a moment to see how you were. And you're obviously fine. Have you heard how Logan is doing?"

"As it happens, I have. I talked to Robert this morning and apparently Logan was up and about and doing his chores when the damn reporters descended on the place and sent him into hiding."

"That was a very brave thing he did yesterday."

"He had to do something. He's in charge of the bloody animal that attacked me," she said coldly. "He's so insolent, it makes me furious."

"Do you know anything about his background?"

"Not really. He arrived on the island when I was not in residence. I have an idea he came from Argentina. But he's not Spanish, although with those dark looks of his, he could be."

"No. He's definitely English." Skye glanced at his watch and stood up. "I'm on my way, ma'am. I don't want to tire you. By the way, I saw the *Caroline*. She seemed to be heading this way. She was making heavy weather of it."

"Charles is so gallant." She actually simpered.

Foxcroft was waiting for him in the villa's airy, sunlit livingroom.

"Did the towel get off?" Skye asked him.

"It left Barbados last night in a diplomatic pouch. The experts at the Yard have already started to run the tests."

"Fast work. When will you know the results?"

"In a matter of days for the PCR test, where the chances of identical results from two different people are as high as one in two thousand. It'll take up to a month for the definitive test, RFLP, where the odds are one in a million. But if the PCR results are positive, you can be sure the Yard will move in on our lad. God, but wouldn't it be wonderful to close that file after all this time? What made you suspect Logan?"

"The way he cursed the Princess for being a spoiled, drunken brat. It struck me he must have known her in another life."

"Lassiter was part of her set. Until he ran out of money."

"That fits. And in the heat of the moment he spoke in the rich, clarety voice of an Oxford man. Completely different from the way he usually grunts out words."

"Lassiter went to Oxford."

"Well, we'll soon know, one way or the other."

Foxcroft merely nodded, but his eyes were bright with anticipation. "Can I ask why you don't want Princess Helen to return to London?"

Again Skye looked a little sheepish. "I was a bit premature on that. Will you take a raincheck?"

It took Foxcroft a moment to sort out the unfamiliar idiom, then he nodded, and Skye went on. "I'll tell you this much. It doesn't involve the Princess, it's you and your men that I don't want to see leave."

"No more do we. We want to be right here when those DNA results come in."

Foxcroft got to his feet to escort Skye to the door.

Skye glanced in at the kitchen where the cook and the maid were beginning to make preparations for the evening meal. "I don't know whether you know it or not, but all the staff are voodoo worshippers."

"I know. It's my business to know."

* * *

Skye's route back to Whistling Frog took him past the stables and he stopped to see how Elizabeth was making out with her new horses. The cold bloods seemed to have settled in, but two of the thoroughbreds paced restlessly behind the railing Elizabeth had erected to separate them from the other horses.

"It's those blasted drums," Elizabeth told him. "They've never heard them before and it makes them crazy. I galloped both of them today, but it doesn't seem to have done any good."

Sun Dancer and Belle were standing together near the tack room. Sun Dancer was eyeing Skye as if wondering whether they were going for a ride. The two horses stood still as he went over and patted them on the neck. Their ears pricked up and they whinnied softly when he went into the tack room and came out with a handful of grain pellets. Leaving them crunching their treat, he waved at Elizabeth and went back to the jeep.

* * *

Overfine, carrying a plastic shopping bag, came out of the villa as Skye cut the engine. "The fish boats be back and Agatha does want some bonito to grill for dinner."

Handing him the keys, Skye said, "Tell Sebastian I'm coming down to see him after he's sold his fish." He looked at his watch. It was just after six. "Say around quarter of seven."

Overfine was back with the jeep before it was time

for Skye to leave. Lights were coming on in the villas as he drove to the fishermen's camp. There was no electricity in the camp, but hissing gas mantle lamps provided adequate, if harsh, illumination. "The fish was still running good, but the sea got too rough," Sebastian told Skye as they walked the short distance to the beach.

The fishermen's camp was in a protected cove and normally little wavelets washed gently over the sand, but tonight white-capped waves broke against the shore, threatening an ancient manchineel tree that grew just above what had been the high water mark.

"I remember you once saying that you have known Adrienne since the day she was born," Skye said.

"That be so. Her daddy and I does be friends back when I live in Grenada."

"Do you know who Penelope's father is?"

"I know. Does it be important for you to know?"

"Yes."

Staring out at the darkening sea, Sebastian said, "Marcellus Thomas."

So there it was. The PM was Penelope's father. The PM who had just received a new heart. A young new heart that was a perfect match. Adrienne knew. That was why she had let out that soul-searing scream in the garden when she overheard Lord Fraser talking about what a miraculous match it was.

Skye waited for Sebastian to ask him why he wanted to know, but the fisherman's face was expressionless as he continued to stare out at the sea. Skye thanked him and left him alone on the beach. The drums began to beat as Skye drove home.

* * *

After complimenting Agatha on the delicious grilled fish, Skye took his coffee out on the patio. Listening to the pulsing drums, Skye thought that this was how the plantation owners in their Great Houses must have felt when the rhythmic chanting began in the slave quarters and cane fields burned in the night.

Skye shook his head when Overfine came out to ask if he wanted a liqueur. "What's with the drums, Overfine?"

"Adrienne's new *loa* tole her he's ready to come down."

"When? Do you know?"

"Not for sure. Maybe tomorrow night."

"I don't like it, Overfine. There's so much tension in the air things could get completely out of control. You know these people; is there any danger of an uprising?"

"No. People live good here. It just be that heathen religion. Adrienne say her new *loa* be more powerful than Baron Samedi. It be silliness."

Brave words, my friend, thought Skye. But you've got the wind up, just the same.

* * *

The whistling frog that lived under the oleander bush stopped its bleeping, telling Skye it was almost midnight. The drums were still throbbing when he went to bed. As usual, Myra had done a turn-down service that would have put a five-star hotel to shame. Picking a bougainvillea blossom off the pillow, Skye placed it on the dresser. Old man Kelly would have heard from Brenda Fewster by now. Skye had played the Astro card and the way ahead was clear for him and Erin. He wondered where it would eventually lead. As for himself, he had a feeling he might be falling in love.

Chapter Seventeen

Skye, eyes burning after a night of sleep made fitful with thoughts of Penelope's possible fate, wakened as sunlight filtered through the drapes to invade his bedroom. Switching off the air-conditioning, he opened the French door. The only sound was a tropical nightingale churring its serenade to the bright new day from its perch on the bare branch of a plumeria. Overfine was cleaning the pool; Skye waved at him and said he would be ready for breakfast in half an hour.

* * *

"I just found this under the front door." Overfine handed Skye a single sheet of paper as he sat down at the table.

The brief printed message was from the Manchineel Company, apologizing to the homeowners and renters for the disturbance caused by the voodoo "activity." It asked for their understanding and forbearance for another 24 hours, promising that after tonight was over, Manchineel would return to its "normal, tranquil ways." It also stated that the regular weekly cocktail party at Sugar Mill that had been scheduled for that evening was postponed, due to the "circumstances." The note ended with the suggestion that everyone would be well-advised to remain indoors tonight.

Skye put the sheet of paper aside and looked up at Overfine. "It looks like tonight is when Adrienne's new *loa* will make his appearance."

Overfine, his face tight with disapproval, nodded.

* * *

Skye spent the morning with a text book on organ transplants he had bought some months after Jocelyn's death. This was the first time he had been able to bring himself to read it. As he read, he was surprised at how basic an operating room for the retrieval of organs could be. Of course that was because there was no need to worry about keeping the victim alive. For example, it would be a simple matter to conceal a set-up like that on a boat the size of the *Caroline*. He closed the text book with a snap as his thoughts began to race.

Penelope could have been smuggled aboard the *Caroline* the night she disappeared. Maybe that was where Glessop and Edwina were going so late at night. Princess Helen's insistence on having lunch on board the yacht would have put a crimp in their plans. But there was no time to waste; the PM could turn up his toes any second. Pollock, or someone, had improvised brilliantly.

That was why Captain Morton had made such a hash of sailing into the anchorage at Tobago Cays. To give them an excuse to put the passengers ashore and sail out of harm's way. That would also explain the floatplane. Its role would have been to fly the heart to the clinic in Boca Raton. The yacht could create a stretch of calm water for it to land and take off on, by sailing in a wide circle. If Glessop and Edwina were hidden somewhere on board, they could have done the operation while Pollock and his guests were having champagne and caviar on the beach. Skye groaned aloud at the thought of the heart being cut out of a beautiful young girl so that a dying politician could live. That explained why the clinic had carried out those tests. It was a ruse to get a sample of Penelope's blood.

Had the PM told someone of the biological connection between him and the girl? Was any human being capable of such a monstrous act? The PM had never had anything to do with Penelope so maybe there was no emotional involvement. But still. A small entourage of advisers had accompanied him to the States. Maybe one of them had somehow learned of the connection and set things in motion. One thing was certain. It wouldn't have been Adrienne.

Trying to convince himself that it was just a theory, no matter how diabolical, and that Penelope was probably serving lunch in some high class restaurant at this very moment, Skye put the textbooks away. He was due at the Rastoks for lunch.

As the jeep began the long descent down to Nick's Plaza, Skye looked out over the harbour and blinked when he saw that all the yachts had gone. To his surprise there was no sign of the *Caroline*. The Highness would be disappointed. Where was the *Caroline*? Why was she still in the area? With those questions running through his mind, Skye turned off on the road that led to Banyan.

Young Patrick Kelly and the social worker cum private eye, Brenda Fewster, joined them for lunch, which was served on the patio. The Rastoks' villa was located on the beachfront and it was difficult to talk against the boom of the surf.

"Looks like we're really in for it," Skye remarked as he held Mary Rastok's chair.

"What about your plane?" Mary asked.

"No problem. There won't be any wind, just very heavy seas. I've hauled the whaler out of the water. On my way here I saw that all the yachts have left. They'll be heading for the hurricane hole on Marigot."

"You'd think they would let them use the hurricane hole on Frigate," Mary said. "It's so much closer."

"Not a chance. The people who own that island like their privacy."

Patrick was following the conversation avidly, his eyes, green like his mother's and his only feature that was not pure Kelly, darting from Skye to Mary. Skye could tell that while the boy might have started out admiring him, he now resented him, jealous of the time his mother spent with him and undoubtedly aware of how they felt about each other. Maybe there was something he could do about that. Skye refused a second glass of wine and as coffee was served to end the meal, said to Patrick, "Your mother's learning to fly. She's going to be a great pilot. Would you like to go down to the airport and take a look at my airplane? Maybe go up for a flight."

Patrick immediately jumped up out of his chair, but Brenda Fewster started to protest. Smiling at her, Skye said, "Why don't you come too?"

"Patrick is certainly not going up in that!" Brenda Fewster stared at the trim little airplane with alarm. "It's only got one engine, and no member of the Kelly family is allowed to fly in single-engined airplanes."

***

Patrick, sitting in the pilot's seat while Skye leaned in through the cabin door to show him the controls, scowled his disappointment but made no protest. The poor kid is probably used to having his life circumscribed by the restrictions imposed by the Kellys to safeguard their young heir, thought Skye.

"Hang in there," Skye straightened up and walked across to the wooden shack on stilts that was the Manchineel control tower. He climbed partway up the short ladder and poked his head through the trapdoor into the room where Henry Armbruster presided amid an array of dials and switches and squawking radios.

"I thought I'd like to get in a little twin time," said Skye. "Is the Baron free?"

"It is for a couple of hours. It's booked for a charter to Barbados but that's not until five o'clock. Have her back by four-thirty." Armbruster levered himself out of the chair and followed Skye down the ladder. "For you it's only three hundred dollars an hour."

"Do you see that airplane over there?" Skye asked Brenda Fewster, pointing to the Beech Baron. When she nodded, he asked, "How many engines does it have?"

"That's what we're going up in," Skye grinned when she said "Two" through tightly compressed lips.

Erin laughed her infectious laugh.

* * *

With an excited Patrick sitting on two cushions in the co-pilot's seat, and Erin and Brenda in the seats behind, they took off and headed northeast. As Skye had predicted, there were flotillas of yachts, motoring under bare poles, heading for Marigot where they would find shelter in a deeply indented, mangrove-lined bay. The black-hulled *Caroline* was not among them. She was an ocean going vessel, built to withstand the mountainous waves that could be encountered during ocean crossings. Skye turned and flew a reciprocal southeast course.

Half an hour later, they spotted her on the horizon, a thin plume of blue smoke trailing from her funnel. Not that it mattered, but Pollock would never suspect that Skye was at the controls of the twin-engine Baron. The Baron bore the livery of Manchineel Air, and anyone seeing it would assume it was on either a scheduled or a charter flight. It also would be completely natural for a charter flight to take a closer look at the beautiful yacht. Keeping well to one side, Skye flew past at one thousand feet. The *Caroline*'s speed had been reduced even more until she was barely making way, and she was pitching heavily. The stabilizers might moderate her rolling, but they couldn't do anything about the pitching. If Skye's nagging suspicions were correct, it would be impossible for anyone to do surgery while she was being tossed around like that. As it was, Pollock and his crew must be taking one hell of a pounding. They were obviously prepared to ride it out, but why?

When he had left the yacht well behind, Skye turned onto a course that would take them back to Manchineel.

As they disembarked, Patrick gravely thanked Skye for a "thrilling experience." Erin fondly tousled her son's hair and winked at Skye. Even Brenda Fewster seemed pleasantly exhilarated by the flight.

Erin invited Skye in for tea, but Mary Rastok met them with the news that Agatha had phoned to say that Skye had visitors and would he come home as quickly as possible.

Skye's visitors turned out to be Sebastian and his son, Joshua. They were having tea in the livingroom where the devout Agatha fussed over the fledgling clergyman. Joshua wasn't entitled to wear the reversed collar as yet, but he was dressed conservatively in a dark blue suit. Skye was a little taken aback to be embraced and called "brother," but he was genuinely glad to see Joshua. He noted with some amusement that Joshua's voice had deepened to a baritone that could belt out "Hallelujahs" with the best of them.

The solemn look on Sebastian's weathered countenance told Skye that this was no social call. Telling them to bring their tea, he suggested they move out to the patio. Once outside, Sebastian nodded grimly at his son to begin.

"A member of my flock in Barbados," Joshua intoned. "A good Christian lady, has a sister who works here on Manchineel. That sister, I am sorry to say, has turned away from the church, and has become a worshipper of heathen gods. But the two sisters remain very close, and confide in each other. My lady was so upset by what she heard that she consulted me. After I heard what she had to say I knew I had to fly over here and inform you."

Skye was tempted to ask, "Why me," but merely nodded and continued to listen intently.

"Tonight's ceremony is going to be a very powerful one," Joshua went on. "Adrienne will try to invoke her new *loa*." His thick lips turned down as he said the word.

"That's what I understand," Skye murmured. "But how does it affect me?"

"She is going to burn some of Mistress Jocelyn's remains as a sacrifice to the *loa*."

"But that's not possible! I scattered her ashes on the water."

"Adrienne claim her new *loa*, Lord Barracuda, find the pieces for her. She have the urn too."

Jesus. Adrienne must have been spying on them when he and Overfine scattered the ashes. She was an expert diver; it would be a simple matter for her to retrieve the urn if she knew its approximate location. But the bone fragments! And there were teeth too! "I can't let that happen!" Skye was on his feet.

"It won't," Joshua said. "I won't let it."

"Do you have any idea where Adrienne is?" asked Skye.

"We never find her," said Sebastian. "She always go away by herselves before she become mambo."

"I guess that means another visit to the tonnelle," muttered Skye.

Joshua shook his head. "It's not the tonnelle. Tonight it's the cemetery. Sacrilege!"

"Be the first time in a long while they use the cemetery," Sebastian rumbled. "Adrienne planning powerful medicine."

The first bats of the evening fluttered past and the voodoo drums began to talk.

"Nothing to be done till after dark," Sebastian said with the air of one who knows. Skye had heard the rumours that Sebastian sometimes appeared as Baron Samedi at ceremonies held on other islands. It probably explained why he was able to exert such complete control over the fishermen's camp, including the macho lobster fishermen.

Sebastian put down his empty cup. "I hear tonight be quick." Frowning, he said, "Adrienne not even invite Baron Samedi. Joshua and his men be by the cemetery along about nine o'clock."

"This could be dangerous," Skye protested. "I can't let them get involved ..." His voice trailed off as Joshua glared at him. This was an argument Skye couldn't win.

"You was lucky dat other time," Sebastian told him. "But it not be so easy this time. Adrienne watch for you."

"I know. Your men won't be armed, will they?"

Sebastian shook his head. "We don't want dat kine of trouble."

* * *

Knowing that Overfine would ask to accompany him, Skye forestalled his request by telling the butler to stay behind and guard the villa. Overfine protested that that was what they paid the security guard for, but without much conviction, since they both knew the ineffable Jackson would discreetly fade into the night at the first sign of trouble.

* * *

There was no moon to light Skye's way as he drove without headlights. As he went past the stables he saw Elizabeth's horses moving restlessly around the paddock; the new arrivals were still penned off at the far end, the thoroughbreds neighing and snorting as they trotted back and forth behind the railing. It was no wonder they were spooked. The drums were beating incessantly, and earlier the night would have been filled with moving shadows as people, blindly answering the summons of the drums, streamed past the stables and up the hill to the cemetery. A jumbie bird floated by in its curious owl fashion with its body seeming to bob up and down between stationary wings.

Skye drove past Elizabeth's house, guided by the fact that the gravelled surface of the road was lighter in colour than the surrounding vegetation. A few hundred yards further on, he pulled over to the verge and stopped. Joshua materialized out of the darkness as Skye stepped out of the jeep. He told Skye that things were moving quickly and that Papa Legba was no longer at the gate. The noise of the drums and the chanting of the worshippers made it unnecessary to lower their voices. Skye followed him down the hill.

There was no cross in the cemetery. There was always a cross when a voodoo ceremony took place in a cemetery, either at the gate or in the centre. It was to honour Baron Samedi, the "keeper of the cemeteries." What was Adrienne thinking of, insulting the powerful *loa* in this fashion?

Attired in his shabby black coat and battered bowler hat, Papa Legba was sitting in the middle of the throng, a benign smile on his face as he smoked his pipe. He had certainly managed to intercede with the gods tonight. A young woman, possessed by Damballa, slithered on her belly through the grass. Another woman, skirt hiked up above her hips, lay on her back across a tombstone, jerking spasmodically as if copulating with an invisible lover. Seizing the opportunity, a man stepped out of his jeans and entered her. Joshua hissed his disapproval. Skye ignored him as he scanned the lurid scene, looking for Adrienne.

Torches flickered and smoked, casting long shadows which seemed to move and sway with the dancing and undulations of the celebrants. Peering through the smoke, Skye thought he had located the mambo, but when the woman in the white dress stepped out of the shadows, he saw it was Annette, a light-complected young woman who lived in the native village. Her *loa* was Erzulie, a pale, almost white, goddess, who alone among the loas possessed beautiful gowns and jewellery. It was revealing and rather pathetic that wealth and beautiful things were associated with lightness of skin.

A "horse" mounted by Ogun, the god of war imported from Nigeria, stumbled out of the gate, brandishing a decapitated red cock, the god's favourite offering. Four men chased after him, to bring him back into the cemetery. Skye and Joshua moved out of the way to avoid being splattered with blood. The men rushed past them in pursuit of the god-possessed worshipper, then suddenly spun on their heels and sprang at Skye and Joshua, pinning their arms to their sides.

"Jes' hol' strain, man," one of the men holding Skye muttered, his breath heavy with rum fumes. Skye looked at Joshua and shook his head. Their captors might be full of rum but their grip was iron hard, the grip of men who laboured with their hands.

A murmur rippled through the crowd as Baron Samedi, this time carrying a cane, slowly made his way to the peristyle. With a start, Skye realized it was Sebastian behind the dark glasses. If Adrienne was disconcerted by the *loa*'s unexpected appearance, she gave no sign of it as she came out from behind the altar to greet him. She had designed a special costume for the occasion, a body stocking made from fishnet hung with silvery metal fish. The outfit clung to the spectacular contours of her body. Adrienne greeted the uninvited *loa* courteously, bowing with a slight inclination of the head that was much less obsequious than the obeisance with which she had greeted him at their last encounter. The *loa* frowned at this lack of respect. Adrienne led him to a hastily vacated chair, a demeaning distance from the altar. All this was meant to prove that her god was mightier than even the dread "keeper of the cemeteries."

Sebastian, in his guise of Baron Samedi, said something to Adrienne. She listened attentively, but shook her head and retreated into the darkness behind the altar. Sebastian must have tried to use his power as Baron Samedi to persuade Adrienne to give up what was left of Jocelyn's remains, but had obviously failed to convince her. Now Adrienne's assistant came forward, genuflected before the altar and reverently placed the burial urn and a black iron crucible on the altar cloth. Skye cursed and struggled vainly to free himself as the assistant poured kerosene into the crucible and lit it. Then Adrienne re-appeared, bearing a silver tray, probably "borrowed" for the night from one of the villas. She tilted it towards Skye, and his chest constricted and he kicked out at the legs of the men holding him when he saw the little fragments of bone and teeth on it.

"Jes' be still, man. It be ober soon." Another blast of rum-laden breath enveloped Skye.

Adrienne genuflected toward the altar, holding out the silver tray. Her face was transformed with a look of ecstasy as she called out to her *loa*. Suddenly the drums picked up a new beat, a rolling thunder that underpinned their pulsing rhythm. Then Skye recognized the sound for what it was — the sound of galloping horses. They were coming fast and as the thunder of their pounding hooves grew louder, the drums faltered and fell silent, and people began to cry out in fear and wonder. The men holding Skye and Joshua released them and ran off.

Stampede! The new thoroughbreds must have gotten so badly spooked that one of them had crashed through the fence and into the night. Once the fence was broken the other horses, obeying their herd instinct, would follow. A shout of fear went up as the herd burst over the brow of the hill and flowed down the gully, heading straight for the cemetery. Everyone was scattering, dragging those worshippers who were still possessed, out of the way. The horses were tightly bunched with the big thoroughbreds well out in front, an unstoppable river of horses. The lead horse was the high-strung chestnut gelding, his eyes were wild and his nostrils flared. Sun Dancer, running easily within himself and looking as if he was just out for an enjoyable night run with his own kind, was tucked in behind the chestnut.

Jesus! Skye stared in disbelief as Adrienne, glorying in the power of her new god, stood directly in the path of the oncoming stampede. Raising her arms, she commanded them to halt. Her arms were still raised as they swept over her, knocking her to the ground and trampling her under their steel shod hooves. Then they were gone, leaving in their wake a peristyle in ruins, a splintered altar, offerings pounded into the ground, and the bloody pulp that had once been Adrienne.

Fighting his way through the fleeing crowd, Skye ran to Adrienne's mangled body and felt for a pulse. She was so badly pulped that her wrist was the only place he could find to try. Incredibly, there was a flicker of life. Her eyes were open and she was mumbling something through the bubbles frothing from her mouth. Skye pressed his head close to hers and heard something that sounded like "halt." Was she still trying to stop the stampeding horses? Then, incredibly, he clearly heard her say, "Love you, Skye."

"I love you too, Adrienne."

Something that might have been a smile twisted what was left of her mouth, then a gout of blood gushed forth and she was gone. Gazing down at her, Skye realized that what he had said was true, he did love this strange, gifted person. Not the way he had loved Jocelyn and might come to love Erin, but love just the same. He looked up as he heard a voice. It was Joshua, hands clasped together, praying over her.

"You're with your own gods, now," Skye whispered as he gently laid her head on the blood-soaked grass. The fragments of Jocelyn's bones and teeth lay just beyond the spreading circle of blood. Skye gathered them up and looked around for the urn. It was there, at the base of the splintered pile of wood that had once been the altar. As he retrieved it, Skye saw the dent in its side where a horse had trod on it. He would leave it that way. As he unscrewed the top and placed the fragments inside the urn, Skye decided he would take it home to Bridgeport and bury it there in the garden.

Joshua had finished praying. Warren and two other young fishermen were standing beside him, gazing in horror down at Adrienne. They looked both sheepish and frustrated as they explained how they had been taken out of action by two of Adrienne's followers who had pulled guns on them.

"Nobody expected gun play," Skye consoled them, thinking as he spoke that the stakes had been raised. As he stood looking down at Adrienne, Sebastian, his Baron Samedi persona cast aside, joined them. The six of them were alone with the body.

"So dis be the end of that little chile," said Sebastian with a sorrowful shake of his head. Turning to Skye, he said, "I see that she get back to Grenada."

It was by far the best solution. Relieved, Skye nodded and took one last look at the woman who had loved him, and walked back up the hill to his jeep.

Most of the horses had found their way back to the stables. Elizabeth was shepherding them into the paddock while the Rastafarian groom repaired the broken fence.

"Is it true that someone was killed?" a badly shaken Elizabeth asked.

Skye leaned out of the jeep's window. "I'm afraid so. Adrienne."

"Oh, my God. My horses killed her."

"She killed herself. She was in a trance and thought she could stop the stampede. She had plenty of time to get out of the way. Everybody else did." Skye looked at the horses, most of them covered with lather and dried sweat, and said, "Some of your horses are still out there."

"Just the three new ones. Belle led the others home."

Skye tucked the urn out of sight under a rear seat and climbed out. "I'll help you round them up."

Skye rode Sun Dancer and Elizabeth rode Belle with three extra halter shanks draped over her withers. Fortunately, the three horses had stayed together. Elizabeth was sure the pounding surf would keep them off the beach and drive them inland. She was right. They were standing beside the road leading to Beaufort. One of them whickered gently as Skye and Elizabeth rode up. They stood still and seemed relieved to be once more under the control of humans as the halter shanks were snapped on. With Elizabeth ponying two of the thoroughbreds and Skye ponying the chestnut, they set off for the stables.

The chestnut shied violently, almost jerking the shank from Skye's hand, as a dark shape, like some monstrous bat, swept over them. It was a Twin Otter, equipped with floats. It had to be the same one he had seen that day on Tobago Cays. Throttled back so as to be almost noiseless, it was flying without lights, and at almost tree-top level. As Skye fought to control the rearing chestnut, the plane disappeared from sight below a headland.

"It looks like he's going to land on Frigate," said Skye as the chestnut snorted once, flexed its neck and settled down.

"I've seen planes flying at night like that more than once. I figure it's the drug trade and that's something to leave strictly alone."

"Whoever is at the controls is some pilot," Skye muttered with genuine admiration. "A night landing like that is not for amateurs."

Elizabeth nodded approvingly as she saw that the groom had started to hose down the sweat-stained horses. "I feel awful about Adrienne," she said, slipping down from the saddle. "If there's an inquest will you testify as to what you saw?"

"There won't be any inquest. This is Manchineel, not England. Her body will be on its way to Grenada first thing in the morning, and that will be the end of that."

Chapter Eighteen

B efore breakfast Skye assembled the three members of his household staff and explained how Adrienne had been killed.

"She foolish to trust them heathen gods," Agatha pronounced. "But I does be sorry, jes' the same."

Later that morning Skye spun the dial of the safe and removed the urn. Holding it in his hands, he sat on the bed. Shortly after Jocelyn was killed, a friend insisted that Skye take counselling for his grief. He gave it up after two sessions, figuring he could deal with it better on his own. But he did learn there are three stages of grief — anger, then inconsolable loss, and finally the plateau of acceptance. Incredibly, Skye had been angry at Jocelyn for dying and leaving him alone. God knew she hadn't intended to die, but there it was. Then the emptiness of being deprived of his partner of ten perfect, if admittedly self-centred, years. Now there was acceptance. "Thank you for those years," Skye murmured as he kissed the urn and placed it back in the safe.

Replacing the Jill Walker painting of a chattel house that hung in front of the safe, he saw Overfine coming across the lawn with the portable phone. It was Lord Fraser with the news that the PM's condition had suddenly and unexpectedly taken a turn for the worse. "According to what the doctors told Sir George we may lose him. His body is rejecting the heart."

Or the heart is rejecting him, thought Skye as he handed the phone back to Overfine. Could it possibly be that, when he thought Adrienne was still trying to stop the horses, she was really commanding Penelope's heart to stop beating? As a rational man he couldn't accept that possibility. But, wait, what if the PM learned that Adrienne had placed a curse on him? Maybe one of his advisers had made a point of telling him, for purposes of his own. If the PM was already burdened with guilt because he had sacrificed his daughter in order that he might live, the additional shock might be enough to send him into a downward spiral. He was from the islands, and no one from the islands was immune to the power of voodoo. Even if he was completely innocent, the shocking news that it was his daughter's heart beating inside him could kill him.

Whatever the reason, the PM was dead by nightfall. Flags, which unlike the days of Empire, were not taken down when the sun set, were lowered to half mast at the company's headquarters, the school, and many of the villas. The transplant clinic in Florida issued a statement regretting the PM's passing, saying it was unexpected, but that everyone knew the risks involved and that if the transplant hadn't taken place the PM would have died in any event.

"I wonder what that means for Manchineel?" asked

Erin, whose exposure to the Kellys had attuned her to the political ramifications of any new development.

"It's a bloody disaster, that's what it is," Lord Fraser growled. Erin and the Frasers were with Skye in Whistling Frog's livingroom. "That damn socialist, Humphreys, will do his best to milk Manchineel for every last penny."

"Maybe Manchineel should secede. It seems to be the thing to do these days." Skye had spoken lightly, but there was a sudden gleam of interest in His Lordship's eyes. "You may have something there. Too late to do much about it now, of course, but later? Who knows?"

"Will he succeed automatically? Shouldn't there be an election or something?" asked Erin.

"No. He's the deputy prime minister. Although Marcellus was personally popular, his government was a shaky coalition between his party on the right and the socialists. Humphreys despises everything this island represents — wealth, privilege, fame. I think the man would destroy it if he could. But his fellow legislators won't let him go that far. They know the tremendous contribution this island makes to the country's economy. But that won't keep them from imposing a punitive tax. Say a 20-percent value added tax. What would that do to your renters, Skye?"

Skye thought before replying, "With the kind of people who come here, I don't think it would make all that much difference. This place is unique and has so much to offer that people will pay almost any price to spend time here."

"I hope you're right," Lord Fraser muttered without much conviction. Marcellus Thomas had been a good personal friend of his and it was obvious that he was feeling the loss.

Skye decided it was time to change the subject. "I

read in the paper that the Names had scored an important court victory. Will that let your friend Pollock return to England with his yacht?"

Lord Fraser shook his head. "No. I'm afraid it doesn't help him at all. That case dealt with the Feltham syndicate. It was so risky that none of those in the know invested in it. It was mostly sold overseas — a lot of Americans and Canadians invested in it. The court found that the company was grossly negligent in insuring some appalling risks and in failing to lay off some of the risks with other insurers. But Charles wasn't a member of the Feltham syndicate. Poor Charles was a member of a number of earlier syndicates where there was no question of concealment or fraud on the part of the directors. Just a series of disastrous and unexpected losses. But," Fraser added after a pause, "the insurers have made a blanket settlement offer to all the investors. They will accept 60 percent of the amount outstanding in full settlement. Unfortunately, I suspect that only a few of the investors will have enough remaining financial resources to act on the offer. The James people have made it clear that they will vigorously pursue those who do not settle in the courts. I'm afraid we're in for another round of suicides."

"Is Charles going to take up the offer?" asked Skye.

"I don't know. He's in awfully deep. If he does, he'll have to act quickly. The offer expires next Wednesday."

"That's only four days from now. That seems like awfully short notice."

"The offer has been out there for a week. Even so, I agree it's very short notice. The UK government has put the gun to their head. Unless James of Leeds can come up with a balance sheet showing assets equal to at least 75 percent of liabilities by the end of the month, their licence will not be renewed."

"Which puts them out of business."

"Out of the insurance business, yes. After more than three centuries. From then on their only business will be to hound the investors into paying."

* * *

"Robert seemed awfully down tonight," said Erin after the Frasers had taken their leave.

"It's understandable. He's very concerned about what will happen to Manchineel. So am I, for that matter."

"Did you know the Prime Minister?"

"Oh, yes. He spent a lot of time on Manchineel. Too much time some of his constituents thought. He liked to enjoy himself and he was treated royally here. He also visited Robert at his castle in Scotland more than once. The Company had him in its pocket."

"Those poor Names. Imagine having to come up with all that money by next Wednesday. I wonder what Charles will do?"

"He'll have to think of a way to come up with hard cash. Assets like a luxurious yacht and masterpiece paintings can't be sold overnight."

"Robert thinks he has money in a numbered bank account."

"Yeah. Well, it's his problem. Not ours."

"You don't like him very much, do you? Is it because of the way he came on to me?"

"Before The Highness decided he was the new flavour of the month? Probably that's it," he said teasingly.

"He wouldn't have gotten anywhere. Men like that just want to boast that they've bedded Erin Kelly. But they don't succeed. I don't believe in recreational sex. Besides, as you know perfectly well, I only had eyes for you."

"Really? Right from the start?"

"Right from the start. I couldn't believe it was happening. Not with what was in our background. I never thought anything could possibly come of it."

"It took me all of twenty-four hours. Not to feel something, but to realize what it was I was feeling. I couldn't see it ever happening either." Skye paused. "Tell me, if you don't believe in recreational sex, what kind of sex do you believe in?"

"Why don't we drive down to the beach and find out?"

The jeep's headlights were reflected on the water swirling around the base of the first row of palm trees. Incoming waves crashed and boomed against the shore.

"In all my time on the island, I've never seen anything like this." Skye braked to a halt. "And this is on the Caribbean side. Think of what it must be like over on the Atlantic coast. Let's drive up to the lagoon. It's bound to be quieter there."

He eased the jeep into low gear and they crept forward, watching for any sign that the encroaching sea had undermined the road. But it held firm.

"Look over to the right, Skye. Two o'clock. There's someone in the trees. See that flash of white?"

"It's a bandage. And who do we know has a bandaged arm?"

"None other than the genial Logan. Look, there's the clinic's jeep." As they emerged from the Aisle of Palms, Erin pointed to the jeep with the red cross parked beside the little thatched hut that was used by picnickers.

Skye doused the lights and cut the engine. The boom of the sea was fainter now, held back by the seaward arm of the shallow lagoon. Skye wondered if the surging waves would eventually invade the lagoon and wipe it out. His ears caught the sound of an outboard and he saw the dark, unlit shape of a pirogue heading for the open sea through the narrow outlet between a jutting headland and an islet of bare rock marked on the maps as Turtle Island.

"I know you told me how seaworthy those little boats are," Erin said when Skye pointed it out to her. "But won't they get swamped?"

Skye shook his head. "They'll get tossed around something fierce, but they won't capsize." After a pause, he said, "The place is crawling with people tonight. Maybe we should postpone our lovemaking session."

"Something's bothering you, Skye. I can tell. Can you share it with me?"

"It's all conjecture on my part. I have no proof of anything and it may just be my imagination running away with me."

"So I'm not to worry my pretty little head about it," Erin said tartly. "Is that it?"

Skye laughed. "You know better." After another pause, he went on. "Okay, I'll try it on you, and you can tell me if you think I've lost my mind. If I'm right, there's a thriving trade in body parts going on in this area and Pollock's right in the middle of it."

Erin listened intently as he told her of his suspicions, beginning with his sighting of the three slain bodies on the beach on the day of his return to Manchineel.

"Pretty far fetched, isn't it?" he said with a little laugh after he finished recounting his theory about Penelope's disappearance.

"It's terrible," she said. "And frightening, but not far fetched. Not at all. Especially when you consider the availability of supply. All those homeless street people. But you can't do anything about it by yourself. It's a police matter. You should go to the police."

Skye gave a snort of laughter. "The gallant Captain Robertson? He wouldn't have any part of it. Besides, it's possible the St. Vincent police are turning a blind eye to the operation in return for a payoff. But I know someone I can talk to."

Chapter Nineteen

"So it's body parts instead of drugs?" Foxcroft said musingly after Skye finished telling him what he suspected was going on. They were in the gazebo on Serenity's lawn, sheltered from the morning sun. "I must say, though, your theory about Penelope and the PM is a bit of a reach."

"I agree. But has there been any trace of her?"

"None. But I'm not sure that proves anything." After a thoughtful pause, the police inspector said, "All right, let's suppose your theory is correct and there is a ring trading in human organs, what do you propose to do about it?"

"Try and stop it, of course. I can't just stand by and let them go about their business undisturbed." He decided against adding that breaking up the ring was in some way linked in his mind to what happened to Jocelyn. "The only problem is," he went on, "I don't know how or where it's going to come down. All I know is that if Pollock's involved, it's got to be soon. He's got a chance to make a favourable settlement with the James people, but that window closes on Wednesday. He must be cursing that underwater volcano that's churning up the ocean. There's no way surgeons can operate with those seas running. Maybe they'll move the operation onshore. If Glessop and Edwina are also involved, as I'm almost positive they are, they could use the medical clinic here on Manchineel. But on second thought I don't think that's very likely. Too much chance of being seen. Or," Skye stared thoughtfully at the inspector.

"Or what?"

"Or they could anchor in some sheltered bay." Skye's eyes grew bright. "How about Hurricane Hole over on Frigate. That's it! That's what they'll do."

"You may be on to something. And you think Logan may be in on it?" As always, Foxcroft's voice quickened at the mention of Logan.

"There's clearly some connection between him and Edwina. I've seen them together a number of times, including last night down at the Aisle of Palms. And I don't think it's sexual."

"If Logan is Lassiter it won't be. According to his profile he didn't really like women, or sex. One of his friends said that if anything he performed only the occasional boff out of politeness. It was gambling and drinking for our boy."

Skye got to his feet. "Let's put it to the test. Let's try to find the *Caroline* and if she's within range of Frigate, you'll treat this seriously?"

"Absolutely."

* * *

On the way to the airport Skye asked, "Can I assume

that you and your men have some official status in these parts?"

"We do. We have to in order to carry out our responsibility for the safety of Her Royal Highness." Foxcroft, smarting at the thought of Princess Helen's lacerated leg, grimaced as he said this. "My fellow officers and I are fully accredited members of the local police force and are authorized to bear arms. Speaking of firearms, do you still have your Glock semi-automatic?"

As the officer in charge of HRH's security, Foxcroft would know about all the weapons registered to the villa owners. When Skye nodded, he said, "An excellent choice of weapon."

* * *

After take-off Skye circled to gain altitude before approaching Frigate. Foxcroft, equipped with a pair of high-powered binoculars, occupied the passenger seat behind him. As they flew parallel to Frigate's western coastline, he said, "That inlet is a real hurricane hole. The water is remarkably calm."

"Do you see any boats?"

"No."

"There'll be some there all right. The cigarette boat is always there. But they'll be hidden. Probably in the mangroves."

"It looks like someone has been doing some logging. Look over there on your left."

Skye looked where Foxcroft was pointing and saw a bare patch where trees had been felled. "You don't log palm trees," he said. "That'll be to conceal the *Caroline*. Her hull may be black but her superstructure's white."

The large boulder that sat in the middle of the field with its smaller fellows grouped around it like so many court attendants, making it impossible for an airplane to land, was still in place. But moving them would only be a few minutes work with a backhoe.

"I have an idea where the *Caroline* might be holed up." Skye veered to the right and set a course for Carriacou. Foxcroft moved over to the right hand passenger seat. The roiling sea was awash with whitecaps, reminding Skye of a lathered horse. Like that chestnut thoroughbred the night Adrienne was killed.

"I don't want to get too close," he said, altering course to take them well south of the island. "See that long headland sticking out into the sea? Put the glass on it as we go by."

"Thar she blows!" Foxcroft's excited voice rattled in the microphone.

Looking to the right, Skye saw the yacht tucked in close to the sheer cliff of the headland. Without binoculars he couldn't make out the details, but there was no mistaking the rakish black-hulled yacht. White spume leapt up her sides as she was pounded by the surf. Those on board would be having a rough ride, but she seemed to be securely anchored. Skye continued flying south as though heading for Grenada.

"There's no reason for her to be taking a pounding like that unless your theory is correct," said Foxcroft as he lowered the binoculars. "When do you think they'll make a run for Frigate?"

"Not until tonight. They'd be too conspicuous in daylight, out there all by themselves on those heavy seas. Anyway, I'll come back in the late afternoon in a different airplane to check on her whereabouts. Want to come along?"

"Definitely. You and I have some planning to do if we hope to interdict this operation."

"I have a few ideas." Skye flew east for a few minutes over the ocean then headed back to Manchineel.

* * *

A yellow Islander, a charter airplane that made frequent stops on Manchineel, was parked in front of the terminal. As he taxied past Skye saw Erin, holding Patrick by the hand, Brenda Fewster, and the Rastoks, standing by the gate. What the hell was going on? As soon as he reached his parking spot, Skye cut the engine and jumped out.

As Skye strode up to the gate, Erin moved away from her little group and motioned him to join her.

"Patrick has had a heart attack. A severe one. He wants to see young Patrick and me. We're leaving right away. I was waiting for you to get back so I could tell you."

"Jesus. Is he going to be all right?"

"It's too early to tell. But it's a bad one." Erin handed Skye a card. "Here's where you can reach me. We're staying in the Kelly compound. Will you call me tonight? Six o'clock your time. I should be back from the hospital by then."

"Of course. I've no reason to love the guy, and every reason to hate him, but I'm sorry."

"I'm glad to hear you say that." Seeing Foxcroft coming across the tarmac, Erin gave Skye a sharp look. "I hope you're not getting involved in that organ business? I couldn't bear it if anything happened to you."

"I'm just doing as you suggested. Bringing the police into it." Changing the subject, Skye asked how she was getting back to the States.

"The Kelly jet is on its way to Barbados to pick us up."

Flying in the Kelly jet, staying in the Kelly compound. It sure looked as if she was being drawn back into the Kelly orbit. Skye kept this thought to himself as he kissed her and held her close. "Promise me you won't do anything rash," she whispered against his shoulder.

"I'll be careful."

"Not good enough." She lifted her head to look at him. "But it's all I'm going to get, isn't it? Oh God, Skye, I'm scared."

"Don't be. I've convinced Foxcroft that something is coming down and the police will take over from here."

Erin looked highly skeptical, but managed a smile over her shoulder as she and young Patrick and Brenda filed out to the airplane.

"He's a bit young to be having a heart attack, isn't he?" Foxcroft was standing beside Skye as they watched the Islander trundling down the runway to begin its take-off run.

"Not with his lifestyle," Skye answered. The STOL Islander lifted off, using only a fraction of the runway. Skye and the Rastoks waved as it flew overhead. "Old man Kelly would have a fit if he could see what his precious grandson is flying in," Skye murmured. As he watched the airplane fade from sight, he admitted to himself that he felt a certain sense of relief that Erin was out of the way. She would have been appalled at the role he was determined to play, and would have done everything she could to dissuade him.

* * *

"When do you reckon this operation will take place?" asked Foxcroft. He and Skye were seated in two deck chairs at the far end of Whistling Frog's pool.

"Tomorrow night," Skye promptly replied.

"How can you be so certain?"

"Convergence. Think about it. The deadline for the deal with the James people is this coming Wednesday. It has to be a night operation. You can't have an airplane, almost certain to be a Twin Otter with fuel bladders, land

and take off from Frigate in broad daylight. Especially since it's supposed to be impossible for a plane to land there. When you're dealing with human organs time is of the essence, as our lawyer friends say. So you would want the shortest interval of time between har... ah, retrieving ... the organs and getting them on their way to where they are going to be transplanted. All this presupposes that I'm right about there being a body parts ring and that Pollock is in the centre of it," Skye added after a thoughtful pause.

"Why else would the *Caroline* be hiding out over on Carriacou?"

"No other reason that I can think of," Skye agreed.

"What kind of a force are we dealing with?"

"Let's see." Skye began to count on his fingers. "Four, maybe five, guards on the island. A crew of four on board the *Caroline*. Glessop — we can forget about him if it comes to a fight — Edwina, and one, maybe two, extra surgeons. If this is on the scale I think it is, old Glessop couldn't possibly handle it by himself. I wouldn't be surprised if some of the crew are surgeons. A couple of them, in particular, looked very professional, including the captain. We can ignore the medical people. They'll be preoccupied with their work."

"So we have to deal with six or seven men," the inspector mused. "That's not too daunting a prospect."

"I think they rely on secrecy and concealment rather than force. Besides, they wouldn't want to split the proceeds, enormous as they may be, too many ways. And some of the guards will be needed to shepherd the victims onto the boat."

"You think they are being kept underground?"

"Yes. Under the ventilator I saw. There are probably more at other places on the island. The fishermen talk about how they used to live in the caves, sometimes for a week or more, when the fish were running."

"All right. Let's count our assets. I can spare two of my men. Do I take it that you are planning to come along?"

Skye stared at him in astonishment. "Of course. It's my show. Besides," Skye played his trump card. "I know the *Caroline*'s layout. I've had two tours of her. Have you ever been on board her?"

Foxcroft shook his head. "Her Royal Highness was adamant that we remain behind. I didn't like it, but I couldn't come up with any convincing arguments when she pooh poohed any possibility of danger. In retrospect, I gave in to that lady all too often. But back to the matter at hand, I agree that knowledge does make you rather essential to the operation. I assume you know how to use the Glock?"

"I checked myself out at a gun club."

"Good. I can probably second some police officers from St. Vincent. We have very good relations with them. Scotland Yard broke up a yacht hi-jacking ring a few years ago and made sure the local police got the lion's share of the credit."

"I have a better idea."

"What's that?"

"The fishermen. In the first place, their pirogues are the best if not the only way to get to Frigate in this sea. No ordinary boat could survive Commotion Channel, and they're all gone anyway. Secondly, they know the island. The St. Vincent police don't. And they're armed, in case fishermen from the other islands try to muscle in on their fishing grounds. They're a perfect strike force."

"I see what you mean. But will they do it? I realize they hold you in very high regard. But still."

"They'll do it. But not for that reason. More than

anything else in this world they want to get Frigate back, so they can use it as a base the way they did before the Frigate Company took it over. Also the guards let one of the fishermen spend a whole day caught in a leg trap before releasing him. They want revenge for that. Remember, they're a macho bunch. Speaking of traps," Skye went on, "that could be our biggest problem. The whole island is booby trapped."

"If we're dealing with leg traps, that's not a problem. I have metal detectors. Can you set up a meeting with the fishermen?"

"I'll talk with Sebastian first. In fact, I'll do that right now." Skye looked at his watch. "Meet me at the airstrip in an hour and we'll see if the *Caroline* is still at anchor."

* * *

"I've had my talk with Sebastian. They're on," Skye told Foxcroft. He was doing a walk-around inspection of the Baron before taking off. Satisfied, he motioned Foxcroft to climb onboard.

"He realizes it could be very dangerous, I trust?" Foxcroft buckled himself into the right hand front seat.

Skye didn't reply until he had completed the instrument check. "He knows that. I didn't have to tell him, although I did. I also explained that if the people who own the island are found guilty of criminal acts, the island will go back into limbo, like it was before." Skye smiled "Then I had to explain what in limbo meant. He thought I was talking about the dance. As I thought, they'll run any risk to get that island back."

"I'll provide them with walkie-talkies and automatic weapons."

"Walkie-talkies are fine, but I think you'll find they want to stick with their bolt-action rifles. And clubs." Skye propped the cabin door open to let in some air as they taxied down the runway, the propellers barely ticking over.

"Clubs?"

"Yeah. The kind they kill fish with." Skye swung the Baron around and advanced the throttles as they began their take-off roll.

"Clubs. Bloody good, that," Foxcroft said as they levelled off at six thousand feet and Skye throttled back. "I was worrying over the fact that we don't have any silencers, but a club can take a man out without alerting the others."

Minutes later they were off Carriacou. "She's still there," Foxcroft confirmed, focusing the binoculars.

"That's all we need to know." Skye began to fly a wide circle that would take them south of Grenada and then back to Manchineel. "We'll do another fly-over in the morning to see if she's still there. If she isn't we'll have a pretty good idea where she is."

"When can we meet with the fishermen?"

"Anytime we like. They can't fish in these rough seas, and they're just sitting around in camp, playing cards and dominos, bored out of their skulls. Sebastian and I agreed we would take six of them, which will give us a force of ten. We'll go over in two longboats. I have to make a phone call at six, but apart from that, I'm free. Why don't we meet them at Tamarind at seven o'clock? They can walk there from their camp."

Skye kept well out to sea as they flew past Frigate.

"What about the possibility of a leak? There could be a mole in that camp."

"Sebastian and I discussed that. The fishermen keep very much to themselves, and, apart from selling fish and purchasing supplies, have almost nothing to do with the rest of the island. Sebastian does have some doubts about one individual who goes with one of the maids. He will assign two men to make sure he doesn't contact anyone."

"He seems to have those people completely under his thumb."

"He's their Alpha leader." Skye lowered the flaps and lined up for a landing.

* * *

"He's awfully sick." Erin's voice was subdued.

"Will he recover?" asked Skye.

"They won't know that for at least three days. But his heart has been badly damaged. It's sad to see him lying there with drips in his arms, and tears in his eyes. He's like a little boy who doesn't understand why this has happened to him."

"Has Patrick seen him?"

"Not yet. I wanted to see what I would be exposing him to first. But it's all right. He's sedated with Demerol, but he's conscious and lucid. He held my hand for the longest time and kept on apologizing for the way he treated me. It was kind of touching. I'll take Patrick in to see him tomorrow."

"I miss you."

"I miss you too. Will you call tomorrow?"

"Of course. But let's make it earlier. When will you get back from the hospital in the afternoon?"

"Probably around five."

"Okay. I'll call you a little after five."

Erin was instantly suspicious. "You're getting yourself mixed up in that organ business, aren't you?"

"It's all right. I won't take any chances." Even to himself, Skye sounded unconvincing.

"Why don't you let the authorities handle it?"

"I am. You saw me with Foxcroft at the airport. He's in charge and he knows what he's doing. I'm just along for the ride."

"Hah. I know there's nothing I can do to stop you, but for God's sake, Skye, take care."

"I will," Skye, grateful for the way she had accepted the inevitable, promised.

As soon as he rang off, Overfine began to serve the early supper Skye had ordered. He was halfway through it when the sound of a jeep's engine coughing into silence announced the arrival of a visitor.

"Eating rather early, aren't we?" asked Lord Fraser, surprised to find Skye at the table. Skye waited until Overfine had gone back to the kitchen before saying, "Agatha wanted to go to an early prayer meeting tonight. Sit down and have a drink while I finish."

Before Fraser could reply, Overfine came back with a glass of Glenlivet and water on a silver tray. Fraser accepted it with a pleased smile.

"I dropped in to see if there had been any word on that Kelly fellow," he said as he took an appreciative swallow.

"I just finished talking to Erin. You knew she's gone to see him?" Fraser nodded, and Skye continued. "Apparently there's been a lot of damage to his heart and he's not out of the woods by a long shot."

"Is Erin coming back?"

"Back here? To Manchineel? We haven't discussed it. I imagine it depends on how long she feels she has to stay in California. I think she might leave once it's clear he's out of danger."

"It's hard to know when anyone is out of danger. Look at what happened to the PM."

When Overfine began to serve the dessert, Lord Fraser finished his drink and got to his feet. Relieved that he would not be late for his meeting with Foxcroft and the fishermen, Skye accompanied him to the door.

Impulsively, Skye asked, "Where did Logan come from, Robert? Do you know anything about his background?" Did he detect a slight stiffening of his friend's shoulders, or was he imagining things?

"He just showed up at the door one day, looking for work. Said he was good with animals, which I soon found out was true. They took to him right away. Why do you ask?"

Skye shrugged. "Just idle curiosity. He's such a mysterious, Heathcliffian character, I got to wondering what made him that way."

"He's different, I grant you that. But he's good at what he does. Damn good."

Settling himself behind the wheel, Lord Fraser looked at Skye. "I wouldn't want to lose him, Skye."

"I can understand that."

Chapter Twenty

"The most important question is, can your boats make it to Frigate?" The sullen roar of the surf underlined Foxcroft's words as he looked at Sebastian.

The grizzled fisherman looked at Warren who nodded. Skye expelled a sigh of relief. "It's a go, then," he said. "Assuming we find in the morning that the *Caroline* is no longer at Carriacou."

"It will be a rough, wet ride," Joshua cautioned.

"We'll be wearing wet suits," Foxcroft told him. "Now, where do we land?"

All eyes turned to Sebastian, who remained silent for a few moments as if pondering various options. Finally, he said, "We bes' lan' on de windward side."

The whites of the fishermen's eyes shone in the dark as they stared at each other. Landing their frail, wooden craft on the rocky Atlantic coast in these ferocious seas would test their strength and skills to the limit. But none of them demurred, or looked away.

"No one would think we'd be crazy enough to attempt to land on the Atlantic side. Is that it, Father?" asked Joshua.

"Dat's it."

"Well, they'd be right," said Joshua with a little laugh.

Skye spoke up. "If we land near the mangrove swamp I know of a way to get across it." He told them about the plank pathway laid across the roots of the mangroves.

"Dat be new after I was las' dere," said Sebastian.

Foxcroft looked at his raiding party and was well satisfied with what he saw. With the exception of Sebastian, they were young and fit. And although he might be advanced in years, Sebastian's powerful physique attested to his ability to keep up with any of them. The two Scotland Yard detectives were seasoned police officers; Detective Goodwin, in particular, had taken part in a number of drug busts in London. And, as Skye had predicted, and Sebastian had confirmed, the prospect of getting "their" island back had immediately brought the fishermen on side.

"After we land and cross the mangrove swamp," Foxcroft said, "we will have to take out the guards. According to Skye, there are four, maybe five, of them. But there may be more. We'll have the element of surprise in our favour. They won't be expecting anyone to try and land under these conditions. Especially if, as Sebastian says, we come in from the windward side. Assuming we dispose of the guards, we still have to board the yacht."

"Anchors," said Joshua. When Foxcroft looked at him, he explained. "Their tines will catch on the railing and we can haul ourselves up on a rope. We'll wrap the anchors in cloth so they won't make a noise."

"Perfect," Foxcroft murmured. He handed a walkie-talkie to Joshua and showed him how to use it. "If we find the *Caroline* has left Carriacou we'll go on active status. I'll be in touch as soon as Skye and I get back.

"Do you think there'll be another landing tonight?" Foxcroft asked after the fishermen had melted back into the night, and the two Scotland Yard men had driven off. "Of an airplane, I mean."

"It's possible. It's also possible that the airplane may already be on the island, hidden away in one of those old fish plant buildings. We could drive up in the hills and keep watch for a while if you like. There's nothing much else to do until tomorrow."

Driving without lights, Skye carefully manoeuvred the jeep onto a patch of bare ground and parked facing south. The dark mass of Frigate Island loomed at them across the white-capped turbulence of Commotion Channel. The perfume of a night-blooming flower wafted in through the jeep's open window.

Skye smiled to himself as he sniffed the fragrant air; sitting here with a stern-faced Scotland Yard detective was a far cry from the times he and Erin had parked to make love. Since Foxcroft remained silent, Skye let his thoughts dwell on her. Until Robert had asked about it, he had assumed that Erin would return to Manchineel, but what if, for one reason or another, she didn't? Would he go charging into the Kelly compound and make off with her? And then there was Patrick III. Definitely a complicating factor.

Skye knew he could neutralize old man Kelly. The old fart loved to wrap himself in the Stars and Stripes and pose as an ultra-patriotic American. But he was guilty of the most unpatriotic act an American citizen could currently engage in — trading with America's favourite bogeyman, Cuba. To make it even worse, the mine, operated by a Canadian front company, had once been the property of an American company before being expropriated when Castro came to power. If Kelly's "treason" became public, not only would he be disgraced, but he could be facing a jail term.

Skye's musings were cut short by Foxcroft's urgent whisper that there was a light on Frigate. The light that he had spotted was just a faint, diffused glow.

"They've turned on the landing lights," said Skye as he climbed out and focused his binoculars. "They're really dim, but they'll show him where to land."

The Twin Otter, its pontoons making it clearly recognizable, was coming in from the south. Skye couldn't hear its engines over the surge and roar of Commotion Channel, but he followed its long gliding approach. "That's a seaplane," Foxcroft exclaimed. "He can't land on land."

"It's an amphibian. It has retractable wheels."

The plane disappeared from view as it touched down. The lights immediately blinked out.

"The pieces are falling into place," Foxcroft muttered. "But you know, Skye, it's as consistent with the drug trade as with your theory about human organs."

"I guess we'll find that out tomorrow, won't we?" replied Skye, switching on the ignition.

* * *

"She's not there," Skye and Foxcroft said in unison. There was no sign of the *Caroline* at her former anchorage, and the waves swept unimpeded to dash against the headland.

"I wish we could fly close enough to Frigate to make sure she's there," said Skye as he banked the Cessna and headed for Manchineel. "But we can't take the chance of alerting them. Can you see anything?" he asked Foxcroft who was peering through binoculars.

"Not from this distance. There seems to be a lot of green at the base of the cliff, but that could be the mangroves. They seem to grow like weeds in Hurricane Hole."

"More likely it's the *Caroline* under a canopy of palm fronds. Well, let's alert the troops." Skye dipped his wings as he roared over the fishermen's camp.

* * *

"There's a lot to be done before nightfall," Foxcroft said as the propeller swung to a stop.

"Telling Overfine that he can't come is one of them," said Skye, looking at his servant standing beside the Whistling Frog jeep.

"Maybe I can help," Foxcroft said. "I assume you trust him?"

"Completely."

Overfine hadn't said anything about Skye spending so much time lately with the Scotland Yard inspector, but he was certainly aware of it. His eyes held a question as the two men walked up to him.

"You know something is going on, don't you, Overfine?" Foxcroft leaned forward from the rear bench seat as they drove away.

Overfine looked at him in the rearview mirror. "Yes, sir."

"Mister Skye and I are trying to put a stop to what we believe is a very serious crime."

Overfine glanced sideways at Skye who said, "He already knows something about it. I told him."

"That shows how much Mister Skye trusts you, Overfine. This has become a police matter," Foxcroft went on, "and I've organized a force to deal with it."

"Mister Skye be going?"

"Yes. He knows some things the rest of us don't."

"Listen to me, Overfine," Skye interjected. "You're not cut out for this kind of work. I'm not either, if it comes to that, but there will only be one of me. I'm asking you to understand and accept that having you along would hinder rather than help us."

"Okay, Mister Skye."

"Thanks, Overfine." After a pause, Skye went on, "There are a lot of ways you can help us between now and then."

* * *

The strategy session took place that afternoon at Princess Helen's villa, Serenity. Glessop's idea of pain management was lashings of booze and morphine every six hours so Princess Helen was safely tranquillized. The detective who would stay behind sat in the sun-filled livingroom, while Skye conferred with Foxcroft and the two other detectives in the guard house.

The guard house, a circular building with thick walls and armour-plated windows, was a combination command post and arsenal. It was also, Skye guessed, meant to serve as a bunker in case of an attack. One of the rooms was equipped as a kitchen; closed doors concealed the other rooms but undoubtedly they contained beds and other living accommodations. Although he was sure there would be a tunnel connecting the guardhouse with the villa, Skye couldn't spot any door or exit leading from it.

"I'm not much of an artist," he muttered in frustration as he tried to sketch the *Caroline*'s decks.

"Tony Goodwin is a dab hand at drawing," Foxcroft said. "Just describe it to him and he'll sketch it."

Skye thought back to the dinner party on board the

Caroline and retraced his steps from the gangway up a flight of stairs to the main salon with its fabulous art, dinner in the fantail salon, up to the bridge, down to the diningroom, which was an extension of the main salon, and then up a staircase to Pollock's office.

"Obviously there are some parts I didn't see, such as the galley and the crew's quarters. They would be up forward."

Goodwin asked for the approximate dimensions of each room as he drew. "That's the only place they could be," he said. "There isn't room for them anywhere else."

"Where do you suppose they'll set up the operating room?" asked Foxcroft.

"Most likely in the main salon and diningroom," Skye replied. "That's where there's the most space. Although," he added with a thoughtful frown, "I went up a set of stairs to get from the gangway to the salon. That means there could be a whole deck I didn't see."

"What you're saying is that we'll have to board her not knowing where the target area is," Foxcroft muttered.

"We'll have to pick up a guide," said Skye. "One of the crew who can lead us there."

A phone, the one without a scrambler, suddenly rang. It was the detective in the villa saying that Overfine had arrived with a suitcase for Skye. Skye looked at his watch and nodded. Overfine had waited until Agatha and Myra were having their afternoon siesta.

Foxcroft took the suitcase from the detective at the guardhouse door. As Skye had ordered, it contained his wetsuit, which fortunately was black, flippers, a snorkelling mask, the Glock semi-automatic, and several clips of ammunition.

"We need a map of our route," Foxcroft said after Skye had stored his paraphernalia in a closet.

"Give Joshua a call and have him bring Sebastian

here to meet Tony."

Detective Goodwin who had been applying finishing touches to his sketch, looked up when Skye mentioned his name. "Sebastian knows every inch of that island and Tony can draw it," said Skye.

"Good plan," said Foxcroft. "But I don't want to bring him here. Tony and I will pick him up in the jeep a half-mile down the road from the camp. You know," he added thoughtfully, "they could be operating on board the *Caroline* right now."

Skye shook his head. "I don't think so. That Twin Otter is going to make a lot of noise when it takes off. It's a very different matter from ghosting in for a landing. They'll want to wait until the early hours of the morning when everyone over here is asleep. And they'll want the shortest possible time between retrieving the organs and flying them out."

"Well, we can't make a move until it's dark, in any case." Foxcroft picked up the walkie-talkie. "We'll rendezvous here at six o'clock."

* * *

"Patrick wants me to come back to him." Erin's voice was little more than a whisper.

"I trust you told him where to go."

"No, I didn't. Not yet. I thought it might kill him. The doctors want me to encourage him — give him a will to live. After young Patrick left, he got all teary-eyed, telling me he loved me, and promising to change his ways, which he'll have to anyway."

Nonplussed, Skye stared at the mouthpiece. This was the last thing he expected. Finally, he asked, "Does he know about us?"

"He hasn't mentioned it. But I'm sure he does. The family knows, and the Dragonlady would have been sure to tell him. But that hasn't stopped him from wanting me back. The family is being extra-nice to me. They're afraid that with my record of sobriety for over a year, I could regain custody of my son. As I'm going to."

"They could use our affair against you."

"'Affair?' Is that what we're having? They would never bring that up. It would open up the subject of your wife's death. You would think they'd go ballistic over our affair, as you call it, but they haven't said one word about it. I get the impression they're frightened of you. You really spiked their guns, as you said. They must think you're still on the case, trying to prove that it was Patrick who crashed into your wife."

"That must be it."

"I don't hear you pleading with me not to go back to him," Erin said with some asperity.

"That's because I think the whole idea is ludicrous. Unthinkable. But then maybe I'm wrong. I hope not."

They hung up just as Overfine came in with a steak sandwich and a glass of milk. Skye glanced at his watch. When he finished the sandwich it would be time to join Foxcroft and the others.

Chapter Twenty-One

The usually phlegmatic Foxcroft was visibly excited. His eyes shone and he paced up and down the guardhouse as if unable to stay still.

"Are you always like this before going into action?" asked Skye, whose own adrenalin was beginning to kick in.

Foxcroft ceased his restless pacing and smiled rather sheepishly. "It's not that. I've just heard from the Yard. They'll be sending the DNA results shortly. I'm to wait for them."

Skye looked at his watch, a waterproof Rolex. Ten minutes after six. "I hope they're quick about it. We haven't much time."

"I have to wait until I receive the report."

"Jesus, Alan, any delay could cost lives."

"I realize that. But it's an order. Besides, we're almost bound to run into Logan tonight and it's imperative for me to know if he's really Lassiter. I want him taken alive.

Let's get into our wet suits while we wait."

As always it was dark by six-thirty. Foxcroft raised Joshua on the walkie-talkie. As agreed, the fishermen had taken the boats around to Tamarind Beach. Joshua was elated at the way they had handled in the rough seas. Foxcroft congratulated him, and told him there would be a slight, unavoidable delay.

The minutes crawled by. Skye kept looking at his watch and glaring at the inspector who studiously avoided meeting his eyes. At seven o'clock Skye could stand it no longer. "Christ, Alan ..." He broke off as the red scrambler phone began to ring. Foxcroft scooped it up, his face breaking into a triumphant grin as he listened.

"We've tracked the evil bastard to his lair," he said as he put down the phone. "Thanks to you."

"You can tell me as we go." Skye was already out the door where Goodwin and Henry Dalton, the other Scotland Yard detective, were waiting for them in the jeep. "We've got him, men!" Foxcroft shouted as he jumped into the back after Skye. "Logan is Lassiter!"

Goodwin pounded the steering wheel with excitement, and Dalton, grinning widely, gave two thumbs-up. For the first time Skye realized how obsessed the Scotland Yard detectives were with bringing the infamous Lassiter to justice. Having the aristocratic wife killer at large was the most conspicuous failure in the Yard's long history, and now there was a chance to erase it. Both detectives nodded agreement when Foxcroft said Logan/Lassiter was to be taken alive at all costs.

"Getting the test results so soon was fast work." Skye held on to the edge of the bench seat as they bounced over a pothole.

"They worked around the clock. It's the PCR test that the courts in England haven't accepted yet. The

RFLP test that they do accept could take another fortnight. But the PCR is good enough to hold him on suspicion."

"If he's mixed up in what's going down tonight you won't need that to arrest him."

"That's true." Foxcroft sounded almost surprised, as if the thought hadn't occurred to him. He was so fixated on the pursuit of Lassiter that he seemed to have forgotten everything else. Once again, he gave Skye a sheepish smile. "I do know why we're here," he assured him as Goodwin geared down for the rough track leading to the beach.

The two longboats were pulled up on the narrow strip of sand that was all that hadn't been sucked out to sea by the advancing waves. The fishermen were naked to the waist and their jeans, already soaked through, were plastered to their legs. The guns and equipment in the jeep, encased in waterproof wrapping, were hastily stowed in the pirogues, and all hands strained to push the boats into the raging surf, bows first to keep the outboard motors from being ripped off the stern.

A wave smashed against Skye and he fought to hang on to the gunwale. In the interval before the next wave hit, they managed to get the boats afloat, and Sebastian shouted at Joshua and Warren to jump on board and get the motors started. The others braced themselves for the onslaught of the oncoming wave. When it passed and both motors were turning over, he yelled at them to get aboard. Joshua and Warren threw the motors into gear and the sharp prows sliced into a following wave, sending white water foaming over the gunwales. Except for the two steersmen, every man was given a pail and set to bailing furiously.

The full force of the roiling sea hit them as they moved away from the coast and into Commotion

Channel. Squinting through a curtain of spray at the towering waves, Skye couldn't think how they could possibly survive. Without interrupting the rhythm of his bailing, he stole a look at Sebastian. The veteran boatman caught the look and smiled serenely. The noise was indescribable as the booming waves picked the little boats up and tossed them around like a sea lion balancing a spinning ball. But Joshua and Warren kept them quartering the waves, not giving the angry sea a chance to hit them broadside and flip them over. Their course would take them east of Frigate and force them to come about and head back. On the way back they could still meet the waves at an angle, but the tricky part would be coming about.

The propellers raced as each succeeding wave lifted the boats and sent them corkscrewing down the trough. It was their small size that was saving them. Not long enough to straddle two waves at once, they were able to swoop down the trough and ride up the crest of the wave in front.

The following sea was fast pushing them past the rock-ribbed north coast of Frigate. Shouting at Joshua and waving at Warren in the other boat, Sebastian ordered them to steer southeast. This exposed more of the hulls to the waves and both pirogues rolled dangerously. Estimating the distance to the dark mass of Frigate, Skye figured he and his companions could swim to shore if they capsized. Sebastian would have known this, which explained his decision to run the risk of turning onto a more southerly course. The foreshortened angle of attack to the waves meant more water pouring over the gunwales, necessitating even more frantic bailing.

Joshua and Warren were performing outstanding feats of small boat handling, watching the waves and turning the bow slightly to port as each swept past, then quickly returning to course. Suddenly they were out of the channel and in the lee of the island. The waves were still huge and boisterous, but less turbulent than in the narrow confines of the channel, and their deafening boom slackened off. Sebastian pointed shoreward and Skye tensed. He was not alone. Down toward the stern, Foxcroft and Goodwin exchanged glances, and a burly fisherman crossed himself.

"Stop bailing and hang on!" Joshua shouted. Seconds later he pushed the tiller hard over and the bow began to swing. Despite the furious bailing, several inches of water remained in the bottom of the boat and the turn was agonizingly slow. Too slow. Skye gasped for air as a wall of water crashed over the boat. He felt the boat lifting beneath him and prepared to kick out from under the hull when it overturned. Half filled with water, the boat keeled over, then sluggishly settled back. The wave rolled on, leaving the dazed men to survey the damage.

Joshua pressed the starter again and again, then shook his head. The motor was swamped. Sebastian reached for the oars that had been secured to the thwarts. With two men rowing and the others bailing, the pirogue limped toward the shore. Warren's longboat had fared a little better, although it too had lost its motor. Gradually the freeboard increased as the water level inside the boat fell. Skye began to think they might make it after all, but now the question was, how were they going to get ashore through the surf? The sound of the waves crashing against the rocks was growing louder and louder and more and more unnerving.

The pebble beach just north of the frigate bird colony was to be their landing spot. The waves were behind them now, hurtling them forward in a wild roller coaster ride. Sebastian said something to his fellow rower and they rested their oars. Sebastian looked over his shoulder at the rapidly approaching land.

"Hang on!" he shouted and then "Now!" He and the other fisherman backwatered furiously against the tug of a cresting wave. When it hit the beach and began to recede, they pulled for the shore, but couldn't reach it before another wave picked them up and flung them on the beach with a crash that stove in the longboat's timbers. The men scrambled over the sides, and struggled to haul it further up the pebble beach.

"It's no use," panted Skye when the wrecked boat refused to budge. "Let's get our stuff out of there and leave her."

Warren's boat didn't quite make it to the beach. The same wave that sent Joshua's pirogue crashing on the beach, overturned it, spilling its passengers and cargo into the water. The water was shallow and the men stood in the surf, grabbing their clubs and throwing them onshore, then picking up the waterproof container with the rifles and ammunition from the ocean floor. Shaken, the little group stood on the beach, watching the capsized longboat being carried out to sea.

"That was some ride," said Skye. He turned to Sebastian. "I'll see that your boats are replaced."

"Time for dat later."

Skye removed the plastic wrapping from the Glock pistol and slapped the seventeen-round magazine into its grip. "Okay. Let's unpack our equipment and move off."

The plastic sheets and empty containers were hidden behind some large rocks and the raiding party prepared to set off. Goodwin was to lead with the metal detector. Foxcroft had Dalton and Warren bring up the rear, separated from the main body by a hundred yards. They were to be a second line of defence in case of any surprises. Foxcroft opened a can of black shoe polish and handed it in turn to each of the white men to smear on their faces.

As they formed up, Skye warned that since the little beach was one of the more accessible places on the island, it could well be booby trapped. He reasoned that the traps would be set close to shore in order to prevent unwelcome visitors from penetrating inland.

"Jesus!" Goodwin jumped back as a man sprang out from behind a casuarina tree. A fisherman walking behind Skye stepped to one side and hurled his club, striking the man in the head. It had no effect and the figure continued to bob up and down.

"It's a dummy." Skye went over to inspect the figure. Mounted on springs screwed into the trunk of the casuarina, it was fashioned from a wooden log, surmounted by a cutout plywood face painted in a demonic design.

"He's the first of the welcoming committee," he said as he rejoined the group. "But you can bet he won't be the last. Heads up, everyone."

The casuarina pines gave way to an almost impenetrable growth of sea almond trees. Sebastian tapped one of his men on the shoulder and he began to hack a path through the thickly entwined branches with his ever-present machete. Despite being burdened with rifles and clubs, the fishermen refused to be parted from their machetes, which were almost extensions of their arms, and wore them looped from their belts.

As the machete wielder neared the end of the sea almond thicket, Skye told him to stop. He nodded at Detective Goodwin to go ahead with the metal detector.

"Hold it!" Goodwin called out as the detector began to click. Cautiously moving forward he swept the detector from side to side. The clicking intensified as it was moved to the right, and faded away when he took a few steps to the left. The others followed in single file with one of the men staying behind to guide Dalton and Warren around the trap. They were in the open now, with tufts of eel grass growing in pockets of sand. Down by the shore the sea still thundered and crashed.

Large gauzy clouds began to float across the sky, as if in a parade, diffusing the too-bright moonlight. Looking up at their silently drifting amorphous shapes Skye was put in mind of the angel paintings by Chagall. He decided this wasn't the time nor the place to share this bit of artistic insight.

"That helps," Foxcroft said as the light dimmed, as though controlled by a rheostat.

"It sure does," Skye agreed. "It will help keep the frigate birds from taking wing." If they took off and began to file in agitated circles over the breeding colony, it would almost certainly raise the alarm. The plan was to skirt around the colony, but there was a limit to that since it was located close to the edge of the swamp.

The raiding party was some distance inland when they encountered the swamp. First, the ground under their feet became spongy, then brackish water was lapping around the arching roots of the mangroves. Led by Goodwin, they waded in. In the clearing off to the right, the frigate birds began to stir and cackle. Foxcroft handed his night vision glasses to Skye. Some of the birds were standing up on their nests and calling uneasily to one another. A couple of them were flapping their wings, but Skye saw that their feet were firmly gripping the side of the nest. They were disturbed and anxious, but reluctant to take flight.

Skye motioned Goodwin forward and they moved on, stepping with care through the shallow stagnant water. They stiffened as one of the birds took off, croaking hoarsely. Holding his breath, Skye waited for the others to follow as he swept the colony with the night glasses. Some of the adult birds were bounding up and down but were discouraged by the lack of light from taking off. The pilot in Skye nodded understandingly as he and the others crept forward. As the distance increased, the birds began to quieten. The question now was whether any of the guards had been posted near enough to hear the racket and report it. Maybe he was lying in wait, ready to cut them down with a Kalashnikov AK47 as they emerged from the swamp.

Standing ankle deep in water, Skye looked back at the rookery. The plank pathway had ended directly across from it. With the night glasses it was easy enough to pick it out. But should they use it? Walking along it certainly would be a lot easier and faster than slogging through the swamp and climbing over mangrove roots, but it was likely to be booby trapped and there was always the possibility of that AK47 waiting for them at the end of it.

Foxcroft was obviously thinking along the same lines. When Skye pointed to the plank pathway, he shook his head and said, "Too risky. It's too exposed."

Clambering through the mangroves was a fetid, mosquito-infested nightmare; the arched roots were slippery and difficult to straddle. Skye and Foxcroft tucked their semi-automatics inside their wet suits and were able to use both hands to work their way over the roots, but the others, especially the fishermen encumbered with rifles and clubs, and tormented by mosquitoes buzzing hungrily about their heads, made heavy going of it. More than one slid helplessly off a root into the clinging, gooey mud. Gradually the ground beneath their feet became firmer, the trees more widely spaced, and then they were walking on dry land. Land, Skye knew, that had been created by the mangroves themselves as their roots trapped sediments over the centuries.

Now that they were in more open country, Skye, his mind filled with the horrors that could be taking place on the *Caroline*, was tempted to race ahead. But anytime now they could have their first encounter with the enemy. With Skye and Foxcroft in the lead, and Dalton and Warren bringing up the rear, the little band advanced cautiously. With a thrumming of springs, another figure jumped out from a tree. Although this time they were prepared for it, the men were still startled and waited with tense trigger fingers to see what would happen. The tails of the long frock coat flapped as the figure bounced on its springs.

"It's an effigy of Baron Samedi." Peering in the dark, Skye went over for a closer look. Apart from the frock coat draped over its shoulders, the effigy was made of wood. As he took another step forward Skye felt the ground giving way beneath him and desperately tried to jump backward. Then he was falling through the air to land with a jarring thump. His first thought was relief that he hadn't been impaled on sharpened sticks. Looking up, he saw Foxcroft peering anxiously down at him.

"Are you all right?" asked the policeman. When Skye replied with a shaky, "Yes," he said, "Hang on, we'll get you out."

The pit Skye was in was too deep for anyone to get out unassisted. Like the fisherman caught in the leg trap, the Frigate goons would undoubtedly let anyone who blundered into the trap remain there until they saw fit to haul him out. It was all designed to give Frigate the reputation of being an island to stay away from.

Sebastian's face replaced Foxcroft's at the top of the pit and he lowered the rope from one of the anchors. He had knotted a loop at the end of it and Skye placed this under his arms and, planting his feet step by step on the wall of the pit, walked up the side as his companions pulled on the rope.

"Playful little buggers, aren't they?" Foxcroft muttered as Skye hitched a knee over the lip of the pit and scrambled to his feet.

"At least they were considerate enough not to line it with stakes," Skye replied, stooping to examine the lattice work of thin boards that had covered the hole. It was strong enough to support the clump of grass that had been placed across it but would break as soon as a person stepped on it. Straightening up, he said, "We're way behind schedule. We've got to step it up." The sound of the pounding surf had receded as they progressed inland and they were keeping their voices low.

Crouching to take advantage of the scant cover provided by the occasional bush and shrub, they moved on. Goodwin, in the lead, suddenly sniffed and looked back at Foxcroft with a knowing look. Then the others caught the unmistakable sickly sweet smell of marijuana. A guard on a marijuana high wouldn't be at the top of his form.

A cough betrayed the location of the guard. It was a guard all right; he had an automatic rifle slung over his shoulder. Foxcroft inched forward on his belly. Something must have alerted the guard for he started to turn in Foxcroft's direction. He froze when Foxcroft in a calm, cold voice told him he was covered and to come forward, adding that any attempt to touch his gun would be his last move.

The guard was black and young. And very frightened. He stood stock still as Goodwin relieved him of his rifle and patted him down for any other weapons. He was carrying a walkie-talkie but no other guns. His eyes were wide as he stared down at the semi-automatic .45 in Foxcroft's hand. It was equipped with a silencer and was the only weapon so equipped. If there was to be any shooting, Foxcroft would do it first.

"We need information, and we need it fast," Foxcroft said. "First, how many armed guards are there?"

"Four. Beside me."

"If we find you've lied to us, we'll come back and shoot you."

Some of the fear went out of the guard's eyes. At least he wasn't going to be summarily executed. "I not lying."

"What about the boat?"

The prisoner's face registered surprise. "One guard and the crew."

"You know what's going on there, don't you?"

"Not me, mon. It none of my business."

"But something's happening tonight. Isn't it?"

"Something. Yeah."

"Where are the other guards posted?"

"Roving, mon. Roving."

The guard's walkie-talkie began to crackle. Goodwin quickly handed it to him. "Tell him everything's fine."

"Everything's cool, mon," the guard said into the transceiver.

"All right, mon. Stay alert." The walkie-talkie clicked off.

"What can you tell us about the boat?" Foxcroft demanded.

"Nothing. Never seen it before."

"That fits," said Skye. "Normally everything would be done out at sea. What about the airplane?"

"What I know is that it can land on water or land. That's it, mon."

"That's the one," said Skye. "Let's tie this guy up and get ..."

He stopped short as a voice from the darkness ordered them to drop their guns. There was the click of a safety being switched off and a man stepped out of the shadows. "I can take you all out if I have to," he said with quiet assurance. It was true. The assault rifle he was carrying could mow them down in one continuous burst. But there was also a good chance that he himself would be cut down by their return fire, and he seemed to realize this. "Drop your guns. Now," he ordered, but this time with less assurance, as if trying to think of a way to extricate himself from the situation.

"You drop your gun." The barrel of Dalton's rifle dug into the small of the guard's back. "I want to hear that safety being switched on. Do it!" Dalton prodded him with the rifle until with a muffled curse he switched on the safety and lowered the gun to the ground.

"Good work," Foxcroft said to Dalton as he surveyed the two prisoners with satisfaction. The older one, the one who had gotten the drop on them, looked to be brighter and more knowledgeable than the marijuana smoker. Foxcroft had Goodwin gag the younger one and tie his hands behind a tree, telling him not to use handcuffs so he could be released when someone found him. Turning to the second guard, he asked, "What's your name?"

"Eustace."

"Well, Eustace, you're going to be our guide. You know the location of all the booby traps, right?"

Eustace nodded.

"Well, you're going to make sure we don't fall into them, because if we do, things will not go well for you. Not well at all. Understood?"

Again Eustace nodded.

Eustace professed not to know where the other

guards were, although he grudgingly acknowledged there would be three of them.

"Let's empty his rifle," Skye suggested, "and let him carry it and walk well in front of us. If the other guards see him, they might call out and reveal themselves."

"You heard the man, Eustace." Foxcroft quickly emptied the rifle and handed it to the guard. "Start walking."

With an apprehensive Eustace in the lead, and Dalton and Warren once more well to the rear, they pressed on. Skye's tactics paid off. Seeing Eustace coming down the path, a guard stepped out from a bush to ask where he was going. Eustace jerked his head back to warn him, and the guard gaped at the sight of the raiding party. He raised his assault rifle to fire, and Foxcroft shot him, the Sonic suppressor dampening the sound of the shot to a muffled "spit."

Turning to Eustace, Foxcroft asked, "Do you know a man called Logan?"

Eustace, shocked by the death of his comrade, hesitated, then nodded.

"Is he on the island tonight?"

"Yeah, mon. I saw him earlier. With that fat doctor and the good-looking nurse from Manchineel."

Skye and Foxcroft looked at each other. For the first time here was proof positive they were on the right track.

"Look, mon," Eustace was saying to Foxcroft. "I know where the other guard is. I'll lead you around so you won't have to shoot her."

"Her?"

"Yeah. She's my woman. She's the cook, but she has a gun."

"We certainly don't want to kill anyone we don't have to. But that still leaves a guard at the boat."

"You leave my woman alone and I'll help you fool him."

"Done."

"We go this way." Eustace headed off to the right, toward a stand of trees. A few yards inside, he stopped and pointed to a log lying across the path. "There's a pit on the other side," he said. "Go around it."

"Looks like we can trust him," Skye said in a low voice to Foxcroft as they carefully stepped around the log. Screened by the log, the pit was open. Anyone stepping over the log would have fallen in. As the trees began to thin, Skye recognized where they were. Increasing his pace to catch up with Eustace, he asked, "Where is the ventilator?"

The guard gave him a surprised look. "You bin here before?"

"With Mr. Baker."

"I heard about that. I was off island that day."

Probably collecting some more victims, thought Skye, looking to where Eustace was pointing. The ventilator was still there, but it wasn't working. The doomed souls who had been held there were probably awaiting their fate on board the *Caroline*.

"Is Baker on the island now?"

"Not so far as I know. He don't spend much time here."

"We haven't far to go," Skye said as he fell back to join Foxcroft.

They stayed inside a screen of trees as they made their way up the rising ground. Skye knew the fish plant buildings and the landing field with the moveable boulders were somewhere off to the left, but the trees blocked his view. Another procession of Chagall clouds floated past, obscuring the moon. Eustace waited for them at the top of the jeep track leading down to the water. They were following the route that the hapless organ "donors" would have taken.

"The road is safe," he told them. Looking at Skye, he added. "The guard down by the yacht is the guy who drives the cigarette boat."

"Will Logan be on board?" Foxcroft demanded.

"I don't know for sure, but I expect so. I ain't seen him anywheres else."

"Everyone remember he's to be taken alive," Foxcroft warned.

"That may not be possible, Alan," Skye replied. "He'll be armed with an assault rifle and one of those things can take out a squad like ours in seconds."

"According to his profile on file at the Yard," Goodwin put in, "he's a flaming coward."

"Then if he runs true to form, he'll cut and run," said Skye.

"We can't let him get away again," Foxcroft muttered. "Not when we're this close to nailing the bastard." He detailed Dalton and Warren to split up and cover as much ground as possible in case Logan tried to flee.

"You don't need me any more," Eustace suddenly pleaded. "Why don't you tie me up and leave me here?"

"Oh, but we do need you," Foxcroft said softly. "You're our stalking horse, old boy. Start walking. And this time, if you try any tricks you get shot."

"I'll probably get shot anyway," Eustace mumbled as he reluctantly started down the track.

They were horribly exposed but there was no alternative; the jeep track was the only way down to the water. Suddenly, shockingly, the night was rent with a burst of automatic fire. Wordlessly, they stared at each other, surprised to find their numbers intact.

"Don't shoot. It's me." Dalton was coming down the trail toward them. "He had the drop on you and was ready to shoot. I had to take him out." Dalton was visibly shaken but his voice was steady. Once again, Foxcroft's strategy of having a rearguard in place had paid off.

"Where was he?" Foxcroft asked, looking at the black cliff face.

"He was on that ledge." Dalton pointed to a narrow ledge about thirty feet from the top of the cliff. "He fell off when I shot him."

"How do you suppose he got there?" wondered Foxcroft.

"Be easy enough to climb down a rope," Skye replied. "It sure gave him the jump on us."

"Except for Dalton here." Foxcroft clapped the detective on the shoulder as if to assure him he had done the right thing. "It seems we have lost the element of surprise. And we still have to deal with the crew."

"And Logan," muttered Skye.

Foxcroft looked at Eustace. "I take it you have no ambition to be a hero?"

"Not me, mon. All I want is to live through this night. Me and my woman."

"Hand me your gun."

"Sure thing, boss." Scarcely daring to believe his luck, Eustace lifted the rifle over his head and eagerly handed it over.

"Can you contact your woman and persuade her to leave her post?"

"No problem. Especially when I tell her what happened to the other two."

Foxcroft instructed Dalton to escort Eustace to the top of the cliff and then let him go.

"Why did you do that?" asked Skye as he followed

Foxcroft down the dirt trail.

"He was of no further use to us once we lost the element of surprise."

"That may be. But he's still part of what's going on here."

"Small fry. Besides, he can't get off the island and we can pick him up whenever we want. Logan can't get off the island either," Foxcroft added with a ferocious grin.

Concentrating on negotiating the rutted and rock-strewn trail that zig-zagged its way down the cliff, and on the lookout for any further ambushes, they failed to see the one-man kayak slip out from under the palm fronds on the far side of the *Caroline* and glide across the inlet.

Chapter Twenty-two

Skye, desperate to put an end to the hellish business on the *Caroline*, broke into a dogtrot down the treacherous slope. Pulling up at the bottom, he swore under his breath as he saw that the yacht, draped under a canopy of palm fronds, was anchored a few hundred feet from the shore. They must have moved it away from the base of the cliff after the drugged victims had been loaded on board.

"Looks like we swim for it," he said as Foxcroft pulled up beside him.

"We've still got to find a way to get on board her," Foxcroft muttered, staring at the strange sight of a huge pile of palm fronds floating on the water. In the dark it looked sinister and forbidding.

"We can still grapple her with the anchors and rope," Skye replied. Turning to the fishermen, he said, "When we get close you can stand on our shoulders in the water and heave the anchors over the railing. Right?"

They nodded, and Foxcroft warned, "Keep your weapons dry," as they slipped into the water.

Swimming on his back and holding the Glock aloft, Skye was painfully aware of just how exposed they were. Any second now he expected a stream of bullets to dance a deadly path across the water. Was it possible they hadn't heard the shots that cut the guard down and that we still had the element of surprise? The boat's hull was soundproofed, but surely the shots would have been heard by anyone standing on an open deck? His question was answered with a burst of gunfire from the boat. Skye saw the flash as the bullets ripped through the palm fronds and, rolling over on his stomach, emptied the Glock at the spot. There was the sound of breaking glass and the shooting abruptly ceased.

The young lobster fisherman, the one called Peter, who had been swimming next to Skye, was virtually decapitated. Skye stared in horror as the body, weighted with the anchor he was carrying, began to sink beneath the surface. He had wrapped the rope around his waist and there was nothing Skye could do as the body slowly disappeared from sight.

Who would be the next to be cut down in a withering hail of bullets? There was no point in turning back; they were equally exposed either way. They were getting close to the boat now, soon they would be in the shelter of the hull, but who knew what would be waiting for them at the top?

Off to the right, Goodwin held Foxcroft upright in the water and Foxcroft raked the *Caroline* from bow to stern. Bullets whined and clanged against metal amid a crescendo of shattering glass. The bullets ripped the curtain of palm fronds and a large section fell into the water, exposing the *Caroline*'s hull and bullet-riddled lower deck.

Skye blinked when he saw the narrow fibreglass platform on the *Caroline*'s transom. Just above the waterline, it was used by swimmers for easy access to the water. He might have seen it before, but it obviously hadn't registered. It would make boarding the boat much easier, and do away with the need for the cumbersome anchors, but it was also bound to be under surveillance. Still, things were very quiet on the boat and there was no sign of activity. It was worth a chance. Skye, his shoulders taut with tension, headed for the platform and the others silently followed after him, pushing aside the palm fronds floating in the water. No shots rang out and moments later they were clinging to the platform and staring wordlessly at each other. If anyone looked over the stern, they would be like fish in a barrel.

Suddenly from up above them came the sound of a woman calling out. A woman in pain. "Logan? Where are you Logan? I'm hurt. Help me Logan. Logan?"

"I hope we haven't killed the bastard," Foxcroft muttered. "I didn't want to shoot but we were sitting ducks out there in the water." Keyed up at the prospect of being so close to his prey, Foxcroft said, "Let's board her," and scrambled onto the platform.

One way or another, they were committed. Telling the surviving fishermen they could get rid of the anchors, Skye lifted himself onto the platform. Crouching beside Foxcroft he slipped a fresh clip of ammunition into the Glock. There was a door in the transom but Foxcroft said he had tried it and it was locked. The top of the transom was out of reach, but Skye said, "I'm taller than you, and if you kneel and I stand on your back, I think I can reach it."

Foxcroft looked as if he wanted to argue the point, but looking up at the transom, knew that Skye was right. He dropped to his knees and Skye, standing on his back, gingerly straightened up. He was able to touch the top but couldn't get a grip while holding the Glock. He tucked it into the belt of his wetsuit in the small of his back and tried again. Now if anyone was waiting for him at the top, he would be completely helpless. For someone who had discovered that life could once more be sweet and fulfilling, he was sure putting it at risk. He hauled himself up until his head was just below the top of the transom and paused there. When he looked over the top would he be staring at the muzzle of a gun? Taking a deep breath, he cautiously pulled himself up.

"I could shoot you," came a woman's voice as Skye dropped onto the deck. "But I'm not going to. It's over."

Reaching behind for the Glock, Skye finally spotted her. She was lying on the deck propped up against, and partly hidden by, a set of steps leading to the upper deck. She could have shot him all right. A semi-automatic lay by her side.

The top of her white uniform was stained with blood and her face was ashen. Keeping one eye on her, Skye leaned over the stern and beckoned the others to follow.

Looking down at the wounded crew member, Skye recognized her as the blonde who had smiled when he laughingly took her hand at the gangway the night of Pollock's party. Kicking her gun out of reach, Skye looked around the deck. It was like the aftermath of a battle. Spent bullets and cartridges littered the deck. The motionless form of a dead crew member lay beside the railing further up the deck. That would be the one who had shot Peter's head off and who in turn had been shot by Skye. It was a jolt to see the body of a man he had killed, but now wasn't the time to worry about that. Foxcroft and the others were swarming on board,

Sebastian bending back over the stern to help the last man up.

"Where's the captain?" Skye asked the blond sailor. She was in pain but she was fully conscious. The blood was coming from a wound high up in her chest, just under her left shoulder.

"Down below. She's a doctor."

Detective Goodwin, who seemed to be a jack-of-all-trades, produced a first-aid kit from somewhere on his person and knelt beside her. Cutting away her shirt, he began to dress the wound. She smiled gratefully up at him.

"And Pollock?"

"Locked in his office. He always does that when this is coming down."

Foxcroft had her tell Sebastian where Pollock's office was located and sent him off to stand guard outside the door.

"The bullet is still in there, but at least we've stopped the loss of blood," said Goodwin as he finished taping a gauze bandage in place.

"How do we get to them?" Skye asked.

"You know the dioramas in the fantail salon?" Skye nodded, and she said "If you press the brass nameplate of the one of the *Bismarck* sinking the *Hood* a door will open in the bulkhead. Behind it are steps leading down."

"You finished with her?" Goodwin was filling a syringe from a small vial. "I'll give her a shot of morphine for the pain."

"Almost." Skye unclipped a two-way radio from her belt. "This is how you communicate with the people in ..." Skye hesitated before saying "surgery" for want of a better word.

"Yes."

"So they've been warned?"

"Not unless they've heard the shooting, and I don't think they will have. The lower deck is completely soundproofed. I was trying to help Jim," she jerked her head in the direction of the dead seaman, "and I was hit as I was bending over him. I must have passed out for a bit."

"I have a question for her." Foxcroft held Goodwin's hand as he was about to insert the needle. "Do you know where Logan is?"

She shook her head, the motion making her wince. "He must be on the boat somewhere. He'll be hiding someplace." Seeing the irresolute look on the inspector's face, Skye said, "C'mon. We got to rescue those people. We can look for him afterwards." Moving quickly, he headed for the fantail salon.

Skye pressed the nameplate of the beautifully detailed model of the famous naval battle and a portion of the forward bulkhead slid noiselessly upward, revealing a short flight of metal steps. At the bottom of the stairs a red light glowed beside a green door set flush in the wall. The door was thickly padded with insulating material. Skye looked gravely at his companions crowding around him. "Prepare yourselves for what you are about to see." He switched on the radio and handed it to Foxcroft, saying, "You're the one with official status here. Tell them to open up."

Foxcroft took the radio and barked, "This is the police. Open up. I say again, open up."

As the seconds ticked by with no movement from behind the door, Foxcroft again barked into the radio, "You have thirty seconds to open the door. If you don't, we will shoot it out and that means all of you could be killed. I'm starting to count."

The radio buzzed with what could have been the

sound of a scuffle, then Glessop's fruity tones quavered, "Don't shoot. We give up. Don't shoot. We are going to open the door."

"Are you armed?"

"Of course not. This is a hospital."

"Some hospital," Skye muttered.

"Edwina's going to open the door now."

There was the sound of two deadbolts being drawn back, then the knob turned, and Edwina stood in the doorway, a surgical mask dangling around her neck and her green gown splotched with blood. Behind her was a sight from the heart of hell. The photos and drawings in Skye's textbook had been pretty graphic but they couldn't begin to convey the horror of the scene in real life.

There were two operating tables. The body of a young East Indian girl was splayed out on the first one. She had been split from the base of her throat to the top of her pelvis in what Skye's reading had told him was the Virchow incision, named after a pioneer pathologist. It exposed the entire contents of both the chest and abdominal cavities. All her vital organs had been removed, leaving only a hollow, pink carcass with splotches of blood on the skin. Captain Morton, still holding a scalpel, stood at the head of the table, eyes wide with alarm above her surgical mask.

Skye heard someone being violently sick behind him, and his own stomach was heaving dangerously, but he swallowed hard and advanced further into the room. The second table must be where Glessop had been at work. So far only the abdominal cavity had been opened. The intestines were piled in a greyish mass on one side of the operating table and the liver was bathed in an oxygenated solution in a plastic container that bore an incongruous resemblance to a picnic hamper.

Horribly, the unconscious victim, a teenaged male, was still alive. His heart would continue to beat and supply the other organs with blood until they were removed. Then his chest cavity would be opened so the lungs and heart could be retrieved. Syringe in hand, Edwina looked questioningly at Skye. He nodded, and she inserted the needle into the arm of what remained of a human being. The young black's eyelids flew open, a soft groan issued from his lips, and he expired.

Foxcroft was placing everyone — the two surgeons, Edwina and the other nurse, and an assistant — under arrest, telling them they had the right to remain silent. The formal language of the statutory warning sounded bizarrely out of place in the macabre setting. He herded them down to one end and, as they moved away from the wall, a final horror was revealed. Stacked in one corner of the room were three completely eviscerated bodies. One of them was a white youth, his skin now an ashen grey. All three were half-propped against the wall, their empty, pink eye sockets staring blindly ahead. Blood dripped from their empty body cavities onto a plastic sheet.

"You ready for the ..." The words died in the man's throat as he opened the door of the adjoining cabin and gaped at the scene.

"You. Come out!" Foxcroft's voice was steely. Without being told, the man, attired like the others in a green surgical gown and cap, raised his hands over his head, and advanced into the room, his bewilderment rapidly giving way to fright.

"He's not carrying," Goodwin announced in some surprise after frisking him.

"There's no need," Glessop, eager to ingratiate himself, volunteered. "They're drugged. So they won't suffer," he added with a simpering smirk.

Skye shot him a look of contempt as he walked over to the open door. Despite what the rogue surgeon had said, he kept the Glock at the ready. But Glessop was right about there being no need. The floor was crowded with naked, semi-conscious bodies. A few pairs of eyes looked dully and uncomprehendingly up at Skye. He remembered what the book had said about leaving a little spark of life in them until the intravenous needle was inserted. One of the babies — thank God they were still both alive — had crawled over to the side of a young girl and was vainly trying to suckle at her unresponsive breast. The babies would be left to the last so there would be the shortest elapsed time before the hearts were transplanted.

There was nothing to be done at the moment except hope that the victims would recover consciousness without permanent damage. Going back to the operating room, Skye looked down at the dead teenager on Glessop's table. "Can his organs still be retrieved?"

"All except the heart," Glessop replied.

"Well, get to work. What about those?" Skye pointed to the containers stacked along a wall.

"They're fine. They've all been properly perfused and oxygenated."

"Good. I'm sure HOPE will be delighted to receive them."

To his considerable surprise, Skye found himself watching the procedures with interest and respect. Captain Morton glanced at him and when he nodded, came over to assist Glessop. As Skye was later to find out, she had signed on as the medical officer on a cruise ship after completing her internship. She had fallen in love with the seagoing life and had earned her master's ticket. Add a dose of larceny, and she was a perfect fit for this inhuman enterprise.

"We better pry Pollock out of his office." Foxcroft studiously avoided looking at the two surgeons bending over the corpse. "After all, he's the mastermind behind all this."

"I'm not so sure," Skye replied thoughtfully. "He's involved up to his eyeballs of course, but somehow I don't see him as the mastermind. Anyway, I think we should leave him where he is for the moment. If I know Glessop, he will talk, but he could clam up if Pollock's around."

Foxcroft blanched when Edwina went past holding a kidney in her cupped, gloved hands.

Seeing his discomfort, Skye suggested, "Let's go topside. There's nothing for us to do until they finish." Turning to Goodwin he said, "When they're finished here, have one of the doctors check out that woman on the deck. You did a good job of bandaging her, but they should look her over."

Foxcroft breathed deeply as he and Skye stood on the open deck. "In my career I've seen murder victims, suicides, crash victims, people dead from drug overdoses, and taken them all in stride. But for some reason, watching an operation is different. I guess it's because I'm a bit of a hypochondriac and I imagine myself under the knife."

Before Skye could make any reply to this piece of self-analysis, there was the coughing splutter of an airplane engine starting up. It settled into a steady roar and the other engine coughed into life. Skye and Foxcroft stared at each other as the plane revved up for its take-off run. Staring up at the cliff there was nothing to see, but soon a change in the pitch of the engines told them it was airborne. Then the black shape of a float-equipped Twin Otter was briefly silhouetted against the thin sliver of the descending moon. It levelled off at a low altitude and headed south.

"There goes your friend, Logan," Skye muttered. Foxcroft gave him a stricken look. "Lassiter can't fly an airplane," he protested.

"No. But he can make someone else fly it. I think your boy has gone south, Alan."

"You may be right, but I'm going to have every square inch of this island searched when it gets light." After a pause while he absorbed the humiliating possibility that Lassiter might have thumbed his nose at Scotland Yard yet again, Foxcroft asked, "What are we going to do with all those people, Skye?"

"We'll lay on an air lift. But there's still a long night ahead of us."

Chapter Twenty-three

S ir George Glessop, still wearing his bloodstained surgical gown, was an incongruous sight as he sat in a leather armchair in the opulent main salon of the *Caroline*. He was in a surprisingly expansive mood. He had waived his right to counsel, saying that since he had been caught in flagrante delicto, a statement would do him no harm and might do him some good. Foxcroft had immediately warned him not to expect any favours. "I understand that, but could I please have a drink?"

Skye persuaded a somewhat reluctant Foxcroft to go along with this request and Glessop, his throat well lubricated, began to talk. The operation that he described was pretty much the way Skye had envisaged it. The donors were kept on Frigate until a sufficient number had been assembled and, in some instances, the individual specifications of the clinics in Florida or Mexico had been met, then they were transported out to a waterborne rendezvous with the *Caroline*. The organs were flown to the mainland in the Twin Otter. The cadavers were kept in freezers on the *Caroline*, which sailed to an area of the Atlantic where sharks were known to congregate, and the bodies were dumped overboard.

"What about the three bodies that were washed up on the beach on Manchineel?" Style asked.

"As you correctly surmised, their organs had been surgically removed. Maybe the sharks weren't hungry that day."

When asked how long the ring had been operating, Glessop had to think back before replying that it was over two years. Last night's operation was not the largest, but it was the first one to include babies.

"And now those two will live," muttered the inspector.

"Yes. And two others will die."

Glessop held out his empty glass. Skye took it from him and walked over to the bar, followed by a worried Foxcroft. "If you keep plying him with liquor," muttered the inspector, "it could invalidate his statement."

"This is it. It will be a long time between drinks for him in prison."

There was a malicious glint in Glessop's eyes as he eagerly accepted the drink. "You gentlemen haven't asked the right question yet."

The moment Skye had been dreading had come. "What is that?" he asked, almost in a whisper.

"Who is the real head of the organization? The kingpin, as the Americans say."

"Who is it?" Foxcroft demanded. "Logan?" A thorough search of the ship had revealed no trace of Logan, which only further fuelled Foxcroft's obsession.

"Logan?" squeaked an astounded Glessop. "Good heavens, man, of course not." Looking at Skye, he said, "It's your good friend, Lord Fraser."

Skye wanted to cry out that it was a lie. A malicious damnable lie. It couldn't be true. But he knew it was true.

"You better tell us about this," Foxcroft said quietly after a stunned silence.

Skye stared morosely down at the carpet as Glessop began to speak. "Robert Fraser was a Name," he said. "One of the biggest. For years he lived handsomely off his investment in the syndicate. He often boasted of earning an annual return of 60 percent. Some years it was close to a million pounds. As the years went by and the syndicate continued to pay dividends, he invested more and more heavily, raising cash by mortgaging his castle in Scotland, his London flat, and other assets. I think the possibility that he might be required to make good on his unlimited liability never entered his mind. When it happened he was ruined."

Glessop paused for a long swallow of his drink. "Fraser has a very strong sense of noblesse oblige," he continued. "It's been bred into him for generations. He couldn't stand the thought of losing the family seat in Scotland and depriving the family retainers of their livelihood. That bothered him more than anything else. The only way to prevent that was to find a way to raise enough money to meet the calls. A seemingly impossible task. Until certain things fell into place for him."

"Your being here on the island and your reputation as a pioneer in organ transplantation," Skye interjected.

Glessop accepted the compliment with a gracious inclination of his head. "That is so. He had brought me there as a personal favour and, needless to say, I was very grateful. I had performed a successful kidney transplant on a cousin of his to whom he was very close and I have no doubt that was why he helped me. All this was before his world collapsed, of course."

"And when it did, he somehow discovered the astronomical amount of money that could be made in the organ trade," said Skye.

"Exactly. That was the second ingredient."

"Is there really that much money to be made?" asked the inspector. "I mean, look at the cost of running an operation like this."

Glessop's smile was condescending. "Let me give you an example. Let's take the two babies. By the way, we purchased both of them in Caracas. We were to receive two hundred and fifty thousand for the heart of the younger one and no less than one million for the other."

"AB negative," murmured Skye.

"Exactly." It didn't seem to surprise Glessop that Skye knew that this was the rarest blood type.

"And the third ingredient was the availability of donors," said Skye. "Homeless youngsters that would never be missed, parents that were prepared to sell their children, and corrupt governments that would supply street kids for a price, or simply to get rid of them. Am I right?"

"Once again, Skye, your surmise is correct."

"I assume Robert owns Frigate?" asked Skye.

"Yes. He acquired it some years back when he was still riding high. His intention was to keep it from being developed, but then he found other uses for it."

"You know, of course, that Logan is really Lord Lassiter?" Foxcroft, returning to his favourite subject, asked as off-handedly as he could manage.

Once again, Glessop was astounded. "Are you serious?" he asked. "Yes, I see you are. Amazing. Of course I never knew Lassiter, but from everything I heard he was the exact opposite of the dour Logan. Another case of Robert helping out a friend. You have arrested him, I take it?"

"No. We damn well haven't," Foxcroft grated.

Glessop's eyes widened, but he wisely remained silent.

Foxcroft consulted the notes he had made. "If that's everything, I'll type up a statement for you to sign."

While they waited, Glessop asked Skye, "I know you suspected something about a trade in human organs, but did you expect to find Edwina and myself in that operating theatre?"

"Yes."

"May I know why?"

"The night Penelope disappeared I saw you and Edwina driving near the waterfront very late at night. She later told me she was driving around to sober you up, but I didn't entirely buy that. Then the next day Captain Morton — or should I say Doctor Morton? — made a hash of sailing into Tobago Cays and got the other boats so stirred up that she took the *Caroline* back out to sea after we were landed on the beach. Shortly thereafter the PM received a matching new heart. Then I learned from Sebastian that the PM was Penelope's father. The timeline told me that if you and Edwina were hidden somewhere onboard the *Caroline*, you could have retrieved Penelope's heart while we were having our picnic. I also saw a mysterious float plane flying north in the direction the *Caroline* had taken."

"Remarkable. What about Robert? Did you suspect him?"

"I tried very hard not to. I just couldn't see him involved in something as despicable as this. And I didn't know he was a Name, so I didn't realize he had a compelling motive. But it's common knowledge that he brought you to Manchineel, and then when we found out that Logan was really Lassiter, and Robert was protecting him as well, I could see how he might be part of this."

"He was more than a part. He was the instigator and the leader. Although he kept himself well removed from the messy bits ..." Glessop broke off as Foxcroft returned to the salon with a brief typewritten statement.

Glessop read it carefully, then signed it with a flourish and handed it back. "Accurate, but a bit terse," he murmured. "Maybe I'll expand on it later. Maybe I'll even write a book. I expect I'll have plenty of time in prison, won't I?"

"This isn't England, Sir George," said Foxcroft, "they hang people here."

* * *

Foxcroft had contacted Dalton by walkie-talkie and he reported that neither he nor Warren had seen Logan.

"Ask them to try to find a boat of some kind and bring it out here," said Skye. "We're too far out from shore."

Warren, familiar with the island from former times, knew where the cigarette boat was likely hidden. He and Dalton sloshed through mangroves on the north side of the inlet until they came across the black cigarette boat in a channel scarcely wider than itself. As soon as they were satisfied it was unattended, they hauled themselves on board and crept up to the front cockpit. Lying on the floor boards, Warren jerked two wires down from under the dash, deftly spliced them together, and pressed the starter. One of the twin engines rumbled into life. Untying the ropes that secured it to the mangroves, they backed the boat out and motored slowly across to the *Caroline*.

With the fishermen acting as crew, it was a simple matter to raise the *Caroline*'s anchors and tow her into position so that her extended gangway could reach the base of the cliff.

* * *

At three o'clock, Skye looked at his watch and said, "It's time to organize the airlift. I've got to get hold of Armbruster at home, but I don't know his number."

"809-456-3440," Foxcroft recited. Armbruster would be part of the emergency response team, and the inspector would have to know how to get in touch with him at any hour.

"We need some STOL airplanes, Henry," Skye said when the manager of Manchineel Air answered the phone. "What do you have handy?"

Armbruster, whose business kept him mentally prepared for an emergency, had come instantly awake. "We've got an Islander on the tarmac here in Manchineel and the Twin Otter and another Islander over at St. Vincent. The rest are over in Barbados. Where are you calling from?"

"Frigate."

"Have you been drinking, Skye? There's no place to land on that island."

"There is now. It's just a matter of moving some rocks. Trust me."

"Okay. What do you need?"

"All three. At first light. I'll pay for it."

"Are you going to tell me what's going on?"

Armbruster listened intently as Skye gave him a brief account of the night's events, breathing "Jesus Christ!"

from time to time as the story unfolded, and a final "Christ Almighty!" when it ended. "I'll round up the pilots and they'll be over Frigate at six-thirty."

"As soon as you've done that, call the medical authorities in St. Vincent and alert them to the situation. They should have ambulances waiting at the airport."

After Armbruster had rung off, Skye sat in silence for a few moments, then said, "I have another call to make, if you'll excuse me."

Foxcroft looked down at him for a long moment, then gave an almost imperceptible shrug, and left Skye alone in the radio room.

Chapter Twenty-four

The planes, flying in loose formation, banked low around the southern tip of Manchineel and headed for Frigate. Skye, standing with the first group to be taken off, watched as the Twin Otter made a low pass over the field to make sure that it was safe to land. Then the planes landed in quick succession and taxied to where their passengers waited.

The rescued victims would be the first to go. They were beginning to shake off the effect of the drugs, at least enough to walk, but were still dazed and apathetic. Two of the women had recovered enough to take over the babies, whimpering feebly with hunger.

When the planes were loaded, Skye sat up front beside Andy Foster, who was flying one of the Islanders. As they lifted off, both babies began to yell as the change in pressure caused their sensitive eardrums to pop. The sound made Skye smile. If they could make that much racket, they would surely survive. Down below, Foxcroft stepped out of one of the abandoned fish plant buildings and waved. He and Warren were scouring the island for Logan. Chances were, thought Skye, it would turn out to be a bootless inquisition. If Logan was on board that float-equipped Twin Otter, he could be anywhere. There was no limit to the places that airplane could land.

They were cleared for immediate landing at St. Vincent where the ambulances were lined up, waiting for them. Reporters from the local newspaper and television station were also waiting for them and approached Skye as he walked away from the plane. Deciding that it was best to get the sensational story straight from the start, Skye granted them an interview, repeating pretty much what he had told Armbruster. If they had any doubts about the wild tale, the proof was right before them in the form of the pathetic figures being loaded into the ambulances.

"That's a wrap, fellas," Skye said as Andy Foster signalled he was ready to leave. Knowing they had been given a career-making interview, they thanked him profusely and hurried away.

Foster dropped Skye off at the Manchineel airstrip where Overfine waited for him with the jeep. Skye looked up at the control tower where Armbruster was busy with incoming traffic. Armbruster waved at him through the window, and Skye gave him a thumbs-up. As they drove to Whistling Frog, Skye answered Overfine's few questions absently, his thoughts dwelling grimly on what lay ahead. He went inside the villa to wash up, then set off alone in the jeep.

On the way he exchanged waves with some people he knew casually, driving by in their jeeps, and stopped to have a few words with Elizabeth riding Belle and leading three other riders. Driving on, he realized that they would know nothing of last night's horrors, nor would they ever be called upon to look at them in real life. It made him feel distanced from the normal, everyday world. He fervently hoped the feeling wouldn't last. And there was probably yet another horror to come.

Arriving in front of Beaufort's massive gate, Skye reached out to press the button of the intercom built into the gate post. "This is Skye MacLeod. Would you open the gate please."

The intercom buzzed futilely for a few moments, then the quavering voice of Ralston, the bagpipe-playing butler, came on. "The master's shot himself, Mister Skye. I will open the gate."

There was a click and the two halves of the gate began to swing open. Robert had fallen on his sword. It was what Skye expected, but he was nonetheless swept with a desolating sadness. Ralston, eyes brimming with unshed tears, was waiting for him in the cobblestone courtyard. He opened the front door and led Skye across the immense foyer, the scene of so many brilliant parties, to the paneled library. As he crossed the foyer's marble floor, Skye saw Lady Fraser sitting rigidly erect in a straight backed chair in the "withdrawing" room.

Lord Fraser was slumped to one side in a leather armchair. There was a star-shaped entry wound in his right temple and blood and grey matter from the exit wound stained the back of the chair. His gun lay on the carpet just below the outstretched fingers of his right hand. Skye recognized it as an ancient Webley revolver and thought how appropriately British that was. Peering down at Fraser's hand, he saw the telltale traces of gunpowder. "It's suicide all right," he said as he straightened up. "Was there a note?" he asked the butler, who remained standing in the doorway.

"Her Ladyship has it, sir. It was addressed to her."

"I'm so dreadfully sorry." Skye lightly brushed his lips against Lady Fraser's forehead.

She gripped his hand. "He was terribly fond of you, you know. I think he thought of you as the son we never had."

"I will miss him terribly."

"I don't know what your phone call was about, he wouldn't tell me, but it distressed him terribly. He paced around the house like a caged animal, then went into the library and closed the door. And then ..."

Sky glanced at the envelope in her lap. "Could I see the note?"

Wordlessly, she handed it to him. The envelope was addressed to "My Dear Wife and Lifetime Companion." The note inside read: "Fiona, please forgive me. I have no choice. I cannot escape what I have done. I have always loved you. Robert." There was a postscript: "You mustn't blame Skye. He did us a great favour at what must have been at great cost to himself."

"Did you know anything about his business affairs?" Skye handed her back the note.

"Nothing whatsoever. I think Robert wanted to protect me from that side of life. He was old-fashioned in many ways. Is that what this is about?"

"In a way, yes. Fiona, you must prepare yourself. It's going to be ugly. Very ugly. I'll do everything I can to help."

"For God's sake, Skye, what happened? Tell me."

She would soon know the shocking truth in any event, and it was best she hear it from him. Skye sighed, and gave her a sanitized version of her husband's criminal activities. Sanitized or not, it left her shaken with disbelief and shock. Skye went in search of Ralston and found him still standing beside the library door. Skye told him to find Lady Fraser's personal maid.

"Are there any sleeping pills in the house?" Skye asked the tear-stained maid when Ralston escorted her into the foyer.

"Yes, sir," she replied, choking back a sob. "His Lordship sometimes had trouble sleeping."

I bet he did, thought Skye grimly. Taking Lady Fraser by the arm he helped her up the broad circular staircase. When she saw the maid heading for the master bedroom she shook her head. "I'll never sleep in that bed again."

The maid opened the door of one of the guest bedrooms and said to Skye, "I'll take care of her now, sir."

Seeing no sign of Ralston, Skye let himself out the front door. As he drove away, he heard the wailing drone of bagpipes. Ralston was playing a lament for the fallen lord.

* * *

At Agatha's insistence, Skye drank a glass of juice and ate a piece of toast. Carrying a cup of coffee over to the phone, he tried to call Erin, but was told that Ms. Kelly was out and could not be reached. Skye didn't push it. She would be at the hospital, and he didn't want to disturb her there. The adrenalin that had sustained him until now suddenly drained out of him. He was powered out. Leaving word that he was to be called in two hours, Skye headed for his sleeping quarters. As he crossed the lawn, he saw an Islander gaining altitude as it climbed away from Frigate. They were still evacuating people from the island. Or maybe they were ferrying in police to take it over.

* * *

"I came by earlier but told them not to wake you. You needed the sleep." Foxcroft, amazingly, still looked and sounded alert and brisk.

Skye, refreshed if not completely restored by his nap, invited him to join him at the table and have some lunch.

"You didn't find Logan, did you?" he asked.

"I did not. One thing is certain; he's not on Frigate." He paused with a forkful of salad halfway to his mouth. "We found a kayak hidden in some bushes. He could have used that to make his escape from the yacht. What do you think happened after that, Skye?"

"He could have skirted around Dalton and Warren, your two sentries, sneaked up on the pilot who would be waiting to fly the organs out — and probably getting the wind up over all the shooting — and forced him to take off at gunpoint. That plane was probably equipped with fuel bladders, so they could be long gone."

"Thanks," Foxcroft said bitterly.

"You're welcome. Seriously, that might be worth following up. You could find out the range of that particular aircraft and draw a circle in South America. Of course, they could have refuelled somewhere, but at least it's a start."

"I'll get on it. Thanks again. This time I mean it." Foxcroft smiled as Overfine placed a bowl of callaloo soup in front of him. "My favourite."

"Mine too."

"I've just come from Beaufort. Dreadful business."

"Yes."

"That was the call you made from the yacht, wasn't it?"

"Yes. Thank you for letting me make it."

"He will still be disgraced in the eyes of the world."

"True. But this way he's not here to bear the shame. I felt I had to give him that choice.

"What about the guard, Eustace, and his girlfriend?" Skye asked as Foxcroft rose to leave.

"They gave themselves up. They couldn't get off the island with those seas running, of course. Incidentally, the seas are subsiding. Apparently that underwater volcano has stopped erupting."

"It'll flare up again. One of these years there'll be a new island in the Caribbean."

When Skye returned from seeing Foxcroft to his jeep, Overfine was holding the phone. Placing his hand over the mouthpiece, he whispered, "It's Her Royal Highness." He was obviously impressed by the fact that she had placed the call herself.

"Skye, what's this I hear about Robert being dead?" she demanded.

"I'm afraid it's true. To make it worse, he committed suicide."

"Cook says she saw you on the telly. Some wild tale about human organs."

"It's wild all right. But it's also true. It's why Robert killed himself."

"I want to know everything. You get your ass over here, Skye MacLeod."

Skye managed a wan smile as he put down the phone. The Princess was addicted to American detective stories and occasionally liked to pepper her language with colourful colloquialisms that struck a jarring note with her English accent.

Serenity's gate was open, and Skye saw the police jeep parked over by the guardhouse as he drove up to the villa, but there was no sign of Foxcroft.

"Just what have you been up to, Skye? Shanghaing my guards and leaving me unprotected." Princess Helen's words were severe but there was a twinkle in her eye. With her bandaged leg propped up on a footstool and a gin and tonic on an end table beside her, she seemed to be revelling in the excitement.

"Detective Burrows was on twenty-four hour watch," Skye pointed out.

"Fat lot of good he would have been if someone had tried to abduct me."

"Well, they certainly couldn't have done it by sea, and doing it by air would have been too conspicuous."

The Princess laughed. "You're always so plausible, Skye. Now tell me about poor Robert.

"That Names business again," she murmured when he reached that point in his narrative. "It's ruined so many lives."

"Including lives who were not Names," Skye added.

In describing the raid on Frigate, he extolled the role played by Foxcroft and the two detectives although there was no need to embellish the truth. He spared her a description of the horrors they had uncovered on the *Caroline*.

"Robert and Charles were very naughty," she said when Skye finished.

"You could say that," he agreed ironically. Her main concern seemed to be that the press would link Pollock with her. Hoping to catch her off guard, he asked, "You knew Logan is really Lord Lassiter, of course?"

"What? Impossible! Absolutely impossible!"

"Not according to the results of the DNA test."

That brought her up short. "They are quite reliable, I understand," she murmured.

"Almost conclusive. This particular test puts the odds of Logan and Lassiter not being one and the same person at one in two thousand. Pretty good odds, I'd say. As I told you earlier, we know he was on board the *Caroline*, but he managed to escape. I'm sure he was in that Twin Otter. The man has a genius for escaping and going to ground."

"I think I know where he'll go."

Skye stared at her. "Where?"

"To a ranch in Argentina, near a place called San Carlos de Bolivar. It's about two hundred miles from Buenos Airés. It's owned by Baroness von der Lin who, for reasons that entirely escape me, has always doted on Lassiter. She would take him in and cover for him."

"Have you ever told the police about her?"

"No."

"Why not then, and why now?"

Princess Helen seemed exasperated by his obtuseness. "Larry Lassiter, foolish and dissolute as he was, was one of us. That oaf Logan most certainly is not. As you saw for yourself, that insolent creature openly insulted me and treated me with contempt."

"Give me those names again." Skye committed them to memory as she repeated them, turned down the offer of a drink, and excused himself. Outside the villa, he spotted Goodwin sitting in the police jeep. The detective climbed out and came over to join him. "Have you had any sleep?" Skye asked as they shook hands.

"Not yet. I've got the watch. But I'll be relieved in a couple of hours."

"What about Alan? Is he asleep?"

The detective shook his head. "No. He's in the guardhouse trying to reach the company in Canada that manufactures Twin Otters."

Foxcroft, finally beginning to look a little worn around the edges, opened the door when Skye knocked. "How is she?" he asked, jerking his head in the direction of the villa.

"She's cool." Skye paused, then said with a wide grin, "Have I got news for you!"

* * *

"He's gone, Skye."

"Patrick? He's dead?"

"Yes. He died a couple of hours ago. I was sitting in the room with him when he went into cardiac arrest and stopped breathing. They came charging in with a crash cart and those paddles, but they couldn't resuscitate him."

"Are you all right?"

"I'm okay. I'm still at the hospital." She gave her little tinkling laugh that, as always, made his pulse quicken, and said, "You'll think I'm crazy but I suggested to the Kellys that we donate his organs. Those that hadn't been ruined by his drinking. I guess I was thinking of bringing some sort of closure. Of course, his parents were horrified and absolutely forbade it. To them it would be a sacrilege."

"Would you like me to come up there?"

"No!" The denial was so vehement and immediate, it rocked Skye. "It's a wonder you're not dead yourself," she went on in a milder tone. "I've been with Patrick all day, but I did catch one newscast. It's so sad about Robert. I really liked him."

"Everyone did."

"I have to go now. The Kellys are coming down the hall. They're absolutely devastated. They're clinging on to each other for support. It's kind of pathetic. I never thought I'd see them like this."

"I'll call you tomorrow."

"It's better if I call you. I'll be on the run all day, making arrangements. I'll call you at noon, your time. Bye."

As always when he needed to think, Skye craved motion, whether it was riding a horse, flying an airplane, driving a car, or just walking. Tonight it would be walking. Closing the front door, he stepped into the soft tropical night and walked down the road to the beach. The island had been under siege by journalists all afternoon, but the lack of overnight accommodation had come to the rescue once again, and the buzzing swarm had departed.

The crashing boom of the surf to which he had become almost inured in recent days had lessened considerably and it was possible to walk along the upper edge of the beach. Looking up at the Southern Cross, low on the horizon, Skye thought of the two beautiful women that were so intimately connected with this island. Patrick Kelly's death could be the crossroads for himself and Erin, but, strangely, it was the times he had spent with Jocelyn that he was remembering. He tried to concentrate on Erin, but his thoughts kept slipping past her to memories of Jocelyn. With a cringe of conscience he realized that he had scarcely thought of Erin in the past adrenalin-driven twenty-four hours. Uttering an audible groan, he turned and headed back to Whistling Frog. He would have a nightcap and go to bed. Tomorrow would have to take care of itself.

* * *

The breakup of the organ transplantation ring shared headlines in the morning papers with Patrick Kelly II dying at 40. Reading what was written about Lord Fraser, Skye knew his decision had been the right one. After breakfast, he drove to Beaufort to comfort Fiona and help her with the arrangements. Erin would be doing much the same thing in California, he reflected. The full enormity of her beloved husband's crimes had crashed down on Fiona, and she was numb with shock. She smiled faintly with relief and gratitude when Skye said he would stand by her and see her through the ordeal. Fiona wanted him to stay for lunch, but he said he had to return home to take an important call. As he drove away, Skye thought about her future. When the dust settled, she could be destitute. Fortunately, he was in a position to help.

The call came precisely at noon. Skye picked up the portable phone and went out on the patio. After some preliminary skirmishing — why did he think of it as "skirmishing"? — Skye asked Erin what her plans were. He heard the sharp intake of her breath.

After a pause, she said slowly, "I'm going to stay on here. Patrick is a Kelly, and I want him brought up as a Kelly. Not the kind his father was; but still a Kelly. I owe that to my son. He has a role to play in the world."

So she's bought into it. "What about your ex-in-laws?"

"Not a problem. With Patrick's death, custody of young Patrick reverts to me. And they're old, Skye. They're turning to me for advice and help, of all things."

She was in control. No need to give her a lever over them by telling her about the old man's Astro involvement. "Have you given any thought to us?"

"A lot. What about you?"

"The same."

"And?"

"It won't work, as I'm sure you know. I understand what you're doing and why you're doing it, but I can never be part of it."

"I'm not asking you to be. I'm asking you to be part of me. No strings. I can handle the Kellys."

"'Tis a consummation devoutly to be wished,'" Skye quoted blithely, his spirits soaring.

"Oh, Skye, you idiot! I love you!" Erin's captivating laugh floated down the line.